LIE
TO ME

LIE
TO ME

OLIVIA
GAVOYANNIS

embla
books

First published in the UK in 2025 by

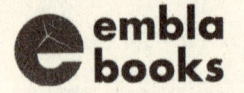

embla books

An imprint of Bonnier Books UK
5th Floor, HYLO, 105 Bunhill Row,
London, EC1Y 8LZ

Copyright © Olivia Gavoyannis, 2025

All rights reserved.
No part of this publication may be reproduced, stored or transmitted in any form or by any means, electronic, mechanical, photocopying or otherwise, without the prior written permission of the publisher.

The right of Olivia Gavoyannis to be identified as Author of this work has been asserted by them in accordance with the Copyright, Designs and Patents Act, 1988.

This is a work of fiction. Names, places, events and incidents are either the products of the author's imagination or used fictitiously. Any resemblance to actual persons, living or dead, or actual events is purely coincidental.

A CIP catalogue record for this book is available from the British Library.

ISBN: 9781471419188

Also available as an ebook and an audiobook

Typeset by IDSUK (Data Connection) Ltd
Printed and bound in Great Britain by Clays Ltd, Elcograf S.p.A.

MIX
Paper | Supporting
responsible forestry
FSC® C018072

The authorised representative in the EEA is Bonnier Books
UK (Ireland) Limited.
Registered office address: Floor 3, Block 3, Miesian Plaza,
Dublin 2, D02 Y754, Ireland
compliance@bonnierbooks.ie
www.bonnierbooks.co.uk

For Edward

ONE

The boat arrived at Igoumenitsa with a jolt, toppling the passengers at the front and creating a ripple effect that spread quickly through the hold. Robert and I lunged for the railing and managed to get there just in time to keep ourselves upright, but there was a flash of white as Vivienne teetered over to make a soft landing on her holdall.

I waited a moment to check that she wasn't hurt, and as soon as Robert stooped to pull her up I took my chance. Not looking back, I skirted around the edge of the confusion and scuttled up the dented metal stairs.

My heels were raw where I'd been pacing around the deck in my ill-fitting shoes, but I barely registered the shooting pain as I pumped my arms and legs, blood pounding and crashing in my ears. I'd been planning this moment for the whole journey, and I couldn't afford to let my nerves get the better of me now.

The passengers on the upper deck were so tightly packed that nobody seemed to have gained enough momentum to hurt themselves in the fall, but a group of Greek traders were shouting and gesturing wildly at the captain, their bags of fruit and vegetables swinging on their arms.

I tried to push my way to the front but I was penned in, and I hugged my handbag close to my chest to stop it being jostled to and fro by jabbing elbows.

Unable to bear the din any more, I hauled myself onto a ledge to get a better view and scanned the dusty walkway below.

The riot of local activity more than made up for the lack of holidaymakers. Forlorn donkeys laden with bulbous sacks were being led around a fleet of battered vans, and the cigarette smoke rising up from the men waiting to board mingled unpleasantly with the odour of the fishermen's crates stacked on the dock.

Shielding my eyes, I scoured the crowd until I found what I was looking for – a group of policemen standing in the shadow of the boat. I had spent so much of the journey worrying about this moment that it felt almost inevitable that they were there, looking up intently at the deck as if searching for me in the crowd.

I ducked down and watched for a few moments to assess my options, and when one of them stepped out of the shadow to greet a trader I saw the glint of a gun at his belt.

A wave of vertigo swept over me and I lowered myself carefully to the ground. I fumbled with my bag, the clasp slipping between my sweaty fingers until it opened with a pop. I peeked inside, and my stomach twisted at the thought of what would happen if the policemen searched me. Scrunching up the canvas tote, I pushed it right down inside the bag until it barely showed.

We'd agreed that I should wait until the boat was far from land and surrounded by churning water before hurling it overboard, but when I got up to the top deck there were too many people around. My only option was to place it on the side and nudge it off, but I was paralysed by the thought of the breeze catching it – forcing me to watch helplessly as it fluttered back onto the deck below.

I clicked my bag shut, cursing myself for losing my nerve, and tried to make my way back to the stairs.

With rising panic, I realised the passengers behind me had already shuffled forward to fill the gaps. Pushing against the wall of hot bodies, I only managed to move a few steps before the metallic clinking of the ramp rang through the air. I tried to weave sideways to escape from the press, but I was slowly shunted towards the front of the deck.

When I reached the ramp I craned my neck to see if I could spot the blond waves of Robert's hair or Vivienne's jet black crop, but there was no sign of them in the crowd.

The midday sun needled my skin as I stepped out from the shade of the boat, and I felt itchy with the thought of the policemen watching me. One of the men waiting to board grinned at me when I looked up, but I pretended not to have seen and tugged my straw hat further down my forehead.

Clasping my handbag close to my chest, I set foot on the dock and looked around for an opportunity to disappear into the crowd. I joined the back of a rowdy group of fishermen who were pushing their way through the people milling around the boat, but when I drew level with the policemen one of them waved and called me over.

'*Kalosorisateh*,' he said, and I couldn't work out whether it was a greeting or a command. I tried to keep my expression neutral as I turned the unfamiliar word over in my head, but I could feel the fear tugging at the corners of my mouth.

'Where are you from?' he asked, switching language when he realised I hadn't understood.

'England,' I stuttered, my tongue sticking to the roof of my mouth.

'So how did you end up on this boat? It's for *agrotes*,' he said, grasping for the word. 'For traders only.'

'Oh, I didn't realise it wasn't a passenger ferry,' I said, studiously avoiding eye contact or looking anywhere near the gun strapped to his belt.

He nodded. 'And you were staying in Corfu?'

'Yes.' I decided it would be safest to stick to an abridged version of the truth.

'Where?' he asked, and I screwed up my face. I was hoping he'd drop the subject, but when he started naming hotels I nodded at one just to make him stop.

'Pelekas is nice,' he said enthusiastically, and I tried to ignore the urgent thrum of my heart. That was the town right next to where we'd been staying. 'And what brings you to Igoumenitsa?' He cocked his head and looked at me more intently.

Realising my roving eyes might draw attention to my nerves, I drew my shoulders back and lifted my gaze to meet his face. He smiled, and I was caught off guard by the way his eyes flashed from green to gold in the sun. He was a lot younger than I had originally thought and couldn't have been much older than me. Early twenties maybe.

'I'm on holiday.' I put my clammy hands in my pockets to stop myself fidgeting.

'In that case, I can tell you the best places to go,' he said, but I was so horrified that I'd almost let slip where we'd been staying that I didn't take in anything he said.

'The best hotels are a ten-minute walk over there,' he was saying when I surfaced from my thoughts, pointing to his left. 'And you can change any money you need with him.' He indicated a lanky man sat on a wall smoking, and then gestured further inland. 'And the best bars are up there in Dimarchiou Square.'

When he'd finished I readied myself to answer more questions, but he just smiled.

'Well, maybe I will see you again later.'

'Maybe.' I edged away.

'Wait. What's your name?'

I hesitated.

'Jean?'

I nodded mutely, my panic spiralling until I realised he'd spotted the scrawled tag I'd attached to my handbag when we left London months ago.

'Well, *ta leme*, Jean. I hope I'll see you again.'

I could feel beads of sweat dripping down my back, but I tried to keep a steady pace as I walked past the money-changer, moving far enough away that he wouldn't try to engage me in conversation. Once clear, I stopped and leant against a nearby wall but my body was still tensed, ready to run.

Lifting my cigarettes out carefully without disturbing the tote, I tried to ignore the slight tremor that had started up in my hands as I waited for Robert and Vivienne to appear.

The crowd of people coming down the ramp was thinning, but just as I began to think I might have missed them they emerged from the hold. They were distinctive even with large shades obscuring their faces, and the searing white of Vivienne's shirt made the battered boat look even grubbier than it had before.

They left their luggage at the top and sauntered down the ramp arm in arm. It was unlikely that anyone in Greece recognised them from the Fleet Street papers, but they still managed to draw the attention of people waiting to board. I tensed as one of the policemen turned to watch Vivienne pass, but he didn't call her back.

When they reached the dock Robert guided her towards a ticket-seller and they reached up in unison to perch their shades on top of their heads.

I watched Vivienne closely.

She gave the man one of her gap-toothed grins and gestured up to the luggage, bringing her hand back to rest lightly on his arm for just a moment. He called over to the money-changer, who stubbed out his cigarette and went to fetch Vivienne and Robert's luggage for them.

I ground the butt of my cigarette into the floor and followed.

Vivienne was too engrossed in looking for something in her handbag to notice me, but when Robert spotted me a deep frown creased his forehead.

'Where the hell did you go?'

Vivienne looked up but said nothing, reaching over to smooth my hat back into place. She looked smart in her striped capri pants despite the heat, but Robert was beginning to sweat in one of his linen suits.

'Sorry I didn't warn you, I felt awfully sick,' I said, which wasn't too far from the truth. Robert rolled his eyes so I looked to Vivienne.

'No need to apologise. Are you feeling better?'

Her voice was clear and brisk as usual, but her eyes flicked towards my handbag.

'Much . . . much better,' I said, my tongue tripping over the deceit.

She gave my arm a grateful squeeze but avoided meeting my eye.

'I'm not surprised you felt sick,' Robert said. 'That was the worst journey of my life. I would rather have endured another night in that dump of a hotel in Corfu.'

'Don't start,' Vivienne said breezily. 'You know we had to leave.'

'We didn't, it was just this one complaining,' he said, gesturing towards me. 'So what your lock was broken? This is Greece, you'd have been perfectly safe.'

'But someone broke into my room during the night,' I protested. It wasn't a complete lie.

'Nothing was stolen, it was probably just a drunken guest walking into the wrong room. You could have put a chair against the door if you were that worried.'

I readied myself to trot out the argument I had already given him, but Vivienne cut in.

'Why don't we just enjoy having a bit of space from the others? We'll be with them all summer, and some of them were really starting to get to me,' she said pointedly.

Robert scowled and called out to the money-changer, who had just returned from fetching their bags. 'Where can we get a taxi around here?'

With some effort the man picked up all their luggage at once and walked Robert across the road to a waiting taxi, Vivienne and I trailing in his wake.

It was a relief to lower myself into a seat after standing on the boat, even if the car was hotter than outside.

Robert joined me in the back and we watched as Vivienne's luggage was squashed into the boot. I offered him a cigarette and he grunted his thanks.

'Where to?' the driver asked, turning to Robert.

I wanted to suggest going somewhere out of town but I knew it wasn't my place, and Vivienne didn't look like she was going to intervene.

'Where would you recommend?'

'I know a good hotel in the centre of town? Very smart.'

'Excellent,' Robert said, and I tightened my grip on my handbag. 'Take us there.' The money-changer shouted goodbye to the driver and slammed the door, sealing in the heat and dust as we rattled away from the port.

The residential area was shallow, hugging the curve of the bay, and everywhere I looked mountains loomed behind the tightly packed buildings, the whole place seemingly held up by an interconnected web of washing lines. After the chaos of the port the backstreets felt deserted, with a few men sat in the shade playing backgammon and a dozen curled-up cats.

Vivienne was silent in the front while Robert and I smoked out of the windows in the back, our bodies braced against the erratic movement of the car. My right hand was still shaking so I swapped my cigarette to the left and wedged my arm against the door.

'Here we go,' the driver said proudly as we pulled up outside what looked like an apartment building in the centre of town. An attractive greying man appeared and greeted the driver. 'This is my cousin, Nikos, he'll look after you.'

Vivienne wandered over to the entrance to peek inside while Robert sorted through some coins to pay the fare. She wrinkled her nose in distaste, but Nikos had already heaved our luggage onto a faded bronze trolley and was wheeling it towards the door.

Robert sighed loudly when we stepped inside. 'See, we should have stayed in Corfu.'

There was an elegant sweeping staircase and a wide marble reception desk, but the rest of the lobby looked more like a family living room. The space had been filled with beige sofas and practical dark wood furniture, and there were framed paintings of religious icons on the wall. 'I bet the money-changer was his cousin too,' Robert whispered loudly, and Nikos politely pretended not to hear.

'Passports please,' he said. I handed mine across the desk, keeping my right hand clamped by my side to hide my lingering tremor. He opened it up and rifled through the pages, taken aback by the numerous stamps from borders around the world. I held my breath when he paused on the fresh entry from Corfu, but he said nothing and continued flipping through to the end.

'You travel a lot,' he said as he finally reached the page with my photo. I stood there silent and uneasy as he made a note of my name in a leather-bound folder and slid the passport back to me across the desk.

'We race internationally,' Robert explained, handing over his and Vivienne's documents. 'We're going to Athens next.'

'Ah, Rally Acropolis?' Nikos said, looking suitably impressed. I nodded and his bushy eyebrows drew closer together as he took in my tatty dress. I shifted and felt the coarse material scratch at my calves. 'You drive too? What car?' he said, aiming the question in my direction.

'Saab. Sometimes I drive to give Vivienne a rest if we're on a long race, but mostly I ride shotgun and navigate,' I blurted, holding my hands up stupidly in imitation of reading a map. 'Vivienne's the real driver,' I clarified, nodding my head towards her.

Nikos gave me a smile that reached all the way up to his kind, crinkly eyes and handed Robert two sets of keys. He gestured for us to follow him into a tiny lift and then along a windowless corridor, the air heavy with the chemical tang of detergent. I didn't want to be placed on a separate floor, so I was relieved when he pointed to two adjacent rooms.

'Your luggage will be up shortly. Please call me if you need anything,' he said, giving a little bow and striding back to the lift.

Lie to Me

'What I need is a lie-down,' Robert said. 'Jean, we'll call for you later.' He unlocked their door and held it open for Vivienne.

We hadn't been able to say much to one another on the crossing so I had assumed Vivienne would be anxious to talk alone once we got to the hotel, but she gave me a quick smile and followed him into the room.

Unprepared for the sudden exposure of solitude, I unlocked my door and stood there, worrying the material of my dress between my fingers. The compact space was dominated by more dark wood furniture, and the walls were cluttered with yet more stylised religious icons. I took a step back when I spotted the door connecting the room to Vivienne and Robert's, uneasy at the thought of them being able to hear my every move.

After a few moments the porter knocked and I took my small holdall from him, tipping a selection of coins from the change I had left. I lifted out my clothes and dumped them in a jumble at the end of the bed before rummaging around for my nail scissors and cutting a tiny slit in the lining.

I lifted the tote carefully out of my handbag and tugged at the tight knot I'd used to secure it. The bag gaped open, and I pulled out the handkerchief scrunched up inside.

The detail on the corner appeared first, where someone had spelt out *Angel* in tight stitches. Who had done this? Was it a wife or mother who had lovingly made this, only for ... I stopped myself. I couldn't think this way.

I pulled it out further, but the material was clean. Maybe it was all a bad dream.

A final tug set it free, and I retched at the coppery smell as the stained corner came into sight.

'No,' I mouthed silently, and the dark patch blurred as tears filled my eyes.

Gathering myself, I quickly scrunched it back into the holdall with the identification card that was hidden in a slim wallet. I wiped my hands vigorously down my dress, though none of the stained material had touched my skin.

I slid the bag right to the bottom of the lining and stuffed some clothes over the top for good measure. When the holdall was safely zipped up I stumbled to the shared bathroom at the end of the corridor and scrubbed my hands vigorously with the coarse soap until my palms turned an angry pink.

When I had finished unfolding and hanging my few remaining items of clothing I lay back on the bed.

I had barely slept, and I could feel my eyes drooping as my body sank into the thick mattress. But before I could start to drift off I hauled myself up, knowing that if I shut my eyes the images from the night before would come rushing back into my head.

I reached out to grab my passport and turned to the photo page. I'd developed an enviable tan since Vivienne picked me up a few months ago and started whisking me around the world to race. With my dark hair I could see why the policeman might have mistaken me for a Greek, but the woman looking up at me from this document faded into the pale background.

I angled the page towards the window. It wasn't just my complexion that had changed. My high forehead and straight nose were the same, but my face was gaunt and I looked naive and wide-eyed now that I'd become accustomed to looking at the dark kohl liner Vivienne liked to wear. I ran my finger over the glossy likeness of the bobbly jumper I had worn as a sort of uniform when I worked at the stables and then shut the document with a snap. I shoved it in my handbag and rummaged around for my cigarettes.

I stared unseeingly out of the window for several minutes, listening for sounds of Robert and Vivienne next door, but there was nothing.

Shame flushed my cheeks as I tiptoed over to the connecting door and pressed my ear against it, but I couldn't make out any sounds coming from their room. When I bent down to look through the keyhole, I found the view had been blocked by the key in the lock.

Needing to move, I paced back and forth and tried to focus on the sound of my steps to distract myself from thinking about Corfu. I ended up in front of the holdall and kicked it with a fury that took me by surprise, sending it scudding under the bed and into the adjoining wall.

Before Robert could rap on the door to investigate the noise I grabbed my keys and rushed to leave. Glancing over my shoulder once to make sure the holdall was out of sight, I hurried downstairs and out into the blistering light.

TWO

Vivienne and Robert knocked on my door at seven o'clock and the three of us ventured out into the receding heat. My afternoon tramping around the dusty streets had left me weary, but the others were back on form after their nap – though I still couldn't get Vivienne to meet my eye.

They were having a heated debate about the upcoming race in Athens, and although my focus was on scanning the crowds for policemen, there was something reassuring about their sparring; my role as witness to their witty back and forth giving me the purpose I'd always craved when I was stumbling around aimlessly on my own.

I hung back as the road narrowed and noticed how the locals turned to stare unselfconsciously as Vivienne tripped past on Robert's arm, a little high on ouzo, her hourglass figure squeezed into a cream sundress. She walked with a carefree swing of the hips that would look ungainly on anyone else, and her cropped hair set her apart from other women with their neat beehives and flipped bobs. It was impossible not to be drawn to her as I had been – like a moth to a flame.

I was helping at the stables where I lived with my father when I first fell under Vivienne's spell.

Lie to Me

He had tasked me with ferrying cleaning materials across the yard when I heard the purr of a motor coming from the bottom of the drive. Lifting my hand up to block out the morning sun, I watched as a forest green racing car swung into the yard and squealed to a stop inches from the barn.

The revving of the engine had drawn out several of the greasy-haired boys I worked with, and there was a collective intake of breath when Vivienne stepped out. Her hair wasn't as short back then, but she was wearing an outfit that I had come to recognise as her uniform style: trousers belted high to accentuate her slim waist, with large shades propped on top of her head.

She crunched across the gravel to the outbuilding that was used as an office, not so much as glancing at the stable hands who had edged forward to watch her arrival. As soon as the door had shut behind her, they vaulted the fence to get a better look at the car and I followed suit.

We circled around, admiring the glossy paintwork as it caught the light.

It was so unlike any other vehicle I'd seen before, with its sleek lines and cream leather seats that looked soft to the touch. I didn't dare stretch out a hand to see for myself – though the boys had already left a trail of grubby fingerprints across the bonnet.

A shadow loomed over me and I froze, waiting for my father to yank me around by the coat to face him. When nothing happened I turned slowly on my heels to find one of the older boys behind me, and he let out a low whistle as he stepped around me to get a better look at the car.

Jolted out of my trance, I climbed back over the fence and collected the grooming tools I would need for my round, though

I hung around to see if the woman came back. As I had feared, my father was quick to notice the disruption and stalked over to shoo the boys away.

Backing away before I caught his attention, I retreated to the other end of the stables and stayed there until his balding head had disappeared. When I ran back to the yard I was disappointed to find that the car had already gone.

The locals looked at me inquisitively as I followed Vivienne and Robert through the cobbled streets of Igoumenitsa in my only smart skirt, and I felt a strange sense of detachment as I thought about how they might see me: a young society woman having the time of her life with her glamorous older friends. This wasn't strictly true, but I had got so used to playing the part that it no longer felt like a charade.

As we walked past the apartments I heard dogs barking to each other from their tiny concrete balconies and snatches of conversation in rapid-fire Greek. My mouth watered at the buttery smell of baklava wafting from an open window, and I was relieved when we finally came across a taverna. The waiter gave us pick of the remaining tables, and I pointed to one tucked safely out of sight behind an olive tree before Robert could answer.

The locals were making the most of the period before the summer tourists arrived, and customers were overflowing from the taverna onto turquoise metal tables perched at jaunty angles on the cobbles outside. The owners had propped up painted wooden planks and draped the building with sheets of thin material that billowed gently in the wind, giving the impression of being in a ship out at sea.

'I think I've worked out who your biggest competition is this year,' Robert said after we'd been served some starters. He scooped up tzatziki with a hunk of bread and folded the whole thing into his mouth, shooting Vivienne a defiant look.

'It would have been Sylvia, but she had the bad luck to wreck her car in the Safari Rally,' Vivienne said, glaring at his poor table manners. 'She's not racing the Acropolis, so we are the competition.'

I saw the Swede's car after she'd crashed and it had a nasty dent. But then none of our cars had been in particularly good health after crossing 3,500 miles of East Africa's worst roads. The route was essentially two great loops with Nairobi in the middle, and it took in everything from jungle tracks to swaying plains with man-high grass, winding rivers and barren mountain roads. It was a punishing race for man and car, but the sponsors stumped up a handsome £500 for prize money so people always came back for more.

We hadn't told Robert how close it was, but if Vivienne hadn't been so sharp we might have gone the same way as Sylvia. I was driving in the early hours of the second morning in the dim light while Vivienne got an hour's rest, but I must have dozed off at the wheel because the next thing I knew Vivienne was shouting and a tremendous boulder was looming in front of us. I froze, thinking for a second that I was dreaming, but Vivienne managed to wrestle the steering wheel around so that we just swerved the solid grey mass. As we passed the boulder it turned its head and I came face-to-face with a bewildered elephant roused from its nap in the middle of the road.

In the end we came fifth in the Safari Rally, and the next month we became the first all-women's team to win the Tulip Rally in Holland, so now Vivienne wanted to make absolutely sure of the Ladies' Championship with a victory in Greece.

'I know she's your friend, but don't you think you should be worried about Marie now that Sylvia's out?' Robert persisted.

'Hardly,' Vivienne scoffed.

'No? Even in her new car?'

'Especially in her new car. It's ridiculous.'

'Do I detect a hint of jealousy?' he said innocently, a smirk playing across his lips.

'No, it's just the truth. And besides, Jean and I are untouchable.' She reached across the table to squeeze my hand and I smiled back gratefully.

After the fear of looking over my shoulder all day, I craved the feeling of containment that I'd come to associate with Vivienne and our rides in her car. I'd got used to the seamless dance of the gearstick as I recited a stream of directions, nothing else to think about but the thrumming metal and the road beneath us.

'I don't believe you,' Robert said, forcefully tearing apart another piece of warm bread. 'Her new Ferrari is a masterpiece.'

'It's all show and no go, it's not a rallying car,' Vivienne said, skewering an olive. 'Don't you think Jean?'

'Without a doubt,' I agreed quickly, and Robert rolled his eyes.

I'd taken up an unofficial role as mediator in their marriage; a role I generally enjoyed. But the nature of our dynamic meant that I was mostly called upon by Vivienne to take her side.

She leant over to stage-whisper in my ear. 'Anyway, I don't think we're the ones that need to worry about being left in the dust.'

At present Vivienne had never beaten Robert at an international rally, but we'd been close on his tail lights for most of the Safari and she clearly fancied her chances. I saw something flash across Robert's face as I stifled a giggle of discomfort, though he continued his train of thought as if he hadn't heard.

'I'd buy a Ferrari in a heartbeat if your protégé wasn't such a sponge. I dread to think how much we've spent wining and dining her.' His tone was light but his smile looked forced, with all his perfectly straight teeth on show.

Vivienne ignored the jibe, but I poured myself another drink for something to do. She had insisted there was no point paying me my retainer and winnings from the races until we got back to England, and because I had no money she had bought all my food and board while we'd been away. At first I'd been delighted, but as the weeks wore on it made me dizzy to think how much it must have cost her.

I got up to visit the bathroom and found that I was a little unsteady on my feet. The bread was the only thing I'd eaten that afternoon, and the cool glasses of ouzo had gone to my head despite my determination to dilute the liquor into a cloudy mix of water and ice.

I swayed a little as I tried to manoeuvre myself between Vivienne and the wall, and she met my gaze for the first time with glassy eyes before looking away quickly and calling the waiter over for more ouzo.

He asked if I wanted another and I shook my head vigorously. It was all right for Vivienne to wake up with the reassuring bulk of Robert by her side, but I couldn't afford to fuel the paranoia that I knew would engulf me in the middle of the night.

When I got back to the table I was relieved to see that it had been covered with small dishes of charred stuffed peppers, tightly rolled vine leaves and hot pittas. We let conversation fall away as we tucked into the feast, and when the last of the oil had been mopped from the plates we ordered coffee and sat back to watch a group of chubby children weaving through the tables with blissful abandon.

'What are we going to do to amuse ourselves while we wait for the others to get here then?' Robert asked, lighting a cigarette.

'I would have suggested motoring about in the mountains to get some practice, but it sounds like the cars won't get here for at least another week . . .' Vivienne trailed off. 'So I wouldn't imagine there's much to be done other than going to the beach.'

'I couldn't agree more,' Robert said. The sun was throwing out its final golden rays before it retreated, and his chain was glinting at the collar of his polo shirt.

'Maybe,' I said when he looked to me for confirmation, though I was filled with horror at the thought.

The only swimming costume I had was a navy school-issued affair, and I had felt like a prude when we went to the beach in Corfu. Vivienne and Robert had stripped off and liberally doused themselves in tanning oil, while I wrapped my towel around me and pretended to bury my head in a book.

'We could go on a hike to the viewpoint?' I suggested, pointing up to the mountains behind the taverna.

Vivienne set her gold earrings jangling as she swung around to look up at them and pulled a face. 'I'd rather spend our time here relaxing around the hotel and drinking.'

'Come on, it would be a fine day out. I bet it's beautiful in the forest,' I pressed.

'I don't think so,' Vivienne scoffed, arching her eyebrow at Robert.

'So that's settled then,' he said. 'You'll come to the beach tomorrow?'

'Fine,' I said, sensing defeat.

Satisfied, Vivienne grimaced as she downed the dregs of her thick coffee before it settled into mud. I had drunk mine when it was scalding hot and the heavy liquid had made me jittery, leaving a bitter taste in my mouth.

The waiter brought us a full plate of figs and I set upon them as if I hadn't eaten at all, peeling them roughly with a blunt knife.

The light had faded by the time we finished eating, and the only other people left were some Greek women of about my age talking in low voices in the corner. They looked like they'd spent the day on the beach – their messy hair tumbled across their bronzed shoulders, and I could see white strap lines peeking out from beneath their bandeau tops.

Robert gestured for the bill, and as he rose to sign his traveller's cheque the women fell silent. I'd got used to his appearance in the way that you do with constant exposure to someone, but I was always reminded of quite how attractive he was when strangers stared openly as he crossed a room.

I waited until Robert was out of sight and turned back to Vivienne, hoping to snatch a hushed conversation while we were alone, but I was startled to find an elderly woman shrouded in black hunched over Vivienne's empty coffee cup.

'Can I help you?' I said, but the woman ignored me. She muttered something in Greek to herself, and before I could say anything else she leant over and plucked my cup off the table.

Vivienne and I watched silently as she held it out in front of her. She turned it three times before flicking the sludge of granules on the floor and upturning it on an empty plate. Unnerved, I went to retrieve it and let out an involuntary yelp as she slapped my hand away.

Robert emerged from the taverna and the older woman muttered something in his direction before snatching up Vivienne's cup and repeating the process.

Vivienne stood up to leave but Robert blocked her way with his arm. 'Hang on a second, I want to see what's going on.'

She sat back down reluctantly and the young women who had been lingering in the corner came over to explain in broken English that the old woman was going to read the patterns in our coffee cups.

'But why?' Vivienne asked, and she bristled when one of the young women told her rather sincerely that this woman was known as something of a fortune teller within the town.

The old woman clapped her hands together, making us all jump, and turned my cup over in front of me before doing the same to Vivienne's.

'This is ridiculous,' Vivienne said, scraping back her chair and throwing down her napkin. 'Come on, Jean,' she called back, but I was fixated on the cup in front of me. The inside was a riot of swirly patterns and fat coffee granules, and there was a blurry shape that looked like a mountain range where she had thrown the remaining sediment from the side.

'The bottom of the cup shows the past,' the more fluent of the young women said, pulling up a chair and taking on the role of translator. She was slim and feline, and I could see the salt caught in the sun-bleached hairs on her arm.

'Oh yes, and what do all those squiggly patterns mean?' Robert said gamely, turning to make sure Vivienne was out of sight before leaning in to rest his arm on the back of her chair. I frowned at him but he pretended not to notice.

'Well, the middle of the cup is the present and the top is the future,' she said, warming to her theme. 'Circles are disappointment and triangles are luck. Big shapes near the top of the cup mean something important will happen soon.'

'That looks like a dog,' Robert said, pointing to the middle. I tilted my head but I couldn't make it out.

'Dogs show loyalty,' the young woman said, and Robert made an 'aha' sound.

'It's a bird,' the other young woman said, pointing to a different blob. 'News or a journey.'

'Good news?' Robert asked.

'Good or bad,' she shrugged.

I strained my eyes to make out the shapes, but I still couldn't see anything apart from the mountain range – and on closer inspection even that looked like a formless mound of sludge.

I held my breath as I waited for the older woman's assessment. When she finally muttered something I looked up and was surprised to see that she had tears in her eyes. She spoke again, sorrow etched into the deep lines of her face, before making the *fthou fthou fthou* spitting sound I had seen some of the Greek elders do and turning away.

Robert's laugh echoed around the empty street. I tried to join in but the tightness in my throat made it difficult to form the sound. 'What was that all about?' he said.

I looked to the young women for reassurance, but their faces had hardened against me. 'It's a ... I don't know how you say,' the skinniest one said, before the other woman interrupted and pointed at the top of the cup. '*Satanás*. It's a spirit.'

'A devil?' Robert suggested.

'Yes, exactly.' They all nodded their heads in grim agreement.

I glared back, feeling foolish that I had let them get to me with their superstitious game. Having stared at the cup for some minutes I was certain there weren't any devils lurking there; maybe this was something the locals had devised to trick visitors into paying them to keep evil spirits away.

I was about to protest, but when I looked down into the cup again two slanted eyes locked with mine above a thin mouth and pointed chin. I scrunched my eyes shut and opened them, but still I saw the shape of the devil, clear as day. Its eyes bore into me, and the sharp lines of two horns curved up towards the top of the cup.

'What does that mean?' I choked out.

'She was spitting on you for luck,' the skinny woman said, dodging my question.

Robert let out another honk of laughter and slapped his hand down on the table but my fingers had gone numb, and a crawling sensation was making its way up the skin on my arm.

'Careful, if Vivienne finds out you're a bad omen she won't let you race with her again. We'll have to keep this a secret between the two of us.' He gave me an exaggerated wink.

I turned around in search of the old woman but she had disappeared, and the street was empty. The sheets draped around the building had been so beautiful in the daylight, but their flapping had become eerie now the babble of chatter had gone.

The young women gestured towards their half-full bottle of wine, but Robert shook his head reluctantly. 'Another time.'

I felt like the strength had left both of my legs, but Robert held out his hands and begrudgingly I let him lift me up. We made our way slowly down the uneven street to look for Vivienne, and eventually found her sitting on a low stone wall under a wispy almyriki tree with her handbag clutched to her chest.

'Do you want to hear what you missed? It was pretty ghostly,' Robert said, but she shook her head firmly. 'That's good because I wasn't going to tell you anyway. Why were you being so odd?'

'I wasn't being odd. I just didn't want to hear any of that superstitious nonsense.' She seemed to have sobered up during her wait outside, and her earlier mischievousness was gone.

'It's not nonsense, Viv, it's their culture,' he said in faux condescension as we picked our way over the uneven cobbles back to the hotel. 'Anyone would have thought you had something to hide.'

'Don't be ridiculous, Robert,' she snapped, and I looked up from my shabby sandals to see a wry smile slide across his face. 'I'm not in the mood for your silly games.'

Robert raised his eyebrows at me but I shook my head at him and turned away, nausea bubbling up inside me. I could feel the heat of Vivienne's gaze searching me out in the dim light of the street lamps, but this time I was the one who couldn't bring myself to look her in the eye.

THREE

I woke from a nightmare tangled in the sheets. The dull thud of metal had ricocheted around my head all night, and fumes burnt my throat as I desperately painted over and over the same spot, never making any progress.

The image continued to loom out at me from the weak light of the hotel room, so I tugged the sheet from under my legs and pulled it over my head. The thin material hung in the air for a moment before floating down to cover my mouth and nose, smothering me. I ripped it off and heard a knock on the door.

I rolled over and waited for whoever it was to leave me alone.

The knocking became more insistent, three sharp raps – a pause – and then it started up again.

'Jean? Are you awake? Let me in.' Vivienne's clipped tones carried through the thin wood of the door.

At the sound of her voice, fragments from the night before came flooding in – the ouzo, the coffee-reader and my violent convulsions over the bathroom sink. I waited until I heard the muffled sound of her door banging shut, and then I let out a quiet groan and buried my face back into the pillow.

After a few moments a loud metallic clink made me grab at my sheets, and the door leading to the other room swung open to reveal Vivienne.

'Sorry I woke you,' she said, not sounding very apologetic at all.

'What are you doing? What time is it?'

'Time to get up.' She yanked the curtains back and set the key down on the window ledge. 'I brought you some tea,' she said more gently, and I assumed she'd spotted the bowl I'd placed by my bedside in case I was ill in the night.

The springs of the bed let out a mournful squeak as she perched beside me.

I squinted as I rolled over to face her and croaked my thanks.

'That's quite all right. And if you're not feeling too awful I have plans for today.'

Gingerly, I took the mug she was offering me and managed a sip of the scalding tea.

'Robert's gone off somewhere in a huff so I thought we could spend some time together,' she said, and all at once it felt like the day might turn out to be fine.

The volatility of Robert and Vivienne's relationship was still a mystery to me; sometimes they were obsessed with each other and never spent a second apart, and at other times Robert would disappear. Occasionally he was gone for days on end before returning without any explanation, and it was that time spent alone with Vivienne I enjoyed best.

Their dynamic took me a while to get used to, and it certainly wasn't what I had once imagined a marriage would be like. Even during the times Robert and Vivienne were glued to one another they rowed constantly, and there was a fierce intimacy to these fights that was uncomfortable to watch.

I tried to arrange my face into a look of disapproval. 'Where's he gone this time?'

'Who cares.' She got up to pull the other set of curtains back so the light came streaming in. 'You and I are going to have some fun.'

She crossed the room to turn on the lamp, and I leant over to make sure I hadn't drunkenly moved my holdall out from its hiding place during the night. I knew I should confess that I hadn't disposed of the bag, but her continued silence over what happened on our last night in Corfu made it clear she didn't want to talk about it.

Oblivious to my discomfort, Vivienne stopped in front of the mirror and twisted this way and that before sighing. 'Well, I'm definitely not coming in here to use this mirror again. The lighting makes me look all lumpy.'

Her belted minidress exaggerated her enviable figure and she knew it, but I played along anyway.

'What are you talking about? You look just like Sophia Loren.'

She laughed and jutted out her hip in the way the actress did in the adverts for her new action flick. We'd seen the florid pink posters at a station in Italy months before, and the likeness between the two women had stuck in my head.

She struck another pose and I pointed back at her reflection in the mirror. 'It's uncanny. You could be her twin.'

Turning to face the mirror, she assessed herself once more.

'You know what I think, Jean?'

'What?' I said indulgently.

'I think you're blind, but I don't care.'

I beamed, and not for the first time I thought what an idiot Robert was.

'Come on, get ready.' I yielded to her surprising force as she grabbed my hands and dragged me out of bed.

'Sorry, I'm still in my nightclothes.' I crossed my arms over my chest. I was very aware of how exposed my sinewy body was under my flimsy cotton shorts and top, but Vivienne didn't seem to care.

'Look how young and beautiful your skin is. Not a mark in sight,' she said, running a finger down my arm. My hair stood on end where her cool touch had grazed my skin, and I was strangely relieved when she turned away.

She pulled open the wardrobe and rooted around the few items hanging up. 'Hmm, this will have to do for now.' She inspected the dress I'd travelled in and tossed it over for me to catch. 'Put this on and then let's get some sun.'

It was well into the afternoon by the time we ventured out and the lunch service at the town's tavernas was tailing off, so Vivienne set about finding a bar despite my misgivings.

I'd been desperate to get her alone the night before, but now the silence was stretched out between us I didn't know what to say. How could I possibly dredge up the murky horror of what had passed between us? Examining the details under the mercilessly bright light of day seemed too awful to think about.

Lie to Me

The whitewashed stones and walls were almost blinding as we picked our way across the cobbles, and I wondered if they'd been freshly done for the summer season. I could smell the horribly familiar odour of paint, but when I ran my shoes along the stones no white pigment came off on the worn leather.

After a few more attempts I tore my gaze away from the ground and focused on scanning the streets for the dark blue of police uniforms, feeling woozy from the heat and the nauseating fumes as we made our way to the port.

'Here we are,' Vivienne announced with a flourish of her handbag when we reached a bar on the seafront.

I breathed in the salt air, though I could still taste the bitter paint fumes at the back of my throat, and I wondered if it was just a hangover from my nightmare.

The time had only just gone four o'clock according to Vivienne's watch, but she insisted on ordering us Martinis from the bemused waiter.

It felt odd being alone with her again after two weeks of Robert's presence keeping us at arm's length. So much had gone unspoken since we arrived in Igoumenitsa, but I didn't know where to start.

'Do you have a cigarette?' I asked, needing something to keep my hands busy. I'd been buying cheap Greek ones from a kiosk, but I knew Vivienne still had a supply of Gauloises she'd bought from France.

'Catch.' She tossed her silver cigarette case towards my head with unnecessary force and I threw up my hand to catch it.

'Good reactions.'

I fished out a cigarette and lit up, distractedly running my fingers along the swirly lettering on the case until she clicked her fingers to get my attention.

I slid the case back, and was about to pass her the lighter when she shifted her chair closer and leant in to light her cigarette off mine. She was suddenly so close that her rose perfume was overwhelming, and I noticed for the first time how her top lip curved up into a perfect cupid's bow.

Almost as fast as she'd leant in Vivienne was lounging back in her chair again, and I crossed my legs in what I hoped was a nonchalant stance as the waiter laid out our drinks.

Vivienne plucked one of the Martinis off the table and handed it to me.

'Here's to an outstanding performance at the Acropolis.' I clinked my glass carefully against hers and took a sip.

The first time Vivienne had given me a Martini on a drizzly evening in London I had baulked at its strength, but in the shimmering heat of Greece the ice-cold mixture slipped down with ease.

We'd been at a party hosted at one of those palatial Chelsea houses overlooking the Thames. It was attended by a bohemian collection of pop royalty, painters, waif-like models, hairdressers, multi-millionaires and one woman who looked awfully like a real member of the royal family.

I'd borrowed one of Vivienne's beautiful cocktail dresses, but on my athletic frame it looked ridiculous. The shiny material hung in voluminous folds around my waist, and

I looked out of place even among such an eccentric group of people.

We'd been there for little over an hour when a spindly man wearing a velvet suit clambered onto the piano and announced that everyone was going on a scavenger hunt. He marshalled us into groups and read off a list of things we had to find, including a beetle and a two-day-old newspaper, and told us to be back in two hours.

I thought that surely nobody was going to traipse out into the rain at the command of this odd man, but when a gong sounded the room came alive. Vivienne took my hand and pulled me over to join forces with a floppy-haired man who looked like he'd walked to the party in his pyjamas, and we splashed through the puddles outside to bundle into the back of his shimmering bronze Jaguar.

It turned out that he may as well have walked to the party because he nipped into his flat around the corner to pick up the old newspaper. But when I suggested going to his garden to find a beetle he snorted with laughter.

'I have a better idea,' he assured me, and I felt silly when he exchanged a knowing look with Vivienne.

After a bit of a drive he pulled up outside an ordinary-looking building in Soho with a swaying queue outside. He promised quite cheerfully that he 'wouldn't be a jiffy' and disappeared inside.

Vivienne explained to me that this was the infamous Ad-Lib Club and was the surest place in town to find a beetle, and I nodded along despite my confusion.

When the pyjama man appeared ten minutes later with another man sporting a dark moptop I realised my mistake. I tried to fluff up my hair while Vivienne shrieked with approval as they jumped over puddles to get to the car.

Even I knew who The Beatles were and I couldn't believe that Paul McCartney might be about to sit in the seat next to me, so I was a little disappointed when he introduced himself as Paul's brother, Mike.

Once we were back on the road Vivienne called out to me from the front seat. 'Jean, I think it's your turn to get the next item.'

'Of course, what is it?'

'A number plate.'

'Very funny,' I retorted, but when I saw the pyjama man's smirk in the rear-view mirror I realised it wasn't a joke.

'Do you have a screwdriver?' Vivienne asked, and he pointed to the glovebox. She rummaged around and handed it to me, and I twirled it around and around in my hand nervously.

'How about that one?' she suggested, and he pulled the car to an abrupt stop. There was a Rolls-Royce parked in the shadows, and the sight of it made my heart sink.

'Surely you're not going to make the kid do that?' our new passenger protested, but Vivienne put a hand on his arm to placate him.

'It's just a game. We've all had our turn.'

The Martinis had made me bold, and I hopped out the car without complaint. I didn't have a jacket, and rain stung my bare arms as I jogged over to my target.

At first it was hard to see where I needed to place the screwdriver in the dim light, but once I'd clicked it into one of the nails and heaved with all my strength the plate began to come loose.

The first three nails came out easily enough, but the wet tool slipped between my fingers as I got to the final one. With much huffing I eventually got that loose too, and as soon as I managed to detach the number plate I secured it under my arm and set off at a run.

I tightened my grip on the sharp metal as a shout rang out behind me, but there was no way I was hanging about to find out where it had come from.

'Go, go, go,' Vivienne shouted out of the open window as I drew nearer, and the car started moving before I'd even opened the door. The wet fabric of my dress was weighing me down and I felt a stab of anger at her, but when I finally managed to jump inside and slam the door behind me the feeling was washed away by sheer relief.

I held the cold metal sheet between my legs, and when Vivienne turned around to flash me a wide grin an electric thrill jolted through me.

Staring out at the shimmering heat in Igoumenitsa the whole rainy affair felt like an odd dream, but when I mentioned it to Vivienne she laughed wryly and told me that it wasn't even close to the wildest party she'd attended on Cheyne Walk.

'Did you enjoy it?'

'I did. I think people assumed I was a stray girl you'd plucked off the street, though.' I was aiming for humour, but my straight delivery gave my words a sour twist. 'The dress you lent me was beautiful, but it looked a bit silly hanging off me, I just don't have your curves,' I added limply.

Vivienne was silent for a few moments, surveying me. 'You could certainly do with filling out a bit. But until then I think we need to get you some new clothes. In fact, I think we should have a look right now while Robert isn't here to slow us down.'

I was too taken aback to object as she wedged some notes under the empty glasses and marched off, and I had to rush to catch up.

Nikos had given us directions to the market, and I heard the commotion as we drew close, but I was still surprised by the thrumming energy of it all when we turned the corner and the stalls came into sight.

The first thing I saw was a group of men who looked like they were being followed around by a bunch of low-flying clouds – though on closer inspection I realised they were giant sponges hung off their body with thin string. Behind them were rows of vans displaying pointy shoes and trinkets, as well as crates stacked with bread and fruit.

Before I'd had the chance to gather my thoughts Vivienne had plunged into the throng. When the traders saw her milky skin they started shouting in their best English, extolling the quality of their jewellery and cloth in a disjointed stream of vocabulary. I struggled to keep up with her long strides, and a thickset man threw his hands up in anger when I tripped and stubbed my toe on a tin bowl, sending its contents spilling across the floor.

I sped up, weaving around a group of children hawking straw bags and found Vivienne admiring a row of dresses hung up in a canvas tent. She plucked one off the hanger and held it up for me.

'It's for her,' she told the woman, and she clapped her hands together.

'*Polý oraía*. Very nice,' she said, pointing towards a tiny makeshift changing room with a scratched mirror.

Vivienne shooed me over and I reluctantly tugged the curtain across to cover as much of the gap as I could.

When I'd managed to wrestle the dress over my head I looked at my reflection and pulled a face. The shapeless garment was unflatteringly loose, and to make matters worse my hair had gone lank in the heat.

Just as I began to pull the dress off, Vivienne whipped open the curtain and made me jump.

'I'm getting changed,' I said shortly, but she waved my protests away. 'There's no point coming to look now anyway, I'm taking it off because it makes me look dreadful,' I added, more bitterly than I had intended, letting my arms fall limply by my side.

She stepped into the changing room and we both looked at our reflections in the mirror, her curvy beauty exaggerated by my pinched features.

'Don't be silly, I have just the thing to go with this.' She pulled the belt from her dress and cinched it tight around my waist. She stood back for a second to admire her handiwork then took off her scarf and tied it around my head, making sure to tuck in the loose strands of my hair.

'There you go,' she said, turning me back to the mirror. 'A bit of makeup and you'll be ready to go.'

I did a double take. I certainly looked better; my lank hair was gone, tucked under the scarf, and the belt even made me look like I had a waist. I turned around to see the dress from the back and noticed that I looked a little like Vivienne if I tilted my head a certain way.

'I'll buy it for you as a treat,' she said, cutting across me as I tried to tell her that I couldn't possibly accept. 'We can't have you going around with that on any longer,' she said, gesturing towards the old dress I'd discarded on the floor. I opened my mouth again to object, but she had already swept out of the changing room.

I hung back to take in my reflection, and by the time I'd re-emerged into the makeshift tent Vivienne was bartering energetically with the seller. She could have paid the full price easily, but she was addicted to the thrill of the chase. I didn't interrupt, and it was only when they shook on a deal that I realised she'd also bought a bright swimming costume for me to wear.

When I tried to pick the purchases off the counter to tell the woman there had been a mistake Vivienne grabbed them and made a joke of hiding them behind her back. 'Don't even think about it, you looked first class in that dress.'

I relented, standing a little taller than I had before. She placed it on the counter for the woman to fold up and then handed the bag to me.

'This is a start, but we're nowhere near done yet.'

We spent the rest of the afternoon pottering between the stalls in search of trinkets. Vivienne was engrossed by her mission to find the best bargain, but I couldn't focus. I kept spotting the navy blue of a police uniform out of the corner of my eye, but when I spun around there was nothing there, and by the time we got back to the hotel I was worn out.

As we walked across the lobby I spotted Robert reading a newspaper in a chair next to the sweeping staircase. He turned to look at us as Vivienne's heels clacked across the tiles, but she didn't give any indication that she had seen him.

We got into the lift and Vivienne hit the button for our floor. She didn't try to stop the doors when Robert hurried towards us, but he caught up and wedged his paper between them before they shut.

None of us said anything as the lift ground into motion and Vivienne ignored Robert, though I could almost hear the crackle of tension between them. The silence continued as we made the seemingly endless walk to our rooms, and I had to fight an urge to pick up my pace.

'See you for breakfast,' I said to nobody in particular when we finally reached the end of the corridor. I fumbled with my keys and hurriedly unlocked the door to my room.

When I was safely inside I hung up the clothes Vivienne had bought me and flopped back onto the bed, waiting for the inevitable argument to start.

Within minutes I heard the snipe of raised voices through the wall and strained to make out what they were saying. This carried on for several minutes, the voices getting louder but no more comprehensible, until something thudded against the wall I shared with their room.

I sat up. Vivienne was constantly bruised from the physicality of being thrown about at speed in a racing car, but I had never questioned whether there might be more to the purple marks that blossomed across her fair skin before.

There was another thud, this time further away, and I thought I caught a muffled moan of pain.

I stood up, unsure what to do, until my gaze snagged on the silver flash of the key Vivienne had left on my windowsill. Tiptoeing as quickly as I could towards the door that connected our rooms, I bent down and looked through the keyhole.

At first I could only see the wall, but as I leant further forward the back of Robert's shoulder came into view. Careful not to make a sound, I shuffled to my right and had to hold in a gasp when I saw Robert pinning Vivienne against the wall.

The viewpoint of the keyhole cut off both of their faces, but I could see a patch of sweat on the back of Robert's white shirt.

I bent down further to try and see the expression on Vivienne's face, but Robert shifted position so the back of his head was blocking my view.

I froze, my breath catching in my throat, until Robert moved again and I saw that they were locked together in a fierce kiss. Before I could react he lifted her up onto their dressing table and slid his hand up her thigh until it disappeared beneath her dress.

Vivienne moaned again, this time louder.

I knew I should look away, but I was frozen. My gaze was fixed on Vivienne as she tipped back her head and parted her lips and I felt a sickening tingling across my skin.

Lie to Me

It was only when Robert lifted Vivienne up and out of my line of sight that I snapped to and managed to pull myself away. I stumbled back to my bed and lay fully clothed in the dimming light.

As much as I tried to block them out, there was no escaping the noises now. I thought I heard Robert make a muffled attempt to shush Vivienne but her groans got louder and louder, and I lay rigidly on my back until they stopped.

It was only later when I was lying awake in the sticky heat that I wondered if she had wanted me to hear.

FOUR

I woke up unsettled by what I'd seen through the keyhole. During the early hours I had convinced myself that Robert and Vivienne would know I'd been spying on them – and when I thought about how long I'd stood watching them I broke out in a cold sweat.

My panic receded a little as the night crawled away and the familiar details of my room came into view, and at ten o'clock I worked up the courage to knock on Robert and Vivienne's door.

Robert let me in with his usual charm, and I perched across from where Vivienne was sat with her morning cigarette glowing between her fingers.

He was on good form as he chatted about the beaches he wanted to visit that day and poured me a coffee, though I'd started to notice that he treated me with the same detached public-schoolboy politeness he reserved for waiters and acquaintances.

Even if his greetings were never particularly warm, today his enquiries about how I was finding the new room seemed genuine enough, though I was convinced I saw a knowing smile flicker across Vivienne's lips as she blew out a plume of smoke.

I had grown accustomed to Vivienne's morning cigarette during the two weeks I'd stayed in their London flat before we went on tour. Vivienne had refused to even get out of bed until she'd had it, but when she was done she had a disconcerting habit of padding noiselessly down the shag-carpeted stairs. She had surprised me one morning while I was still wearing my flimsy dressing gown, and after that I would rush to my room whenever I got a whiff of smoke to avoid the indignity of the interaction.

Our leisurely coffee meant we left the hotel later than planned, and I was glad the bus was so busy that we had to sit apart. I found a seat near the front and stared out the window as we trundled past rows of gnarled olive trees, the potent odour of their fruit mingling strangely with sweat and diesel.

We were deposited some way from the beach and Robert cursed as we hacked our way through the scrubland, weighed down by our picnic. When we finally emerged at the beach our efforts were rewarded with a fabulous view stretching out in front of us: rolling sand and electric blue water framed by towering cliffs of chalky rock on either side.

Robert decided on a spot and unfurled the blanket so I could lay out a selection of doughy olive bread, hard cheese and tomatoes for our lunch.

I'd left Robert in charge of the drinks, and he was struggling with a stubborn bottle of home-made red given to us by one of the local shopkeepers when he let out a short laugh.

'It completely skipped my mind yesterday, but when I went to the American Express there was a letter waiting for me. Apparently the others are fed up of their hotel and want to join us at some point next week,' he said, turning his attention back to removing the cork. 'Though they might regret it when they see what a dump this new place is.'

'Did it say anything else?' I was trying to sound nonchalant, but Vivienne shot me a warning look.

In my distraction the knife slipped on the tomato I was cutting, and I bit back a yelp as a hot flash of pain pierced my finger.

'Not really, they said they've pretty much been doing the same things we have,' Robert said, and I felt my shoulders loosen a little with relief. He went back to opening the bottle, and I hid my throbbing finger. 'They've got the cars, so they've managed to get a bit of driving in. But mostly they're sunbathing and going swimming.'

Vivienne didn't seem particularly interested in Robert's news, but she looked up at the mention of the cars. 'Does that mean we'll be able to drive next week?'

'Yes, thank God. The cars should be coming over on the ferry with them.'

'Well, I guess that's something at least. It's driving me crazy not being able to practise.'

Finally, Robert managed to pull the cork off and it flew across the sand with a pop. While they were distracted by filling up the glasses I checked my hand, hastily wrapping it in a towel when I saw the slick of blood.

I was somehow both reassured and unsettled to learn that the others hadn't had any contact with the police. Either way, I wasn't sure how I felt about the prospect of them bowling in and upending our routine. The group included two couples – Marie and Hugo, and Anne and David – as well as Robert's co-driver Mark, and they all raced and partied and drank as if they were invincible.

At first I thought they were unbelievably polished, like the models and actors who appear to float above the inconveniences of real life. But the more time I spent silently observing them the more I noticed the cracks in their facade.

I was introduced to them at my first international rally in Monte Carlo. The race was 2,500 miles along relatively smooth roads from Lisbon, and even though it was snowy I was able to drive a few stretches with Vivienne supervising.

It would have been a steady introduction to rallying, but the relatively good terrain and stable weather only increased Vivienne's appetite for risk.

We flew through the first half of the course, and I soon understood the addiction these racers shared: the madness and sheer fun of chasing down the competition en route to some glitzy destination, the fleeting promise of glory goading them to push the car harder.

We were making good time, but just after the halfway mark Vivienne dared me to go faster and I lost control on the ice. Vivienne leant over to take control and I shut my eyes, feeling the sickening lurch of the tyres spinning uselessly beneath us, until the car crunched to a stop and my head whacked against the window.

The helmet had taken most of the impact, and I hesitantly ran my hands down my body.

'You're fine,' Vivienne barked, and my eyes snapped open. I followed her gaze behind me and my blood ran cold. A pointy branch had smashed clean through the window at the height of my bare neck, and if I'd been any further back I would have been impaled.

'Jesus Christ,' I gasped, but Vivienne had already jumped out the car and started kicking at the damaged branch.

'Come and help me,' she shouted. Disorientated, I hauled myself out and together we snapped off the branch so we could get going again.

'You haven't got any blood on you,' she said matter-of-factly as she caught me trying to slip my hand under the helmet to inspect my head, and I knew better than to complain about the pain.

My nerves weren't the only things that seemed to have frayed in the crash. The brakes were busted too, and for the rest of the course Vivienne had to ram the car against the cliff face to slow it down on the corners, ripping off the expensive paint job in a hideous squeal of metal against rock.

At one point she cut it so fine that we almost left the road, and that was when I saw Marie and Hugo for the first time. They overtook us unexpectedly with a triumphant wave that sent Vivienne into a foul-mouthed rant, and we set off in hot pursuit, cold air streaming in from the broken window behind us.

We were both watching the progress of their handsome Sunbeam Rapier out in front when they hit some ice – one moment the car was going like mad, and the next it stuttered and slid straight off the steep edge of the road.

Vivienne slowed down and cornered the bend as far from the edge as she could to avoid our car doing the same, and a grim silence descended over us as we rounded the corner and braced for what we might find.

Unbelievably, the car had been caught by two trees, and although it was upside down and the roof had been squashed in, Marie and Hugo waved to show us that they were quite all right.

They hung in the trees for a few moments until Marie threw her weight against the door and the car rolled off and righted itself. I unbuckled myself ready to run over and help them, but they set straight off – the roof slowly growing back to its original height as Hugo shimmied onto the back seats and kicked out the dent with his boots.

Other than those incidents I found the Monte course decent, but I soon discovered it was better loved for its swinging parties than for the race itself.

All the hip hotels like L'Hermitage, Hotel de Paris and the Metropole had at least one cocktail party every night in honour of the event, and Vivienne and Robert went to them all – splashing in the hotel pools with their finery still on and dancing wildly into the night.

Even after dark everything was seen as a test of daring by these racers, although the favoured activities by that point in the day were drinking, gambling and sex. It was the traditional duty of the winner to remove the last garment from the stripper at the Ali Baba, and from there on out it was a race to the bottom.

Vivienne rapped her knuckles impatiently against her glass and I jumped, letting the towel slip from my fingers. I inspected the cut, which had stopped bleeding, and sloshed some water over it to wash away the dried blood. Using a fork, I placed the unspoiled tomatoes on a plate and urged the others to tuck in.

Robert hummed away while Vivienne and I ate our lunch in silence, and my gaze was drawn to a group of athletic young men charging into the sea. They disappeared under the glassy water, resurfacing like seals with shiny slicked-back hair to bob about in the shallows.

When we'd finished the food I had laid out, Vivienne rooted around in the bag to see if there was anything left. 'I fancy something sweet, you haven't hidden anything in here have you?'

I shook my head apologetically, and she turned around to scour the beach.

'You're not going to find an ice cream van here, Viv—' Robert started, but she cut him off.

'Look.'

There was a man selling fruit from a box by the sandy track, and Vivienne ran barefoot to pick something up. She paid with a handful of coins and skipped back over the hot sand to land on our picnic blanket, depositing a flurry of sand and a paper bag of flat peaches between us.

We tore the flesh from the fruit and hurled the stones into the sea, and with our hunger finally sated we pulled our towels into the shade. The other two stripped down to their swimsuits to get some relief from the heat, but I held back.

I had tried on the swimming costume Vivienne bought me in my room with the aim of building up my confidence, but looking at myself under the lurid lighting had only made me feel worse. The front was conservative enough, though the lime green material was a little thin for my liking, but the back was a different story – swooping down low to expose an awful lot of my bare skin.

I looked over at Vivienne in her red bikini. She had fully embraced the trend for two-piece swimsuits after it had raged through France, but she looked decidedly out of place on this quiet beach where the men ogled her curves and the local women tutted behind her back.

When I was sure Vivienne and Robert had shut their eyes I peeled off my dress and lay back, my knotted muscles loosening as the heat of the sand burnt through my thin towel onto my exposed skin.

I must have drifted off quickly and slept for some time, because when I woke with a start the sun had moved over and I could feel the telltale sting of sunburn across the bridge of my nose. I blinked my eyes open to see Robert waving his hand so the shadow danced across my face, and he chuckled when I flicked him with my dress.

I glanced over to where Vivienne was lying and caught her watching me. Her pale skin was framed against the dark material of her hat, and even though we were at the beach her makeup was immaculate – a thick black flick of liner painted precisely across the crease of her eye. I smiled lazily and turned my face away from the sun.

It was Vivienne's makeup that had fascinated me most when I came face-to-face with her for the first time, several years after I'd glimpsed her in the yard. She whirled into one of the stables in a cloud of floral perfume, and I was surprised to find that I recognised her instantly despite the intervening years. I snuck glances at her from the corner where I was sat on a stool, mesmerised by the way her pale face powder seemed almost to absorb the light.

My mother had left when I was very young and the stables were frequented by country men and their ruddy wives, so I didn't have any real-life exposure to makeup before Vivienne, though hers could hardly be described as such. She looked more like one of the impossible porcelain beauties in the copies of *Queen* magazine I saved up to buy from the village shop than anyone I'd seen in person, and she wielded her mesmerising beauty like a sword.

Anyone who set eyes upon Vivienne, men and women, fell under her hold. Even Mr Grant, the red-faced owner of the stables, wasn't immune to the charm she laid on when enquiring into housing her horse there.

'I'm sure we can sort something out,' he said, taking a drag on his cigarette. 'When were you thinking of moving the old fellow here?'

'I brought Maverick with me on the off-chance you might be able to find somewhere today,' she said, batting her heavily coated lashes. 'I'm going travelling soon, and I was really hoping to find him a new home before I leave.'

'Well of course, I'll see what we can do.'

'That's awfully kind of you,' Vivienne said, and he reddened even more when she placed a hand on his arm.

Normally I would have smirked at Mr Grant's embarrassment, but I felt with some certainty that I would not have been able to breathe if she'd turned to look at me, so I didn't even allow myself a smile.

'Actually, you know what, I have an idea,' he said, throwing his hands up. 'We have a few horses we can move to free up some space in the stable next to the barn. How does that sound?'

'Oh, thank you,' she cooed, and he dismissed her thanks with a magnanimous wave of the hand.

He strode over to the door to put his brilliant plan into action and caught sight of me. He flinched as if he'd forgotten I was there, and Vivienne turned to look at me properly for the first time. I wasn't sure if her high, perfectly arched brows were always this shape, or if she was surprised to see me sat there too.

'I can move the horses, if you'd like?' I said, jumping to my feet and hurrying outside before she had time to take in my lank hair and bobbled jumper with her cool gaze. The frosty gravel crunched beneath my feet as I marched across the drive, and when I looked back I was relieved to see that neither of them had followed me.

The squeak of the stable doors brought two of the horses trotting over to greet me, and my favourite nuzzled the skin under my ear. I let him rest his speckled head on my shoulder for a few minutes, and the warm weight of him calmed me before I approached the less friendly horses on the other side of the barn. Their ears slanted back as I opened the door to the bitter cold outside, though they came willingly enough when I offered them some carrots.

Once I'd let them into their new homes I took a detour to the bathroom to smarten myself up, buttoning my coat over my tatty jumper and scraping back my hair to disguise the separating strands.

I took a deep breath and walked back to find Vivienne standing outside the stable with one of the most statuesque horses I'd ever seen.

'Thanks for doing that,' Mr Grant said, appearing at my side.

'Sure, I was happy to,' I said, keeping my gaze on Vivienne and Maverick. 'He's a beauty, isn't he?'

He chuckled. 'Aye, he is.' We watched Vivienne run a hand along his chestnut brown flank, singing him a gentle song as if she was unaware of us standing there.

'Do you want me to settle him in?' I asked, mustering up the courage to introduce myself.

'Don't you worry about it. I'll take care of him today.'

I didn't protest. I was relieved I could turn back to the shelter of the stable without having to interrupt Vivienne's spell, though there was also a small part of me that felt disappointed. A part that took me by surprise.

'Good morning,' Vivienne said in a sing-song voice, waking me from my dream.

'How long have I been asleep?' I said groggily, the woman from my memory merging seamlessly into the one who was lying next to me.

'About an hour. You must have been tired, you were snoring within minutes.'

The stinging on my nose had got worse, and the skin was sore to touch. 'Do I look burnt?'

Lie to Me

'Doesn't look like it.' She lifted her shades. 'You're lucky, I'd look like a lobster if I stayed in the sun for that long without tanning oil.'

'I do feel rather burnt,' I admitted.

When I sat up I found Robert's towel rumpled and vacant, and quickly spotted him standing in his swim shorts by the sea. He had attracted the attention of a young woman in a polka dot bikini and stopped on his way past to chat.

'I've got some oil with me if you want to put some on,' Vivienne said, narrowing her eyes at the woman. 'You can top me up too.' She pushed her bag over to me through the sand and I rifled through it until I found the curvy glass bottle of Ambre Solaire.

I poured some of the golden liquid into my hand and breathed in the subtle rose scent – the one that Vivienne trailed behind her whenever she left a room. I slathered some over my arms and legs and made sure to rub it all in carefully.

Unsure if Vivienne had been serious about topping her up, I pretended I hadn't heard. But when I went to put the bottle back in her bag she stopped me, lying on her front and undoing the straps of her bikini top so that her bare back was exposed. I checked Robert was still distracted and leant over her to rub the oil into her shoulders and then across the top of her neck.

'Don't be shy.'

I tried not to think about what I'd seen the night before as I slid my hand down to do her lower back, too flustered to make sure it was all rubbed in.

'Let's see the swimming costume then,' she said when I was finished. 'Give us a twirl.'

Embarrassed, I stood up and turned around on the spot as fast as I could.

'You wouldn't make a very good model spinning around like that,' she laughed. 'But you've got the legs for it.'

I flushed, suddenly desperate to run down to the sea and submerge myself in the icy water. My legs weren't something I'd ever thought about before, but I supposed I'd developed a certain athleticism from years of working at the stable.

'Do you want to come in for a dip?' I asked out of politeness, but I was relieved when she shook her head. 'I'll stay here and watch, but you go.'

'Suit yourself,' I said, jumping from foot to foot on the burning sand. The pain took my mind off my unease at Vivienne's eyes following me, and it was a relief when my feet met the cool water.

After I'd tentatively submerged the rest of my body I shouted over to Robert, but he continued chatting with the woman on the beach. I was overcome by an urge to splash him, and before I could think twice about it I had swum over and flicked a handful of water at his torso.

The woman yelped and I tried to swim away but Robert dived into the water and caught up with me, shovelling handfuls of water towards me until I started to splutter uncontrollably.

I thought I caught a cold glint of anger in his eyes, but by the time I'd managed to wipe away the stinging water there was no trace of anything but easy mirth.

'Pick on someone your own size next time,' he said when we reached the safety of the shallows. I splashed him again less forcefully and this time he kept his cool.

I waded further into the water until I could no longer touch the seabed and set off in a languid breaststroke.

'Race you to that rock. I'll give you a head start,' Robert said, appearing to dismiss all thoughts of the disgruntled woman he'd left on the beach as he counted to five and dived into the sea in a graceful arc.

Struggling behind, I kicked my legs as hard as I could while he propelled his bulky frame through the water with surprising ease. I had only made it halfway to the towering mass of rock by the time he got there, so I decided to cut my losses and turn back. I was a strong swimmer, but even I didn't like being this far out.

Manoeuvring myself around awkwardly with my arms and legs flailing, I eased into a steady front crawl.

When I got back to the cove I waded through the crystal water until it was up to my waist and watched the fish flit past under the surface. I'd assumed Robert was still near the rock, but when I glanced up he was stood in the shallows looking at me strangely.

'Say, is that new?'

'This?' I pulled at the thin material of my swimming costume.

'It suits you.'

'Oh, thanks,' I said, taken aback.

I realised I'd seen this look before. It was the one he gave to an attractive waitress or a woman he might decide to strike up a conversation with at a bar.

Robert was a terrible flirt – that was no secret, and Vivienne was just as bad – but I'd never even entertained the thought that he might notice me that way before.

'What happened to your hand?'

Before I could reply he'd taken hold of my arm and gently turned it over to inspect the cut, which had started bleeding again.

My arm was tense under his touch, and when he ran his finger absent-mindedly along my skin the hair stood on end.

'It's fine, I'll just splash some salt water on it.' I pulled my arm away hastily and tried not to wince as I sluiced some sea water over it.

I turned back to the shore to see Vivienne stretched out with her hat pulled over her face, but I could still feel the burn of Robert's gaze on the back of my neck. Seized by a sudden restlessness, I waded back out into the sea and set off in a strong front crawl. This time I didn't stop until I reached the rock.

When I got there I checked for sea urchins and pulled myself up. Slowly but surely I scaled to the top, and when I'd heaved myself up I stood so my toes were dangling over the edge. I scoured the water for shadows that might betray anything lurking in the water below – but there was only pure, crystal blue. I took a deep breath and jumped.

My stomach lurched as I flew through the air and I gasped as I hit the wall of cold water, accidentally swallowing a mouthful.

I spluttered, unable to breathe, and my head slipped below the surface.

Flailing my arms and legs around, this time I managed to keep my head up long enough to cough up the water and take a shaky breath.

Lie to Me

Kicking my legs hard, I treaded water until I'd managed to spit out the rest of the water and swam close enough to the rock to grab hold of it if I got into trouble again.

In need of a rest before I attempted to make it back to shore, I lay on my back gulping air and letting the salty sea hold me, newly aware of my glistening skin and the strength of my body.

My panic and shame of the early hours had been replaced by a humming energy – the anxiety was still there, but also a strange anticipation about the potential of summer and what was to come.

FIVE

Our days in Igoumenitsa began to organise into a loop, and it became increasingly difficult to distinguish each cloudless sequence from the next. We would lounge about on Robert and Vivienne's balcony until noon and then catch the bus to one of the sandy beaches to bob in the shallows. When the sky turned pink we knew it was time to return home, and the next day we'd do it all over again.

During the daytime it was easier to go along with Vivienne's pretence that everything was fine. I was distracted by Robert and his high jinks, and I made the most of the temporary oblivion that came with plunging into the icy sea from the rocks. Sometimes it was almost possible to pretend that Corfu had all been a bad dream when the sun was shining, but as the evenings closed in and we went our separate ways I had to face my thoughts alone.

I lay wide awake on my back and listened to the motorbikes whizzing up and down the narrow street. Every night I convinced myself the darkness would never lift, but eventually the dull blue light of dawn snuck up on me and I would quietly let myself out of my room.

As I followed the road down to the sea I pushed away the niggling conviction that I should make the most of the quiet to dispose of the bag. I told myself there was no rush as long as it stayed hidden under my bed.

At the port there was a kiosk with so many newspapers strung up on a thin spool of wire that the colour of the walls underneath remained a mystery. It became my ritual to tentatively awaken the gruff shopkeeper who slept with his balding head in his hands and buy the only English-language newspaper and a few more regional ones before wandering down to the water's edge.

Sitting on the rough concrete, I watched as fish flicked through the glassy water before disappearing into the shadows underneath my legs. I allowed myself this moment of solace until the fishing boats cut through the calm, and then I wandered the streets in search of a *kafeneio* where I could sit and read the papers.

When I found somewhere suitable, I would order coffee and a sweet bougatsa pastry and flick through the thin pages. The news I was looking for was unlikely to make the national paper, so I read that one first to ease me in then turned to the regionals. After looking through the photos I gave the dense print a quick scan for Κέρκυρα, the Greek word for Corfu, and then pored over the text another time to make sure.

Only once did I come across a mention of the island, and in my panic I stared at the innocuous word until the unfamiliar characters blurred together. I didn't know any Greek and the small column had no pictures, so I steeled myself and went up to the man who owned the coffee shop. I pointed at the headline and at first he seemed confused, but I had managed to speak to him using a little English when I ordered my coffee so I persisted.

'What does this say please?' I said, my voice loud and slow.

He knotted his bushy brows together and considered it. It was still early and we were the only two people in the room, and my breath was frightfully loud in the silence.

'Unknown woman killed,' he said finally, struggling to grasp the words.

'Thank you so much,' I said in one long exhale, trying to stop my shoulders from visibly slumping. The relief was so intense that tears sprung to my eyes, and I hastily wiped them away before I let go completely.

The man looked at me oddly and I gave him a weak smile as I turned back to my table.

Once I'd had a moment to process what I'd heard, my elation at the horrible news made me feel a bit sick, but I made myself take a gulp of the fortifying Greek coffee and scanned the rest of the news.

Only once I'd finished checking all the newspapers did I feel calm enough to eat. All of a sudden I realised I was ravenous, and once I'd finished picking at the flaky crumbs I bought three more pastries to take up to Robert and Vivienne's room.

Every day I delivered breakfast with a rundown of what I'd read in the news, watching Vivienne closely as she unwrapped the bougatsas. If I blinked I would miss it, but the only acknowledgement I ever got was a twitch of relief that played across her lips.

We still spent most of our afternoons at the beach, though it felt like our lazy days were numbered. Robert had told the others where we were staying, and every time we returned to the hotel

I expected them to be waiting for us in the lobby with their monogrammed suitcases, Marie's painted lips curled in disdain.

Much to Robert's exasperation I started finding reasons to extend our walk back from the bus stop, veering away from the road to identify the trilling of a songbird or look at a cat curled up tightly in a ceramic bowl.

I was taking one such detour to admire the dainty, purple-flowered branches of a jacaranda tree when I heard a distant wailing. Vivienne and Robert must have missed it because they continued to march along the road but I stopped to listen, the cobbles tacky under my feet with the mulch of fallen petals.

'What are you doing?' Robert called back lazily when he realised I'd dropped behind, but he didn't slow his pace.

Ignoring him, I stepped back against a rough stone wall to let a harassed-looking woman with several squabbling children pass. I waited until their voices had faded and tried to block out the other background sounds. There was the usual chatter from the open windows and the rumble of motorbikes whizzing up and down the adjacent streets, but after a minute or so I heard the wailing cut through the air once again.

'What unfortunate animal have you found this time?' Robert had marched back to chivvy me along and was stood in front of me with his arms crossed.

The sound started up again and I held a finger to my lips to quiet him. It was a bit like the yelp of a dog, but more high-pitched, and it was far too loud to be the cry of a baby. It made my hair stand on end.

Robert wrinkled his nose and cocked his head, hearing it too.

The wails multiplied, and I turned to follow them down a narrow side street. He hung back to call Vivienne over and then I heard the heavy tread of his footsteps following close behind me as he caught up.

After a few false starts we found a path that seemed to lead towards the noise, and as we ventured further into the warren of passages I made out the raw tune of what sounded like a fiddle slicing through the air. This was joined by clapping and chanting as we got closer, broken up every now and then by a blood-curdling wail.

We came up against a few more dead ends before we finally reached a squat stone building on the corner of a small square, its net curtains drawn against the glare of the dying sun. A few moments later a breathless Vivienne arrived and the three of us stood in a row, listening to the frightful sounds.

'I think it's coming from in there.' Robert pointed towards the building.

'This is silly, let's just go straight inside and see what's happening,' Vivienne said, but we ignored her.

I pressed my face up to a grimy window but the net curtains were pulled so tightly across that it was impossible to see what was happening, though I could just make out dark shapes moving around the room.

'It's awfully loud, there must be a door open somewhere,' Robert said in a stage whisper, his attempts to stay quiet redundant against the raucous noise coming from the house. We edged around the corner to find that there was a side door open and tiptoed closer until we could see in.

Lie to Me

My eyes took a while to adjust to the dim light, but from what I could see there was about a dozen men and women wearing sombre suits and long black shawls despite the stifling heat. When I could make out a bit more I noticed that most of them were much older than the energy of their movements suggested, though I was unsettled by the blank expression behind their eyes.

A chill took hold of me as we watched them shuffling around, wailing when the impulse took them and raising their arms in a blind salute. I was so mesmerised by the spectacle that it took me a few minutes to notice the man staring at us from the corner of the room. I squinted, trying to make out his face, and was caught off guard when he stood up and walked towards us.

'What are you doing?' Robert said irritably as I pulled him away from the entrance, but I was too slow. The man's eyes flashed gold as he stepped into the light, but before I could place them he reached out and took hold of my arm.

My heart skipped a beat.

'Jean,' he said warmly, and I recognised him as the policeman from the port. 'This is a nice surprise.' He said it almost as if he was an old friend who had been waiting for me, and I caught Robert and Vivienne exchanging a bemused look.

They waited expectantly for me to say something, and I realised I didn't know his name. There was an awkward pause before he saved me by introducing himself as Konstantin, shaking Robert's hand and giving Vivienne a kiss on both cheeks. She raised her eyebrows at me coyly behind his back and I felt the blood rush to my face.

'So what's going on here then?' Robert said, and I grasped for something coherent to say.

'We met when I lost you at the port. Konstantin's a policeman.' I shot a warning look at Vivienne, but when I turned to Robert I saw that he looked horribly like he might be about to laugh.

I could see why; Konstantin looked much younger out of uniform, and the shirt he was wearing betrayed his slender frame. Without a cap, his snub nose made his face look almost girlish, but his large watchful eyes put me on edge.

'You're just in time,' Konstantin said enthusiastically. He gestured towards the swaying people as another round of howling broke out.

'What in God's name is that?' Robert said.

'*Anastenaria*. It's a holy ceremony. They're praying to the saints,' Konstantin explained patiently.

'They sound like they've been possessed,' Robert joked, and I forcefully pushed away any thoughts of the devil the old woman had found in my coffee cup.

'Something like that,' Konstantin said, beaming at me. 'They're going to walk on fire this evening.'

'Fire?' Vivienne said, her interest piqued.

'Yes. Later we'll set a bonfire and put hot coals there,' he said, pointing to a pile of logs stacked up in preparation. 'And then they'll walk over them – with no shoes.' He left a pause for dramatic effect.

'Won't that hurt?' Robert asked, grimacing at the thought.

'No. The saints will protect them,' he replied matter-of-factly. 'Come with me. It will be a long night so we should have some food first.'

He started towards a narrow street and gestured for us to follow.

'Must we?' I tried to protest, but Robert quickly made the decision for us.

'Let's go,' he said, and the three of us struggled through the dry heat to catch up.

We followed Konstantin through the winding streets until he stopped outside an inconspicuous building and opened the door, releasing a waft of burnt butter followed by something rich and meaty. I stepped inside to find a large living room filled with people chatting, some sat on the floor and others on wicker chairs that had been spaced out around the room.

'Welcome,' Konstantin said, shooing a group of young boys away and pulling the chairs they'd vacated into a semicircle for us. 'Sit down and I'll get you something to eat.'

A group of women in black shawls looked up and gave us a row of gap-toothed grins, the harsh light of the lamp catching in the folds of their leathery skin. I smiled back uncertainly.

'Something to drink,' Konstantin said, reappearing with three perilously full cups of wine that he distributed carefully. I sniffed at the yellowy liquid and it smelt unusually sweet. '*Yamas*.' Konstantin took a quick sip of his own drink before reaching over to chink it against mine. I took a gulp and winced, the bitter aftertaste making my teeth sing.

'It's home-made,' he said proudly.

I took another tentative sip. It didn't taste so bad now that I was prepared, and when I took another I could almost make out a lemony taste.

When Konstantin went in search of some food, I leant over to Vivienne. 'I think we should leave. He's a policeman.'

'Stop it, it will be fine as long as you don't draw attention to us,' she hissed quietly. 'It might be useful to have him onside.'

'What's that?' Robert said, but Vivienne shook her head.

Konstantin returned a few minutes later balancing plates piled high with dips and mezes. I took one from him and cut into the cheesy top of what looked like a hefty block of pasta to find that it was softer, with a potato centre and aubergines underneath. I tried a small forkful, but I couldn't manage such rich food while I felt so trapped in the sticky heat of the room.

Once everyone else had finished their food the chairs were pulled aside and some of the men began a slow tapping dance to the accompaniment of a strange elongated guitar. They started in a line with their hands on each other's shoulders, stepping back and forth, and swinging their legs into low lunges to appreciative whoops from the crowd.

They gathered more dancers from the people watching as the guitar picked up pace, and soon there was a loose circle snaking around the room. Konstantin pulled me up to dance with him and I muddled my way through the steps, apologising repeatedly as I stepped on his toes. We'd each had several glasses of wine by that point, and the movement made me dizzy.

We bowed out of the next dance and Konstantin pulled me towards the kitchen to search for more food.

'So what are the three of you doing here? I still don't really understand,' he said once he'd managed to locate a tray of baklava hidden in the corner of the room.

'We're travelling,' I said curtly.

'So it's just been the three of you in Igoumenitsa for all this time?' I nodded. 'But they're married. Is that strange?'

'No,' I said defensively, desperate to get away from him and his prying questions.

He offered me the box of baklava, refusing to take no for an answer when I tried to decline. I went to take a bite out of one but had to put the whole thing into my mouth to stop the syrup dribbling on my dress.

'I think I would find it odd travelling around with a married couple. They're quite a lot older,' he shrugged.

'I suppose it's a bit unusual but it's nothing untoward,' I said, uncertainty creeping into my voice. I couldn't help but notice the dimples in his cheeks as he wrinkled his nose at the unfamiliar word. 'Let's go back to see what the others are doing,' I suggested, but when I tried to slip away he ushered me back to the dance floor.

My hands felt sweaty in his, and I threw myself into the movements to stop him from noticing that I was shaking.

As the music quickened and the shadows crept along the floor, the crowd seemed to become restless for the main event. Eventually the band ground to a halt and a man shouted something, prompting everyone to move in unison towards the door. Konstantin grabbed my hand and I had to resist the urge to jerk it out of his surprisingly firm grip as he led me out of the room.

When we reappeared at the square the bonfires were starting to die down, the logs collapsing in on one another in a puff of white embers that fluttered perilously close to our bare skin before dropping to the ground.

A man with a chunky stringed instrument was scraping out the monotonous tune we'd heard earlier in the day and a drummer joined in, tapping out a firm beat as the fire-walkers started swaying and dragging their feet along the floor.

I saw something glint in one of their hands and Konstantin nudged me, pointing towards it.

'It's an icon.'

I watched as the woman kissed it and made the sign of the cross in front of her chest. Another woman appeared behind her with a stick of incense, and the heady aroma swirled around me.

I'd hoped to slip away in the darkness, but the more people that joined the circle of onlookers the closer I was forced to stand next to Konstantin. There was music and shouting all around us, but all I could hear was the blood pounding in my ears.

When the last of the logs had burnt down a group of men used long poles to spread out the coals until they formed a throbbing crimson oval in front of our feet. The fire spat violently, but when I tried to back away into the crowd Konstantin grabbed my hand again.

As the preparations drew to a close the fire-walkers began to work themselves into a frenzy, some of them rocking backwards and forwards so violently that I had to avert my eyes.

A few minutes later I heard a shout rise up from the crowd and looked back to see an old man dancing along the hot coals, his steps raising sparks and puffs of smoke. Another man stepped forward to join him, while one woman knelt down at the edge of the coals to pound the steaming ground with the bare palms of her hands.

I looked closely at their blank faces, illuminated just enough by the embers and the moon above to see that they didn't so much as flinch as the fire licked at their bare skin.

The evening wind was starting to pick up, and a sudden gust sent a cloud of smoke from the charred remains of the bonfire across the dancers.

It took a few seconds to clear, but when it did I spotted the old lady who had read my coffee cup stood in the middle of the hot coals, her arms outstretched and her eyes rolling back in her head. I watched her, horrified, until her eyes flicked back to the crowd and a twisted look of recognition lit up her face as she saw me.

Even though part of me knew I should back away, I was transfixed by her slack face. She shuffled closer, and when she reached the edge of the coals she hissed at me, repeating something over and over in a monotonous rhythm before unleashing another volley of Greek.

I put my hands up to placate her, but she grabbed hold of them with her swollen fingers and I yanked them away as if her touch had burnt me.

'What did she say?' I begged Konstantin as the old woman shuffled back into the fold.

'She's talking nonsense. She says you're guilty,' he said with a shrug. 'But God knows what of.'

'Excuse me?'

He lowered his voice and leant in closer. 'She says you're guilty. You've got blood on your hands.'

The ground shifted under my feet.

'Don't listen to her,' Konstantin said, shaking his head in the direction of the old woman. 'Are you OK? You're white.'

I tried to choke out a response but it came out as a cough. 'I'll get you some water,' he said, and I lurched over to the building to lean against the solid stone, my head spinning.

When I'd built up the courage to look up again the old woman was gone.

'Here you go.' Konstantin passed me a cup of water and I downed it gratefully. 'I'm sorry. She thinks she's an oracle, but she's nothing more than a mad lady.'

We were sat close to the scalding remnants of the fire, but I was shivering uncontrollably.

'Are you OK?'

'I'm fine, I think I'm just tired,' I said unconvincingly.

Konstantin shuffled closer and we watched as the fire-walkers showed off the unblemished soles of their feet as they stepped off the coals.

'You look cold,' he said when I continued to shiver. He retrieved a blanket from the building and draped it around me, and I felt a sudden swell of fondness towards him.

Slowly the music came to a halt, and I recovered a little of my strength as I focused on the warmth of his body next to me.

I'd lost sight of Robert and Vivienne in the crowd, but I couldn't face hanging around to look for them. I pushed myself up using the wall and Konstantin scrambled to help me. He held out his arm and I leant on him as we walked past the glowing coals to the road.

Scanning the crowd for the coffee-reader, I spotted her standing on the edge of a group of older men and women. They looked fragile and bird-like in their billowing black garments now they'd stopped dancing, but there was still a crazed look in their eyes.

I tightened my grip on Konstantin's arm and looked the other way.

A heavy tiredness came over me as we walked back to the hotel, and he kept up an encouraging stream of chatter to help me along – though all I could focus on were the woman's words echoing around my head.

Guilty.

'Almost there now,' Konstantin said as we neared the entrance and I nodded, my eyelids drooping.

I didn't have the energy to dismiss his determined offer to help me to my room, and when we reached the end of the corridor he had to take the keys out of my shaky hands and open the door.

'Sit down, I think you've caught a chill. I'll make you a drink,' Konstantin said once we'd got inside. I tried to stop him but he insisted, so I lowered myself down to sit on the edge of the bed.

He went to the kitchenette at the end of the corridor and came back with a strong cup of tea, using one of my well-thumbed magazines as a mat. I mumbled my thanks as he perched beside me on the edge of the bed. 'Will you be OK here on your own now?'

I was desperate for him to stop asking questions and leave me alone with my secrets – but a shameful part of me also wanted to unburden myself of the terrible weight of what I'd done.

He looked on with concern as I slopped some of the tea onto the bed. I think he expected me to say something to reassure him, but I couldn't find the right words. We sat there in silence, listening to the ticking of the clock until I finished my tea.

'I'll leave you to rest,' he said eventually, and panic surged through me at the thought of being alone again. 'Are you sure you'll be OK here?' he said as if reading my mind.

'Yes, I'll be fine,' I said, my eyes prickling. I couldn't afford for him to be around long enough for me to let something slip in my tiredness. 'Please go.'

He didn't look convinced, but eventually he got up and I gave him a meek wave as he pulled the door behind him with a click.

When his footsteps had receded I got off the bed and slid myself along the floor to pull the holdall out from its hiding place. Blood rushed to my head as I stood up, and I had to steady myself against the bed.

I unzipped the holdall, carefully slipping my hand down the lining and pulling out the crumpled bag at the bottom.

Guilty. The word flapped and faltered around my head like a trapped bird.

I'd pushed the memory of Corfu away so forcefully that I had almost slipped into denial, but now I could feel the familiar sensation of the walls closing in on me again.

Breathing hard, I rolled up the bag and stumbled out of the room with it tucked under my arm, straining my eyes in the dark to check for Konstantin's lanky frame. My footsteps echoed in the empty lobby, and when I got outside the only other sound was the distant wail of cats fighting.

I hurried along the street, feeling more conspicuous with every shaky step. Eventually I passed an overflowing bin and paused; I'd been hesitant to dispose of the bag in such a public place, but I didn't think there was much chance of the police searching here.

I held my breath and pushed the bag inside, burying it under the slime of old food and soggy packaging. When my fingers finally scraped the bottom I pulled my arm out and ran, Konstantin's begrudging translation of the old woman's words playing in my head.

You're guilty. You've got blood on your hands.

SIX

I woke early but drifted back into a half sleep, tossing and turning in the rough sheets until I became aware of a knocking on the adjoining door. As I came to, I recognised Vivienne's insistent rapping and scrambled out of bed.

'Wait a second. I'm just getting dressed,' I called out, doing a quick sweep of the room to make sure it was tidy.

A flash of metal caught my eye, and I realised the key was still on the windowsill where Vivienne had left it. I grabbed it and hid it under my pillow – at least this way I could lock the door securely from my side.

Hastily retrieving last night's dress from where I'd left it in a puddle on the floor, I pulled it over my head and opened the door.

'They're here,' Vivienne said, without any attempt at a greeting.

My thoughts flew to the surly policemen with their guns, and I imagined Nikos's look of horror as they filled his pristine lobby with their dusty shoes.

'Marie and the others,' she clarified when she saw my panicked expression.

'Oh.'

'I know, I was beginning to think they'd never come,' she said wistfully.

'When did they get here?'

'A few hours ago. They came on the early ferry.'

She looked at me and cocked her head to the side as if seeing me properly for the first time. 'You look awfully pale. I think you could do with some sweet tea.'

'Yes please,' I murmured.

She got to her feet and walked purposefully towards her room, but I called her back before she got there.

'Wait, Vivienne. Can I talk to you?'

She turned slowly, eyes wide and wary.

'Of course. What's wrong?'

'Could you close the door?'

'It's OK. Robert took the others to find some breakfast and they won't be back for at least another hour,' she said, coming back to sit next to me.

'I feel so guilty,' I said tentatively. 'About Corfu. I can't stop thinking about it.'

I was expecting at least a crack in her composure, or an admission that it had been eating at her too, but her face remained closed and the silence gaped between us.

'It wasn't your fault,' she said eventually, taking my hand in a firm grip. 'It was nobody's fault.'

I felt a sudden surge of repulsion towards her and removed my hands.

'You know what those foreign police are like. They'd have locked us away and left us there to rot. All over an accident.'

'But Vivienne, what if they find out—'

'Jean, look at me,' she cut in. 'There's nothing you can do now. The police will never find out.'

'But—' I said, and she cut me off again.

'You don't have to think about what happened any more,' she said with renewed urgency. 'Promise me you won't.'

'Fine,' I said feebly. She squeezed my hand, and again I felt queasy at her touch.

'Promise?'

'Promise,' I said, this time a little louder.

'Good. I'll go and get you a cup of tea. Do you think you'll be feeling well enough to meet the others for lunch?'

I nodded and she gave me a smile that didn't quite reach her eyes.

'Can I tell you something?' she said, fixing me with a piercing gaze.

'Yes.' I tensed again.

'I don't want them here.'

'How come?'

'Marie and Hugo.' She pronounced their names in the way that Marie did with her thick French accent, rendering her husband's name *Ooh-goh*, and I let out a nervous stab of laughter in spite of myself.

'What did you think when you met them at that party in Corfu?'

'They seemed decent enough,' I said non-committally.

'Oh, come on, that's not an answer. What did you really think?'

I shook my head, but she persisted. 'Hugo first, don't feel like you need to hold back because of me.'

'We didn't get the chance to speak,' I said, thinking back to how his eyes had slid over me as if I was barely there and alighted on someone else.

'He's a hoot, and terribly rich, though God knows how he's managed to hang on to it after all his divorces. Marie must be at least the fourth Mrs Boucher, and I dare say she won't be the last.'

'Surely not.'

'If he doesn't start taking the racing more seriously, she'll take his cash and run. Did you know he's the only man who navigates for his wife?'

'No.'

'He only does it because it's the easiest way to come along for the ride. His partying drives Marie mad because she fancies herself something of a rising star – did you speak to her at all?'

'I saw her from a distance, but we didn't talk . . .' I trailed off as Vivienne marched out of the room to make a cup of tea.

The last time I had seen Marie and Hugo had been excruciating. Vivienne had driven us up a meandering mountain to a holiday house owned by one of her friends from London, and I felt quite sick by the time we'd reached our destination. The house itself was a monstrous white thing with Grecian statues positioned around the drive, and I knew I was out of my depth as soon as we stepped out the car.

In the flurry of greetings nobody noticed me standing there, and the host insisted on dragging Robert and Vivienne away to meet some of her other guests. I hung back awkwardly until they had gone inside and then made my way around to the garden by myself.

There were waiters milling around the lawn handing out glasses of champagne, but they kept passing me by until I went up and plucked one off the tray myself. I tried to catch the eyes of the other guests as I sipped my drink, but my efforts went unnoticed again.

I moved to stand in the corner of the patio and let the hum of voices wash over me until a man in a crisply ironed shirt sauntered towards me.

'Oh, sorry. I thought you were someone else,' he said when he got close enough to see me clearly in the fading light. I could only assume that he was already drunk because he took no shame in looking me up and down with an expression of mild distaste.

'Who are you here with?'

'Vivienne Fenwick.' I could see the back of her head over a sea of lacquered bobs, but I didn't bother pointing her out. The tales of her daredevil racing preceded her wherever she went.

The man perked up considerably at the mention of her name and asked me how I knew her. I tried to bluff my way out of it by muttering something vague about riding but I was out of luck; his sister was a professional showjumper who knew Vivienne from her days competing. We chatted about Vivienne for a few minutes, but when he realised I had only been a stable girl he left with a mumbled excuse about filling up his drink.

Humiliated, I skirted around the pool to where Vivienne and Robert were chatting with Marie and Hugo. Vivienne shot me a quick grin, but the rest of them gave me a disinterested nod and carried on with their conversation.

I looked down and jumped back with a squeal. There was a cheetah lying on the grass.

It blinked open its sad yellow eyes at the sound of my voice then shut them again.

'Don't mind him, he's harmless,' Marie said, hoicking the animal onto her hip.

The cat was a lean, muscly thing, and it had black marks like tear stains running from its closed eyes down to either side of its mouth. Its head lolled back when Marie bounced it on her hip to readjust it, and I realised it must be drugged.

Marie turned away from me to carry on with her story, and I stood silently on the edge of the group while her voice became more and more shrill. I couldn't bear to see the beautiful cat hanging there so limply, so I slipped away to find a lounger at the far corner of the patio where I could lie back unseen in the darkness and stare at the stars. I stayed there for quite some time, listening to the whisper of taffeta skirts as women brushed past my hiding place, until I heard Vivienne calling for me in the crowd . . .

'Here you go,' Vivienne said, drawing me from my memory as she swept back in with a steaming cup of tea.

'Thank you,' I said, wincing as my fingers met the hot china.

'Ah yes, the party. I thought you were going to faint when you saw that poor cat. *Meet my cheetah. I carry him around because I'm an attention-seeking bore,*' she said in her Marie accent, picking up a handkerchief and draping it around her neck as if it was the cat.

The impression was so accurate that a fit of the giggles bubbled up inside me until I could hold them in no more, and when Vivienne joined in I felt the unspoken distance that had hovered between us since Corfu start to melt away.

'She's a complete cow,' Vivienne said, emboldened by my laughter.

'I thought you were friends?' I said, rising to the bait. The hot tea scalded my lips as I took a fortifying sip.

'I suspect she thinks we are too.'

'She's not that much of a drag—' I started, but Vivienne was on a roll.

'And Hugo is far too old for her. It's rather a pity, otherwise I might have gone for him myself. He really is filthy rich.'

'Vivienne!' I exclaimed in mock horror, and she threw her head back with a brassy laugh.

'I know it's been difficult, but we'll get through this together. I promise.' And with that she left the room.

It was almost midday by the time we had both got ready and made our way down to the port, and the seafront was bristling with activity. Pink-faced holidaymakers sipped on their drinks while waiters hovered expectantly, ready to corner passers-by who lingered too long to look at the menus they'd chalked up on their boards.

I heard Marie and Hugo's rapid-fire French before we could see the taverna, but we had no problem spotting them when its striped parasols came into sight. Marie was wearing shorts and a lime green top, and even though they were only a party of two, they had pulled the best seafront tables together to monopolise the shade.

'Hello strangers,' Vivienne called out as we walked up behind them, and Marie jumped up in a tumble of long limbs and coiffed blonde hair. The women threw their arms around each other, and when they finally let go Vivienne bobbed down to greet Hugo, placing a dainty kiss on both of his cheeks. Hugo was as broad as Marie was slight, and despite the hour he was already smoking a cigar.

I hung back. Vivienne had done my makeup and I'd put on the dress she'd bought me at her insistence, but the starchy newness of it made the skirt hang stiffly away from my body.

'No cheetah today?' Vivienne said with some relief, looking around the legs of the chairs as if she expected it to be lurking there.

'*Non*, Hugo wouldn't let me send for him,' Marie pouted.

'Oh well,' Vivienne said breezily, pulling out a chair for me. 'Don't be shy, come and sit down. You remember Jean, don't you?' she said to the others.

'Of course, *enchanté*,' Hugo said. My slight hands disappeared in his fleshy grip, and I stayed behind the table to avoid being pulled into a kiss.

'We've been shopping. The dress suits her, doesn't it?' Vivienne said encouragingly.

'Greatly so,' Hugo said, and Marie shook her head at him in exasperation.

'Did your lovely car get over here in one piece?' Vivienne asked, and I wondered if Marie and Hugo's lack of familiarity with the subtlety of English tones shielded them from the sarcasm in her voice.

'It did, as did yours. I've already found an abandoned coastal road not too far out of town for us to practise on. We could go there tomorrow and do a little warm-up if you like,' Marie said, her eyes gleaming with the promise of a challenge.

Marie was fiercely competitive and, as she liked to tell anyone who would listen, her motto was to '*leeve dangerously*'. She used to be a professional tennis player and got to the semi-final of Wimbledon once, but when she realised she could make more money as a rally driver she never looked back.

She had only been racing a few years and wasn't as skilled as Vivienne, but Hugo was her secret weapon. At first I'd assumed rallying would be little more than a case of slapping a number on a decent family saloon and driving off, but I was woefully mistaken. If you wanted to get anywhere, you needed courage to the point of recklessness, flair – and most importantly, lots of cash.

Happily for Marie, her new husband was a fellow Frenchman who just so happened to be a wealthy marquis. And although he wasn't as passionate about rallying as she was, he was more than happy to buy her cars.

'Challenge accepted,' Vivienne said coolly, calling the waiter over and ordering two glasses of wine.

Despite the shade of the umbrella the heat was fierce, and I wondered how Marie and Hugo were coping so well with their fair skin and golden hair. My new dress was cool enough, but I felt as if the heavy makeup Vivienne had insisted on plastering over my face was trapping the sweat on my skin.

The waiter reappeared and placed the wine next to Vivienne. It had already begun to gather small drops of condensation in the heat, and I had an urge to reach across the table and press the cool, moist glass against my skin.

Robert arrived with Mark and David just as the waiter finished pouring our drinks. Vivienne stood on her tiptoes to return Mark's hesitant hug before turning to David, who made up for his short stature with his loud New York bray. I might have been imagining it, but I thought I saw Robert do a double take when he caught sight of me.

'You remember Jean,' Vivienne said, sliding a glass of wine over to me.

Mark, Robert's watchful English navigator, gave me a considered look before nodding in recognition, but I could tell David was struggling to place me.

'Don't tell me. You're an actress? A model?'

'She's Vivienne's latest *protégé*,' Hugo prompted him, and a look of understanding flashed across David's face.

'Ah, you're part of the circus then. Happy to have you along,' he said, and I gave him a weak smile.

'And what have you done with your lovely wife?' Vivienne said, rounding on David.

Anne was British and rather reserved, and she would have been easy to overlook within the group if it weren't for her tumbling mane of auburn hair.

'The journey tired her out so she went to lie down,' David said, and Vivienne looked unimpressed.

'Poor form from her, I hear the cars got here in better health?' she said, turning to Mark.

'I made sure I kept an eye on them.'

'Thank you, Mark. You're a gem.'

'Say nothing of it,' he said solemnly, pulling off his cap to reveal the bald patch that was creeping across his head.

The six of them fell into an easy patter of gossip about the other teams that would be joining us in Athens, and I felt more at ease among them than I ever had before. My gaze settled on the sailing boats weaving across the glistening sea, and I sipped at my wine until I felt a kind of loosening overtaking me.

'Jean.' David's booming voice made me jump. I had become accustomed to sitting silently on the fringes, so his sudden interest came as a shock.

He leant over and lowered his glasses to reveal piercing green eyes. 'Have you ever been to Greece before?'

'No, not before this trip,' I admitted.

He gave a mock gasp. 'But you're from England, right? How could you miss all this magic on your doorstep,' he said, waving his arms around. 'It takes us an absolute age to get here from New York, but even then it's still worth it.'

I opened my mouth to make an excuse, but he was already racing ahead.

'Wait until you see Athens, it sure is a fine city. The Acropolis, the food, the cobbled streets.' He dived into a long and rambling recollection of his previous trip and I nodded along, murmuring my agreement at the right moments until I heard one of the others mention Corfu.

I tried to tune in to their conversation while keeping track of what David was saying, but it was hard to hear their voices over his. Without warning, he stopped talking and looked right at me, and I realised he was expecting an answer.

'Sorry, I didn't catch that. I think I'm going a little bit deaf from swimming in the sea,' I lied.

'I said, where do the English prefer to travel then? Where did you used to go as a kid?' He said the words slowly and even more loudly than before.

My father loomed large as I tried to dredge up a memory that might serve as an anecdote – as always, the sweet smell of alcohol on his breath. I don't think he had ever been abroad save for the war, and the only holiday I could recall was a week spent in Cornwall with my mother before she left. I was probably too young to have any memories of my own, but I had reconstructed the smell of fish and chips and the salty breeze from a photograph I'd found slipped between the pages of a book in our house.

'We used to go to the coast,' I started, and was relieved when Marie leant over and placed a ring-laden hand on David's wrist, tearing his attention away.

'Vivienne was just asking what else happened in Corfu. I was going to tell her about our unexpected visitors, but really you should tell the story because you spoke to them.'

'The cops?' David said, and I gripped my chair. 'Glad to.'

'What did the police want with you?' Robert said, drawn in by the promise of a scandal. 'When was this?'

'Oh, about two weeks ago. Two boys who couldn't have been a day over sixteen turned up saying they wanted to ask us some questions. We were having a drink so I invited them in and offered them a brew, though they didn't look old enough.'

'Why did they come to the villa?' Vivienne asked, and I was impressed by how composed she sounded. I couldn't have uttered a word without giving myself away.

'Well, their English was appalling but eventually I worked out they wanted to take a look at my car.'

'The Mini? What were they looking for?' Robert said.

I held my breath.

'No idea, they wouldn't tell us.'

'Nothing at all?' Robert pressed.

'They wanted to know if we had any women staying with us, but I told them they weren't for sale unless they gave us a decent price.'

'David, *arrête*,' Marie scolded.

'Anyway, they insisted on getting Marie and Anne downstairs so they could have a look at them, but they didn't have much to say after I'd gone to the effort of dragging them away from whatever they were doing up there.'

'How odd,' Robert said, but I got the impression he'd lost interest.

'The only thing they asked us was whether Anne or I ever drove his car,' Marie chimed in, pointing towards David. 'I told them no, and I wouldn't be caught dead driving that kind of trash, but they didn't ask to see mine. It was still in the garage with yours so I just stayed quiet. I expect they didn't think women could have their own cars.'

'And then they just left?' I said, unable to hold myself back any more. 'They didn't ask where you were going or anything?'

Vivienne shot me a warning look and I knew my tone was revealing, but I was desperate for reassurance.

'I told them we were coming over here and then on to the Acropolis and sent them packing,' David said, puffing out his chest a little. 'I don't think we'll be having any bother from them again so no need to look so concerned.'

'Well done,' I said brightly, digging my fingernails into my thighs under the table.

'I suppose they were looking for something stashed away in the car? No doubt some petty theft from the village,' Robert said.

'I suspect they only questioned us to get a good look at our cars, but you know what these Europeans are like: always suspicious of us Americans.'

'And women,' Marie chipped in.

Keeping my gaze focused on my wine glass, I waited until David had changed the subject and excused myself to go to the bathroom.

It felt like I was floating as I weaved my way through the tables to the restaurant with its rudimentary metal kitchen tucked away at the back.

Locking the door of the tiny bathroom, I stumbled over to the sink and splashed water on my neck to compose myself, making sure not to disturb my makeup.

The body must have been found more than two weeks ago, but Vivienne's car had stayed hidden for all that time. It was the only remaining evidence and now it was back with us – waiting for someone to find it and punish us for what we did.

The rest of the evening passed without incident, and I was relieved to get back to my hotel room. But as I lay in bed I finally allowed myself to think back to our last night in Corfu. Our group had been scattered around the island in different hotels, but none of us fancied travelling anywhere in the heat so Vivienne, Robert and I picked up some cheap wine and took it down to the beach on our own.

We started drinking as soon as we'd laid out our towels, and by the time the sun started to dip, Robert was slurring his words. He grew restless as the evening wore on, eventually announcing that he needed to go to bed and staggering up to their room.

It had been a long day in the sun, and as much as I wanted to make the most of spending time alone with Vivienne, I could feel my eyelids drooping and had to give in shortly afterwards. I didn't like the idea of leaving her alone but she insisted, and there were still scores of families on the beach. As I climbed up the stairs of the hotel lobby I looked over my shoulder to see her lying on her back, a lazy smile on her face as she gazed up at the stars.

When I got back to my room I climbed straight into bed and must have drifted off quickly, but my peaceful sleep didn't last long.

Lie to Me

I woke while it was still dark to find Vivienne standing over me, and I let out a shrill yelp of shock.

'Shh, be quiet,' Vivienne hissed, and I could hear the urgency in her voice.

'How did you get in here?'

'We had the spare keys in our room. I needed to see you.'

'What's happened?' I flicked the lamp on, and I knew instinctively that something was very wrong when her gaunt face came into view.

'There was an accident,' she said, her lip quivering. 'With the car.'

I noticed for the first time that she was wearing her branded Saab driving gloves, and that she was clutching something closely in her grip.

I looked closer. It was a handkerchief, and my stomach turned when I saw the dark stain blossoming across the corner of the material and on the fingers of the gloves.

'What's going on? Are you all right?' I pushed myself up to a seated position, my thoughts flicking guiltily to the number of empty bottles we'd lined up on the beach. 'Why were you in the car?'

'I'm . . . not hurt,' she said, shaking violently despite the sticky night.

'That's all that matters.' I placed a steadying hand on her arm.

'No, no it's not. I lost control. And I didn't see them. There was someone else.'

My heart sank. 'What . . . What happened to them?'

She let out a quiet sob and a tear rolled down her cheek. I'd never seen her cry before, and the sight of it chilled me. 'You have to believe it wasn't my fault, Jean. I needed to go on a drive to clear my head and I took one of the cliff roads. It was so quiet and so dark and I wasn't expecting to see anyone. But then all of a sudden he was in front of me and I tried to swerve but I clipped him.'

'Was he in a car?' I said quietly, and she shook her head.

'No . . . I tried to stem the flow.' She held up a handkerchief and I recoiled. The metallic smell was unmistakable.

'Is he dead, Vivienne?' I demanded, trying to shock her into holding it together.

'Yes. And when I felt for his pulse I panicked.' She dropped her head to look at the floor. 'I didn't know what to do so I took his identification card and left him there.'

For a moment I was stunned. 'We should go to the police?' I said finally, and I was unnerved by the uncertainty that had crept into my voice.

'I can't go to the police, Jean. Once they take a look at the body they'll see what happened.' Her breath was coming in short, shallow gasps, and I recognised the early signs of hyperventilation.

'Slow down.' I emptied the contents of the nearest bag onto the floor so she could breathe into it.

'They'll lock me up in a Greek prison to make an example of me.' Her voice was muffled through the bag.

'Shh,' I said, momentarily lost for words. 'Does Robert know?'

'No, you can't tell him,' she said urgently. 'He's so black and white about things like this, I know he'd push me into confessing.'

'I'm sure he wouldn't,' I said softly.

'Yes he would, you don't know him. Not really,' she said, almost whispering.

I tentatively reached out a hand to rub her back and she looked up at me with watery eyes.

'Please, Jean, you have to help me.'

'What did you do with the car?' I said, my thoughts pinballing around my head as I considered our options.

'It's in the garage with Marie's, but it's got a dent. I wanted to fix it, but you have all our equipment.' She stood up and walked over to the toolbox I'd brought up to my room after our last practice race. It was only a small one but her arms and legs shook even more when she lifted it up. 'I can take the box down with me and fix it now. Paint over the damage.'

'Stop it, Vivienne, you can't go and fix a car now. Look at the state of you.'

She glanced down and seemed to notice that she was still holding the handkerchief. 'I don't know what to do with this. Robert can't find out,' she whimpered.

'Shh, shh.' I placed a hand on her arm.

'Will you help me?' she asked again. I felt like I was on the precipice of a deep pit, but part of me already knew that I'd do whatever she asked of me.

'Of course I will.'

She took my hand in her firm grip, and I tried to quash the strange rush that I got from knowing she had come to me with this and not Robert.

'OK,' I said, trying to take control of the situation. 'Are you sure nobody will come across the body tonight?'

'Yes,' she sniffed. 'It would be hard to see if you were just driving past, especially in the dark.'

'And you didn't tell anyone else you were going on a drive?'

'No.'

'OK. Leave that under the bed with the identification card,' I said, pointing to the bloodied handkerchief. 'I'll go and sort the car. We were going to leave in the next few days anyway, so let's just go to the mainland first thing tomorrow and get the cars moved along later. We can tell Robert someone broke into my room in the night and I don't feel comfortable staying here any more – it's barely a lie.'

It felt odd to boss Vivienne around, but she seemed to be hanging off my every word.

'I can walk to the garage from here. You go back to bed and I'll sort it out. Wake Robert up at six o'clock and then let's get the first ferry.'

'Are you sure?'

'I'm certain, now go.'

'Take this.' She unwrapped her red headscarf and handed it to me. 'It will cover your face a bit.'

'Thank you.'

Vivienne tiptoed out and shut the door softly behind her, our roles reversed as I tied the scarf tightly around my head in the way I'd watched her do so many times before.

Later, when I'd taken care of everything and snuck back into the hotel room in the hazy violet light, I slumped against the door and ripped the headscarf off. I folded the vivid material into the smallest square I could manage and stuffed it in my holdall – not able to throw it away, but not quite able to give it back to Vivienne either.

When we came to Igoumenitsa I brought it with me in the holdall, and kept it pushed under the bed, out of sight. If not quite out of mind.

It was below me now, its paint-tainted smell seeping into my half sleep. A constant reminder of the terrible thing I'd done.

SEVEN

Now that we were all back together the real work began, so we rose early the next morning and set off without breakfast.

I led the charge with Mark, who kept up a reassuring patter as we traipsed through narrow streets heavy with incense escaping from the nearby churches.

Out of the whole group he was the most normal. When he wasn't rallying he worked at a garage back in the West Country to supplement his volatile income, and I felt on a more stable footing with him. Vivienne saw him as a bit of a square but I found his carefully ironed outfits and the burr of his accent endearing, and when he told me he wasn't yet married I felt a swell of pity for him.

A young boy was waiting for us at the garage, and when he saw us he shouted excitedly to someone inside. A man walked out leaning heavily on his stick and ruffled the boy's hair before leading us to a low-ceilinged room where vehicles were lined up under dust sheets.

Each of us gravitated towards our own cars without needing to lift the covers. Hugo and Marie to their Ferrari, Anne and David to their little Mini and the rest of us to our custom Saabs.

Vivienne had been given a baby blue 96 Sport as part of her sponsorship deal. Its sleek lines and two-tone cream interior – along with her star power – had made the model a commercial success. But that didn't stop her from silently coveting Marie's car.

I could see her looking at the Ferrari out of the corner of her eye as Marie and Hugo strained to pull off the heavy tarpaulin, sending a cloud of dust dancing in and out of the shafts of light. Unable to help myself, I turned to watch as the long, low bonnet was revealed.

Like our Saab the body design was simple, but there was something seductive about the Ferrari. The glossy white paint and bold red and green racing stripes exaggerated its sweeping contours, and a handsome pair of fog lamps nestled neatly above the polished aluminium grill.

Transfixed, the young boy slipped from his father's grip as Marie opened the car door to reveal its tan interior. Ignoring the man's protests, the boy ran right up to Marie, and both her and the child giggled as she lifted him up into the driver's seat. The garage owner limped over to apologise, but Marie delighted in showing the boy the speed dials and orb-topped gearstick before giving him a cloth badge with the Ferrari's prancing horse logo as a token and lifting him back out.

While everyone else was distracted, Vivienne walked around to the front of the Saab and tugged off the cover.

We both scrutinised the bonnet, and to my relief I could no longer see where the dent had been among the other minor lumps and bumps from past races.

Vivienne removed a glove and ran her hand over the spot where I'd repainted the car.

'Good job.'

I nodded solemnly and slid into the passenger seat, conflicted by my pride at the competent handiwork.

'Come on, you two,' Vivienne shouted to David and Anne. They pulled a face at one another and got into their Mini, which seemed laughably small with David's sturdy frame inside. I couldn't understand why anyone would pick such a car for rallying, but devotees swore their superior road-holding was just the thing.

Vivienne put her foot down at the same time as Marie, and the roar of the engines ricocheted off the close walls of the garage. The man stooped down to cover his son's ears but the boy pushed his hands away, his face shining excitedly.

The car hummed with anticipation underneath my feet. I absorbed myself in the mechanical process of flicking open as many air vents as I could and folding back my map in preparation for our journey, taking deep breaths of the familiar leather smell.

We followed Marie as she roared out of the garage, the elegant Ferrari 250 GTO logo catching the light.

When we reached the end of the road I looked back through the red dust thrown up by our convoy to see the boy waving us off with his badge clutched in his hand.

At first our progress through the busy streets was slow. The locals parted in admiration as we purred along, but the stray dogs and cats were less minded to get out of our way.

'I wonder why the others were questioned by the police,' I said, wanting to clear the air before the sounds of the engine made it too difficult to talk. 'Do you think the police had a hunch we might have been involved?'

'No. We don't even know if they were responding to the same accident.'

'Surely they must have been? And why were they asking if Marie and Anne had driven their cars? Are you sure nobody saw you?'

'Stop it. People die in road accidents every day.' She said the words quietly but firmly, as if breaking bad news to a child. 'Nobody saw me.'

'But—' I tried again, and she cut me off.

'There was nothing I could have done. Please, let's not talk about it again.' I knew not to push her.

The silence became cloying as we accelerated out of town and the buildings were replaced with trees and the insistent chatter of birds.

Vivienne's refusal to talk about the accident made me uneasy. Part of me felt like I needed to relive the horror of what I'd done to pay a kind of penance, but I told myself there was no benefit in poring over it after the fact. Vivienne couldn't have saved that man, and I knew her silence didn't mean she was suffering the guilt of it any less.

I tried to read her expression out of the corner of my eye, but the canopy of pines crowded in around the car and the two of us were plunged into near black.

Who was I to judge her anyway? I tortured myself during the night, reliving the memories and scratching at my skin, but I had done nothing to right the wrong. Instead, I'd kept Vivienne's secret and helped her to cover it up. The old woman was right, I had blood on my hands – and talking about how guilty I felt wouldn't absolve me.

When we reached a wide stretch of road Vivienne pulled over and freed herself from the seat belt. 'Let's swap, you can do a spot of driving.'

I got out and took her seat. It felt like an age since I'd last got behind the wheel, but when we started moving the familiar choreography of the gearstick and the brakes soon clicked into place.

'We're not going to win anything cruising along like that,' she said when I kept my foot steady on the pedal. 'Look how straight the road is here. Let's get a move on.'

Steeling myself, I nudged the accelerator and felt the shift as the car rose to the challenge.

'Faster,' she goaded.

The speed on the dial crept higher and higher until the lush scenery and the rhythmic ticks of the cicadas fell away, and it was just me and Vivienne and the thrumming metal of the car.

Vivienne whooped as we sped along, and I pushed the car faster and faster until the road became windy and then eased off the pedal again.

'Don't slow down now!' Vivienne cried. 'Use the accelerator to make the back wheels slide out and help the car around.'

I tried to approach the next corner without easing off, but as soon as Vivienne signalled for me to wrench the car around I lost my nerve.

'For God's sake. Pull over.'

The road had narrowed, so I carried on in the hope we'd come across a wider stretch with a bit more room to get out, but Vivienne was done with her stint as a passenger.

'Here,' she ordered, and I reluctantly brought the car to a stop.

I lowered myself out and clung to the hot bulk of the bonnet as I skirted around to the other door. The strip of road between me and the edge looked just about safe to walk on, but the thought of the hidden drop made me feel dizzy.

Vivienne hoisted herself into the driver's seat without stepping out of the car, and when I jumped in after her I could feel my heart flapping.

'Look at that.' Vivienne pointed just in front of the car bonnet and my eyes followed her finger. 'Does that look any thinner than a normal road to you?'

'No.'

'And would you drive as slowly as you just did on a normal country road?'

'No.'

'Have you ever driven into a ditch?'

'No, I haven't—' I started, but she cut me off.

'So it's fine. You'll be killed just as dead if you have an unlucky crash on a mountain as you would on a regular road. You don't have time to loiter at every corner.'

She looked at me sternly and I felt as if I'd been rapped across the knuckles. When I nodded, she turned her attention back to the road.

We soon began a steep incline to the mountain top. A few goats looked up without interest as we motored past, and nausea bubbled up inside me as we wound around the tight hairpin bends.

After another five minutes the road started to plateau, and the trees cleared on one side to reveal a tremendous drop. I wound down my window and was hit by the heady fumes of petrol as I leant out.

'How much space have we got?' she said.

'It's not quite as bad as it looks.' I tried not to think about what might happen if we met anyone coming the other way.

After a few minutes we turned a corner to find Marie's car at a standstill with the hazard lights on.

'That can't be good,' Vivienne said.

We pulled up behind her.

'Easy as you go here,' Hugo wound his window down and called out from the passenger seat. *'Bon courage.'*

My thoughts flew to Anne and her morbid fear of heights. I wouldn't want to be in the car with her when she saw the drop and realised there was no turning back.

Vivienne set her face. 'Anne isn't going to like this,' she said, echoing my thoughts.

We waited until Marie and Hugo had cleared the bend and then followed behind, taking an audible breath as the staggering scene came into sight. On my side the cliff rose up to high above the window, but on Vivienne's there was nothing but air.

Heights had never been a problem for me before, but I could feel a light film of sweat settling on my forehead as the car rattled along the narrow track, each rock a blow to the suspension.

A swallow glided so close to the window that it made me jump, leading my gaze down to the perilous drop. I leant my weight over towards the safety of the cliff and held my breath.

'I would have offered to let you out but it's too late now,' she said in an attempt at levity and I let out a nervous laugh. 'I don't fancy my chances reversing along here.'

'Our car is the widest, isn't it?' I said, as Vivienne wrestled with the steering wheel.

'We'll be fine,' she said, but for the first time in all the months I'd been driving with her I caught a slight catch in her voice. That was enough to make me hold my tongue.

The Ferrari was still out of sight around a corner, but it let out a rev of triumph that blasted through the silence.

'Promising,' Vivienne said, and I nodded. I shut my eyes and prayed under my breath for the road to widen as we inched around the bend.

A few moments later the car lurched to the side and my eyes flew open to find the world tilted at an alarming angle.

I spun around to see that one of the back wheels had gone right off the edge of the cliff, and my sudden shift in weight made the car rock.

The movement was slight, but it was enough to make me squeal.

'What the hell are you playing at?' Vivienne snapped.

'I'm sorry,' I whispered, and before I could think about what I was doing I reached for the door handles.

'Stop it,' she hissed, and I snapped my hands away as if they'd been burnt. 'Do you want to get us killed?'

'We need to try and get out now,' I said, barely recognising my shrill tone.

'And make certain we tumble down the cliff along with the car? Not bloody likely.'

'Vivienne. Can't we wait for David to help?'

'Stop it. You need to stay calm,' she snapped, but I could see sweat beading on her forehead.

'Please. I can pull you onto this side, then we can jump out together.'

'I said, stop it,' she said, slamming her hand on the dashboard, and this time I shut up. 'It's front-wheel drive – when I say go, throw your weight right up to the windscreen and I'll hit the gas.'

'What? No.' I was pleading now, but she ignored me and began to count down.

'Three. Two . . .'

I unclipped my seat belt and braced.

'One.' I threw myself forward so that my chest slammed against the dashboard as the engine roared to life. For a second all I could hear was the three remaining wheels struggling against the gravel, but then the car kicked into gear and we slowly but surely edged back to an even keel.

I let out the breath I'd been holding, but I didn't even have time to gather my thoughts because we needed to take a tighter corner to reach safety.

I shut my eyes as we inched forward, and the sound of our heavy breathing and the rocks under the tyres was unbearable – each one a dull *thunk* – until Vivienne let out a whoop. I opened my eyes to see Marie's car and a solid two metres of ground between us and the edge.

Vivienne pulled up behind her, and when she killed the engine I was overcome with such a violent flood of gratitude that I reached out for her hand.

'Thanks,' I said, suddenly embarrassed as I clasped my fingers around her gloves.

'I'm sorry I was being short. I haven't been handling everything that's happened very well at all,' she said, and I was surprised when she gave me a comforting squeeze with her other hand.

I looked out the window to see Robert around the corner with David close behind, and when the front of the Mini came into sight I nudged Vivienne.

'Look at Anne.'

Her head was slumped against her window, oblivious to the world as David sweated behind the wheel.

When the car stopped Anne jolted awake and looked around, setting Vivienne and I laughing in great hysterical honks. I gulped in the air with the relief of it all until I felt dizzy.

'Unbelievable. That woman could sleep standing up,' Vivienne managed to choke out when she'd recovered her composure.

'Let's go,' Marie called out her window, and Vivienne set off behind her.

As the road began to slope downwards it became wider and the bends less violent, and Vivienne took them at a breezy speed.

Finally able to relax, I looked out of the window and spotted an eagle soaring along beside us, its finger-like feathers fluttering in the wind. My stomach flipped as we jolted over a bump and I let out a little squeal, which delighted Vivienne.

She pushed the car harder and I felt the weight of the past three weeks lifting as we flew through the air, her infectious laugh washing over me.

We found a clearing with a stream when we reached the bottom of the path, and we pulled over to eat the pastries Anne had bought for our lunch.

As we walked to find a good spot there was much hilarity over her ability to sleep through the whole ordeal, and the frenzied laughter made me think everyone had been more scared of toppling over the edge than they'd let on. After all, it wouldn't have been the first accident we'd seen. At almost every race someone would overdo it and run off the tracks, and the finishing area always ended up as a jumble of bent and scraped bodywork and crumpled wings.

Anne put a selection of tiropita and spanakopita down in the middle of a blanket before going back to the Mini and, to much applause, producing four bottles of white wine.

I helped her carry the bottles from the car and we wedged them between some rocks in the stream to chill. The water must have been from a spring further up the mountain because it was deliciously icy on my wrists.

'Hope that's better than what you bought last time,' Robert said, squinting at the label as Anne went past. She didn't rise to his dig, but when she handed out the glasses she kept moving his one just out of his reach so he eventually had to jump up to snatch it off her.

The fright of the journey had supressed my appetite at the time, but as I sat back down and tried to work out which pastry to take I was hit by a violent pang of hunger.

I'd developed a partiality for the spinach spanakopita so I went for a triangular pastry that looked like it might fit the bill and took a bite.

The crisp phyllo shattered in my mouth to reveal the salty tang of cheese and sweet dill, and I let out a murmur of appreciation.

'You'd think nobody had ever fed you before you met us,' Vivienne said, and I tried not to think about how my father was so distraught after my mother left that he often forgot to buy food.

When everyone had taken a pastry and washed it down with a liberal amount of wine there was one left, and Robert and I locked eyes over it.

'You need it more than I do,' he said.

'I don't think I do.' I ran a hand over where my hips had filled out and was conscious of his eyes following me.

'It suits you,' Vivienne said from behind me, and I jumped. 'You look better now, you were such a skinny little thing before.'

'I'm not sure about that,' I said, heat rising from the base of my throat. 'We should share the last pastry, though. You go first.'

Robert shrugged and took a modest bite before handing it over for me to finish off.

'I don't know about you lot, but I feel rather drunk after that,' David announced, lying back on his elbows. 'It must be the heat.'

'Well, I think there's only one way to sort that out,' Vivienne said, biting her lip to hold back laughter.

'What's that?' David said, unaware that Hugo had crawled stealthily along the blanket behind him, beckoning Robert over to help him.

'We'll have to dunk you in the river!' Vivienne shouted, and the others grabbed hold of David's arms and legs and picked him up with grunts of exertion.

'Wait, the keys,' Anne complained, and they allowed her to fish them out of David's pocket before marching him over to where the stream widened and swinging him in.

Vivienne turned to me. 'I think Jean is looking rather hot and bothered as well,' she called out to Robert, and he dutifully returned to collect me.

'No, no,' I protested. 'I'm really rather cool here.' I patted the ground where I was sitting and refused to stand up.

I didn't think Robert would be able to lift me from sitting but he knelt and hauled me up into a fireman's lift, and I was so shocked that I could only shriek with laughter.

He walked around with me until he reached a deep part of the stream and leant down to topple me in, but I caught hold of his top and pulled him in with me.

The wall of water that came up to meet us was astonishingly cold, and we both emerged spluttering and still clinging on to one another. When I realised I had my arms around his waist I let go and started treading water.

'We might as well go for a swim now we're here,' he said, and I followed him downstream, laughing at how our clothes dragged us down.

We swam to a point where the water only came up to our waists and stood on the slimy rocks, surveying one another.

His linen shirt clung to his arms and torso, and I looked down to find that my white polo shirt had gone completely see-through. I couldn't imagine the blue slacks I was wearing would fare any better when I got out.

I crossed my arms self-consciously over my chest and looked defiantly at him. 'Happy?'

'Quite,' he said, and a violent shiver ran through me as his gaze swept over the thin material of my top.

He opened his mouth to say something else but I cut him off. 'Let's get out here, it might be a bit easier where the stream is shallow.'

'Your wish is my command,' he said with a mock bow, and he clambered out first before holding out his hands to pull me up. I could feel the callouses on his skin from where he had tinkered with the scalding car engine, and I quickly let go when I was back on firm ground. When I looked over at Vivienne, she was watching us steadily from under the brim of her hat.

Vivienne had been visiting the stables on and off for a few months when I first saw Robert. It was a brisk spring day but he and Vivienne arrived wrapped up against the fresh breeze, the roof of their convertible optimistically lowered.

He was wearing a deep navy roll neck under his tweed jacket with a pair of shades propped on his head, and it seemed fitting to me that this was the kind of man Vivienne should have.

When she kissed him goodbye I put down the brush I'd been using to sweep the yard and scurried off. I'd taken to loitering out of sight in the stall next to Maverick while Vivienne prepared to go out for a ride, and I had to move quickly if I wanted to get there without her seeing me.

An arrogant older stable hand called Tom had been tasked with looking after Maverick, but I knew I could have done a better job. Tom was the longest-serving worker at the stables apart from me – though I seemingly didn't count because I was a girl, and I was only allowed to be there because it was where my father worked.

I would listen to him trying to engage Vivienne in conversation and baulk at his overfamiliarity. She had become a source of fascination in the months since she'd started visiting the stables regularly, and I knew he stored away nuggets of information from their short conversations to divulge with the other boys when he pleased.

A crowd would gather around him in the evenings and he would relay the things Vivienne had said to him. He told the most extraordinary yarns – that Vivienne had been in the Olympic showjumping team as a teenager, that her husband was a spy and that she had a royal lover.

I'd heard Vivienne tell him she'd been in the national team when I was eavesdropping, but most of his tales were pure fantasy.

The thing that bugged me most, though, was that he made himself out to be her confidant – almost hinting at a romantic interest. Tom was admittedly one of the more attractive boys at the stable and I'd had a soft spot for him when we were younger, but I knew this was a pack of lies. She would chatter to him politely, but in a way that seemed blithely uninterested and almost dismissive. I was tempted to expose him, but I knew the satisfaction I'd get wasn't worth giving my hiding place away.

As I slipped into the stable next door I caught a glimpse of Maverick's glossy chestnut coat. A shy old mare came over to nuzzle my arm, and I heard Tom and Vivienne entering the adjoining stall.

Tom made some remarks about the weather, and I scoffed at his mediocre attempt at conversation until Mr Grant called Vivienne away to meet someone.

'We won't be long, get Maverick ready for when we come back,' he instructed Tom. 'I want him to be gleaming.'

'Yes, sir,' he said, and I heard the stable door shut with a dull thud.

The jangling of Maverick's equipment rang through the air, and I realised I was going to be trapped there for longer than I'd thought.

My father normally expected me to make him lunch at midday at our cottage down the road, but if I stayed in the stall for another forty minutes I'd be late.

As I had got older I'd realised such exacting rules were an attempt to maintain order after my mother left, but his volatility meant I complied out of fear rather than sympathy.

Relief came several minutes later in the unlikely form of Tom's spotty friend, who called around to offer him a cigarette from a packet he'd pilfered.

'Go on then, but I need to be quick. I have to get this one ready,' Tom said, and I heard him bang the gate shut.

When I was sure they were out of sight I shook the cramp from my legs and walked around to see Maverick. He often trotted over for a scratch and a sugar lump, but that day he was pacing around in a circular motion. Tom had already tacked him up to go out, and he was obviously getting impatient.

I started walking away but then I looked back.

The extra bolt to keep the stable door secure hadn't been fastened.

I stopped. There was nowhere Maverick could really escape to apart from the field and he looked like he would appreciate a run. Besides, Tom could do with being put in his place by Mr Grant.

Checking over my shoulder to make sure that nobody was around, I nudged the door ajar and hurried off.

EIGHT

When we got back to town we ordered an afternoon snack of cheese and sweetbreads washed down with ouzo, and retreated to the hotel to get ready for dinner.

I wasn't in any hurry to get dressed when I got back to my room, so I leant against the windowsill to stare out at the ramshackle skyline of terracotta roofs studded with luminous white domes. Further down the road, two men had pulled chairs and a rickety table out of their house to play backgammon under a cluster of deep yellow street lights, but the only sound I could hear was the murmur of conversation between Vivienne and Robert next door. I strained to hear what they were saying until the voices went quiet and the whirr of the pipes started up.

Ignoring the nauseating twist of guilt in my stomach, I tiptoed over to the door and slowly lowered myself down until my face was at the height of the keyhole.

I hadn't peeked into Vivienne and Robert's room since the night of their fight, but whenever I heard the hum of their voices next door the temptation crawled across my skin.

Before I could change my mind I covered one eye and pressed my forehead to the rough wood.

Vivienne was sat in a floral nightgown at her dressing table with her back to me, but I could see her face in the mirror. I'd never watched her put her makeup on before, and I was fascinated by the way she propped her elbows on the dresser to steady her hands as she painted a thick flick of liner from the corner of her eye. For a moment she seemed to be looking right at me and my stomach lurched, but then she looked down at her leather toiletries case and I took a deep breath.

Rummaging around in her bag, she pulled out a small pair of scissors. I took note of the way she held out her fringe in front of her and angled the blades, transfixed as dark tufts of hair fluttered down. Afterwards she swiped a bristled brush across her face, and when she walked out of view I heard her opening the wardrobe with a drawn-out creak.

In my concentration I'd forgotten about Robert, and I flinched as he stepped in front of the keyhole to pick something up and disappeared without a word. A moment later Vivienne came back into view carrying a pile of clothes, which she set down precariously on the dressing table stool.

I kept my gaze trained on her as she pulled off her dressing gown, and a silky cream slip came into view underneath.

The first dress she tried on had a modern cut that exposed the taut muscles of her back, but when she caught sight of herself in the mirror she made a guttural sound of disgust and tugged it back over her head. She went through a few others, pulling poses or winching them in with various belts before taking them off and dropping them to the growing pile on the floor. I couldn't find fault with any of the shimmering embroidery or flattering cuts that she'd discarded, and with each dress my confusion grew.

'Come on, Viv, let's go,' Robert said, and she groaned in annoyance as she unzipped another dress and let the silky material slide through her hands.

'For God's sake, what was wrong with that one? They all look fine. I don't understand what the problem is.'

'None of them are right.'

I couldn't see Robert's face, but I heard the irritation in his voice. 'We're just going out for dinner – it doesn't matter. If you haven't picked out a dress by the time I've finished this beer, Jean and I will go on our own.'

Reminded that I was expected to go with them, I sank down to a seated position and eased myself slowly along the floor so I didn't make the floorboards squeak.

The dress I'd laid out to wear was sprawled shapelessly on the bed, and I sighed as I rubbed the rough material between my fingers. I'd only ever felt a whisper of Vivienne's skirts when the wind blew them against my bare ankles, but now I felt that if I could only try them on I'd have a greater insight into what was going on in Vivienne's head.

My wardrobe door creaked as I wrenched it open, but a quick flick through revealed nothing else inspiring to wear. I hung my drab outfit out of sight and pulled my shoes on hastily before going into the corridor and knocking on their door.

It swung open and Robert appeared. 'Vivienne's taking an age so it might just be you and me,' he said, passing by any attempt at pleasantries.

'Sorry to do this but I'm feeling under the weather,' I said, the lie tripping off my tongue. 'I've decided I'm going to stay here and sleep.'

His brow creased in concern and a flutter of gratitude caught me off guard. 'You do look a bit peaky. Let me have a look?' I nodded wordlessly, and before I realised what he was doing I felt the warm, comforting touch of his hand on my forehead. 'No temperature, which is good. Do you feel shivery?'

'A little.'

I held my breath as he tilted my face up to the light with unexpected tenderness.

'Hmm, too much sun, most likely. Do you want us to bring you something back?'

I hadn't really thought through what I was going to do if I missed dinner, and I had to stop myself from accepting his offer too readily. 'I don't feel up to it now, but it would probably be good for me to eat something later. If you wouldn't mind, I'd be awfully grateful . . .' I trailed off.

'Of course, you rest up. We don't want you getting all skinny again.'

'Not much chance of that happening.' I backed away as I tried to think of something else to say. 'Tell Vivienne I'm sorry,' I called out as I retreated into my room and shut the door firmly behind me.

I was glad Robert had been the one to answer. It was hard enough lying to him, but Vivienne would surely know something was amiss.

I lay sprawled out across my bed and waited.

True to his word, Robert called out that he was leaving and I heard his footsteps disappearing down the corridor. A few minutes later I heard the rattle of the keys and the clacking of Vivienne's heels as she stalked after him.

I pressed my ear to the main door and listened out in case they returned for something they'd forgotten, but the only sound was the chirrup of the birds nesting in the eaves. A tingle of anticipation started up in my fingertips as I crossed the room and clasped the handle of the adjoining door.

Tightening my grip, I turned the handle and stepped through. The room was dark so I left the door ajar; I didn't want any lights to be visible from the street.

I'd been in Vivienne and Robert's room most mornings since we'd been on tour, but it felt different now I was there on my own at night. The heavy wood furniture loomed over me, and out of the window I could see rows of bare masts illuminated by the harbour lights.

As I passed the low coffee table I saw that several maps had been unfurled to cover the Acropolis route, detailed instructions scrawled across them in Vivienne's cursive script.

I walked over to the wardrobe and pulled the door open, but the rectangle of light from my room didn't reach far enough to see inside. I decided that Robert and Vivienne had been out for long enough that I'd be safe to turn on a light after all, so I leant over and flicked the switch.

The wardrobe was vast, but apart from a few of Robert's polo shirts it seemed to be reserved for Vivienne's clothes. There were dresses and skirts hanging up in all patterns and colours, and I couldn't help but step closer and run my hands over the silk and folded cloth.

I stepped back and almost tripped over a pair of heels that had come to rest in a plié where Vivienne had tossed them across the room.

They looked like they'd fit me perfectly, so I tugged off my sandals and slipped my foot into the soft leather. I'd never worn such high shoes before, and their curved shape felt odd against the arch of my foot. Gingerly, I placed my feet on the floor and pushed myself up. They fitted like a glove, but it took me a few laps around the room to master Vivienne's purposeful stride.

Walking over to the pile of dresses she'd discarded, I picked one from the top. It was an emerald green halter neck with straps that tied in a voluptuous bow at the back, and I thought it was the most elegant thing I'd ever seen.

Teetering over to the door, I held my breath and listened intently for a few moments. When I was satisfied that I wouldn't be caught unawares I shimmied out of my skirt and blouse, careful not to stretch the delicate material of Vivienne's dress as I pulled it over my head.

The dress must have been silk because it felt smooth and luxurious like nothing I'd ever worn before, and it was almost as if the material was melting onto my skin as it slid down over my calves.

I smoothed my hands across my thighs and looked up at my reflection. I'd assumed the dress would be far too big, but it skimmed perfectly over my hips and waist. I found a matching headscarf tucked away in a drawer and tied it around my hair the way I'd watched Vivienne do countless times before.

When I'd finished I walked to the mirror and admired my reflection – impressed by how well I'd captured Vivienne's look.

Caught up in my own recklessness, I decided I might as well try on a little bit of her makeup as well. Her leather toiletries case was still open on the dressing table, so I rooted around to find her usual lipstick and dabbed the vivid colour on my lips. Impatient to see what it looked like against my pale skin, I fumbled the shiny bullet as I went to put it down and it bounced off the floor and rattled under the bed.

I brushed away as much dust as I could from the floor and carefully lowered myself down, gathering up the slippery fabric of the dress for fear of nicking it. Reaching out to grab the lipstick, my gaze snagged on something tucked under one of the slats. I craned my neck to get a better look, but I could only make out what seemed to be a crumpled tote bag.

I took hold of a corner and teased it out, hesitantly at first and then more firmly. Eventually it came loose and I manoeuvred myself back out from under the bed, relieved not to see any loose threads on Vivienne's dress.

The bag felt empty, but when I held it up to the light something tumbled out and hit the floor with a slap.

I looked down to see an envelope. The seal was ragged where it had already been ripped open, and when I bent down to pick it up I noticed it was bulging slightly from where something had been stuffed inside.

I tipped it to one side and a tingling sensation crept up my arm as a grainy leather booklet slid into my hand. It was embossed with the unmistakable foil print of a British passport, and as I flipped through I found stamps from Belgium, Germany, Italy and Slovenia.

When I got to the photo page I was half expecting to see my pale face and distinctive shock of dark hair, but that wasn't what I found. The young woman staring back at me was certainly pale, but she had blonde hair and watchful, almond eyes.

I looked for the signature, but it had been scribbled out. I could make out an *A* at the beginning, and then a neat circle carefully printed for the dot of the *i* in the surname, but nothing else.

I looked at her details, which were carefully printed in swirly writing, and did a double take. The woman was two years older than me and born in one of the counties that neighboured mine.

I tried to commit the details to memory before carefully putting it back in place under the bed. I wondered how long it had been there, and whether the woman knew it was missing. Whether we had ever unwittingly crossed paths back at home.

I did a few more laps of the room while I was trying to work out what I'd found, taking long slow steps as I'd observed Vivienne do earlier and swinging my hips from side to side.

My pacing took me right back to the spot where her clothes were heaped on the floor. I tried to imagine crumpling this dress as she had done, but I couldn't; it was too beautiful. I turned around to admire the way it cut away at the back to reveal my shoulder blades, but my reverie was broken when I heard footsteps in the corridor.

Knowing I wouldn't have time to discard the dress, I slipped off the heels and hurried back to my room, shutting the door carefully behind me. I strained my ears for Vivienne and Robert's familiar tones, but a door slammed further down the corridor and the voices went out of earshot.

I made myself take a deep breath, but my body was humming with anticipation.

Robert and Vivienne had worn their watches to dinner so I had no way of knowing what the time was. The cheap bedside clock in their room was off, and my single bedroom hadn't been deemed worthy of even a broken clock. They could have been gone for as little as thirty minutes, but I realised that I truly had no idea how much time had flown by while I was parading around in Vivienne's clothes.

Heart pounding, I let myself back into their room and carefully peeled off Vivienne's dress. For a horrible moment I thought I could smell the sweet soap I had picked up in the town lingering on the material, but I tried to tell myself that my mind was just playing tricks on me. I carefully replaced the shoes and cast my eyes around for any evidence I'd been there before turning off the lights and leaving the room.

NINE

The next morning I woke early and cut myself a delicate fringe with my nail scissors. At first I amused myself by thinking up far-fetched explanations for the hidden passport – that the woman's Greek lover had hidden it under the bed to stop her returning home, or that she'd assumed a new identity to flee the country – but I soon lost myself in my task.

When I'd finished I scraped my hair into a ponytail and inspected my work. I looked much less startled than I had before, and sweeping it over to one side made my jawline less severe. I looked up at myself coyly through my new fringe the way I'd seen Vivienne do and laughed.

The sink was covered in hair. I fished out the dark clumps from around the plug and my stomach turned as I deposited them in the bin.

I was impatient to see Vivienne's reaction to my new look, but I knew she wouldn't be up for hours so I left the hotel and took my normal walk down to the port. The man at the kiosk grunted in recognition when he saw me, and I perused the stands for something to keep me occupied. I was tempted by a Greek magazine with a picture of Marilyn Monroe on the cover, but when I spotted a tucked-away copy of *The Times* I bought it to take to my usual spot on the sea wall.

Too worked up to sit still and look at the water, I began to flick through the newspaper, but it was only after a few minutes that I realised the copy was more than a month old. The vendor must have found it discarded in a hotel lobby, but I didn't have the energy or language skills to quibble with him for my money back.

Vivienne and Robert had copies of *The Times* delivered to their flat in Pimlico whenever they were at home, and I'd become an avid reader in the weeks before we went on tour.

The hefty paper arrived on the doormat with a thunk when they were both still asleep, so I'd collect it myself and take it into the reading room. I didn't particularly like the room itself but it had a splendid view of their courtyard, so I tried to angle my chair so I couldn't see what was behind me. This worked to an extent, but I was always aware of the light reflecting off the two mangled steering wheels mounted on the wall. They were from what Vivienne liked to call her two 'dances with death' early on in her driving career, and she had displayed them proudly like I imagined some posh families might a prized stag head.

I swung my legs over the water as I flicked through to get to the comment pages, but a picture caught my eye. Turning back until I found the right page, I smoothed down the thin paper and craned my neck to get a better look.

I blinked hard. It was a shot of Vivienne and I collecting our trophy for the Tulip Rally, with a write-up about how we'd been the first all-female team to win. Thankfully my drab outfit had been partially obscured, but Vivienne was on full show in a deep

V-neck dress and her hair wrapped in a signature headscarf. We were giggling and clutching our trophy between us – an elegant hand-beaten gold tulip.

I smiled at the memory of the ceremony, held at a grand Dutch hotel that filled its rooms with hundreds of flowers and laid on an extensive cold buffet to mark the occasion. The public paid a lot of money to attend the event, though it was free for drivers, and I spent the evening being spun around four separate ballrooms to entirely different music until I was quite dizzy.

A brass band was even brought in to march through the hotel, though the pomp and grandeur was deflated somewhat when Hugo raced up the steps to pour a cocktail into a tuba passing below.

I stared unseeingly out to sea and tried to imagine how the other stable hands would react if they saw me in the paper, but the only face I could conjure up was Tom's – his face slack with bewilderment as Mr Grant gave him a dressing-down for letting Maverick escape.

Of course, when I allowed the stable door to open I knew Maverick would bolt. I just didn't factor in one of the stable hands leaving the field gate open too.

I heard the thunder of hooves trample past when I was in the cottage preparing my father's lunch, and once I'd put it in the oven I couldn't help but stand on my tiptoes to catch a glimpse of Maverick.

I spied his mane and glossy back through the window, and I smiled at the thought of him frolicking around freely. I turned the oven down and went to get a better look, but as soon as he came into sight I knew something was wrong.

A small animal or a bird must have spooked him because he was tearing around the edge of the field looking for an exit. When he reached the edge of the fence he reared up and ran the other way, and just as I spotted the open gate he made a run for it.

Praying that my father hadn't taken his car out for the morning, I ran to the hall but the key was missing from its normal place on the hook. He was normally quite particular about leaving it there, but sometimes he left it in his coat. I held my breath as I plunged my hand into the large pocket – and let out a sigh of relief when my fingers curled around the cold metal key nestled at the bottom.

Remembering my father's lunch, I ran to turn the oven off and then made a dash for the car. I could only hope the surprise of finding warm food in the oven would temper his fury if he came back early and found me gone.

Looking around to see if there was anybody else I could call on to help, I ran across the gravel and let myself into the car. It was a clunky second-hand truck that my father had owned since I was born, and I had learnt to drive it while I was still a child so I could help ferry equipment and food around the stable.

The car rattled and then jerked forward as I slammed my foot on the accelerator. I spotted Vivienne and Mr Grant coming out of the office as I roared onto the main road, but it was too late to stop now.

This stretch of the road was straight, with tall hedges bordering farmland on either side, and I could see Maverick in the distance. I just hoped I could get to him before he reached the busier road.

I had never meant to put him in any danger, and when I thought about Vivienne finding him gone I felt sick.

The best option would have been to corral Maverick into a corner, but on this road my only hope was to intercept him. Gritting my teeth, I checked there were no vehicles coming the other way and pressed the accelerator to the ground. Veering onto the wrong side of the road, I steered the car wide to overtake Maverick with as much of a gap as I could and tried to put some distance between us.

When I neared the junction at the end of the road I skidded to a stop on the verge and jumped out. Maverick was drawing closer, and the thunderous sound of his hooves striking the road rang in my ears as I squared up to him. He was still moving at pace, but when he drew level I took a deep breath and lunged.

I caught hold of his harness but he didn't stop, and I was pulled off my feet. My knees scraped painfully along the floor but I hung on and he began to slow down.

After a few strides my fingers slipped, but I scrambled to my feet and jogged to catch up. I called out his name softly, and he slowed to a stop and cocked his ears at me. His saddle was wonky where I'd grabbed him, and I could see the sweat glistening on his coat.

As I walked towards him I tried to stay calm. I held my hands up and muttered a string of soothing nonsense, avoiding eye contact as his gaze darted rapidly from side to side.

Lie to Me

I heard the purr of Vivienne's Triumph pull up onto the verge behind me, and I had to fight the urge to turn around as Maverick's eyes alighted on the movement over my shoulder.

I was almost close enough to grab hold of him when his ears twitched. A second later I heard a car hurtling towards us. It was coming down the same lane Vivienne and I had just arrived from, and I threw myself forward to grab hold of Maverick's reins before he bolted. I almost lost my balance as he tried to sidestep me, just managing to get him under control as the car squealed to a halt.

Before I'd registered what was happening Vivienne had jumped in. She spoke softly to Maverick and took hold of the other side of his reins, securing him between us and placing a calming hand on his muzzle. Vivienne appraised me with several short but searching glances, and I wondered how much she would suspect about my part in Maverick's escape and eventual recapture.

Mr Grant waved the driver around us, and when he was out of sight the three of us walked slowly back to the cars, with Maverick trotting alongside Vivienne.

'Did you see how he got out?' Mr Grant asked.

'No. I saw him bolting out of the field from my window and ran to get the car so I could catch up with him.'

'You didn't see Tom?'

'No. He was nowhere to be seen,' I said truthfully, and Mr Grant cursed. He was going to be in much more trouble than I had imagined.

We walked in silence until we reached the cars.

'Are you going to be OK with him from here? I should probably get my father's car back before he misses it,' I said.

'Oh yes, you've done a marvellous job. Thank you,' Vivienne said to me, and I felt a sickening thrill of guilt and excitement. 'I've seen you around the stables. What's your name?'

'Jean.'

'Well, Jean, it's been a pleasure to meet you.' She took me by surprise as she reached out to squeeze my arm. 'I'm sure we'll see each other again soon.'

I picked the newspaper up from the concrete to study the picture again. I was a little disappointed to see that I was listed as Vivienne's nameless navigator in the caption, but even that didn't spoil my good mood. I folded the paper up carefully so the photo wouldn't crease, and almost skipped to the hotel.

By the time I got back the others had congregated in the breakfast room. Everyone had decided to source their own breakfast elsewhere after complaining about the hotel's dry pickings, but it had become routine for us to gather there after we had eaten to set out our plans for the day over pots of strong coffee.

Marie spotted me first and did a double take. Following her gaze, Hugo turned around and his brows knitted in confusion.

I wondered what they were looking at until I caught my reflection in a mirror – in my excitement I'd forgotten about my new fringe.

Sensing a change in the atmosphere, Vivienne looked up and I made myself meet her gaze. Her eyes widened for a fraction of a second before she bared her teeth in a wide smile.

Unsure what to say, I opted for silence and dropped the newspaper down on the table triumphantly, setting the cutlery rattling.

'Steady on,' Robert said. He looked up from the paper he was reading and froze, tilting his head as if assessing my new look.

I was thrilled he'd noticed my hair, and tried to channel Vivienne's calm tone as I sat down and showed them what I'd found.

'Did you know we were in *The Times*?' I said, unfolding the paper and handing it to Vivienne. She studied it silently, a smile playing across her lips. Vivienne was no stranger to press coverage, but this was a particularly flattering picture of her.

'No, I didn't, what a thing to find. Where did you get it?'

'At the news kiosk at the port. Someone must have left it behind in a hotel.'

'It's a very nice photograph. I just wish I could get Hugo to look at me like that,' Marie chipped in with a sneer. This was met with some cruel laughter around the table, although I didn't understand.

I looked at the picture again and the smile froze on my face. In my excitement I hadn't noticed it, but while Vivienne was laughing at the photographer I was gazing up at her intently with lips parted. I was looking on in awe.

'I wonder if the papers will send anyone over to cover the Acropolis,' Anne mused, and I could tell she was picturing herself in her own V-neck dress, clutching a trophy with David by her side.

'I dare say Fleet Street will if they know Viv is going to be there,' Marie replied, already bored with the discussion. 'Though they might struggle to work out who's who now these two have morphed into one,' she added, and I stared intently at the tablecloth.

When everyone had finished drinking their coffee they drifted away one by one with a promise to meet back in the lobby, until it was just me and Robert left.

'It suits you,' he said unexpectedly, as if picking up the threads of a conversation.

Without thinking, I looked up at him coyly through my fringe the way I'd practised that morning. 'Do you think so?'

He nodded, his eyes lingering.

I was suddenly aware of how clammy my palms had become, and I pushed myself up abruptly and made an excuse about going upstairs to get ready for our day at the beach. I made my way out of the room silently, feeling completely detached from reality as I got into the lift and made my way back down the corridor.

I knew something was wrong as soon as I stepped into my room. A cleaner had opened the window, but there was something else. I walked around the bed and froze as a flash of silver drew my attention to the floor. It was a button on a neat pile of clothes.

I stooped down and recognised the green dress that I had tried on the night before at the top of the pile. A piece of paper had been torn off from something and placed on the top, and when I turned it over I recognised Vivienne's cursive handwriting.

Didn't want these any more. Thought you might have had your eye on them . . . V x

I lifted up the silky green material and took a deep breath. To me, the lingering smell of my cheap body soap was unmistakable, but I tried to tell myself it was all in my head.

This must be a coincidence. There was no way Vivienne could have known I was trying on her clothes.

I went to hang them in the wardrobe and faltered. Everything was gone apart from the dress Vivienne had bought me in the market. I ran my hand along the dusty shelves at the back and peered under the furniture but there was no sign of my clothes having been folded and tucked away. They had vanished.

Sitting down heavily on the bed, I began to pick at a hole in the corner of the sheet. I knew it was hypocritical, but I felt uneasy about Vivienne coming into my room without asking first. I tried to reason that she hadn't exactly been sneaking around if she'd left me a note. She was trying to do something nice, but none of it sat right.

I hadn't been particularly attached to any of my old clothes, but I felt vulnerable without them.

It wasn't until I'd pulled on one of Vivienne's structured dresses that I remembered the key for the adjoining door. I didn't think it would have been moved, but I slid my hands under the pillow anyway. I spread my fingers wide and felt right to the back, but the sheets were cool and empty.

Racking my brain to remember if I'd hidden it somewhere else, I stripped everything off the bed and shook out the pillows.

I even slipped my hand underneath the mattress, but to no avail. I wondered if the maid had found it while she was straightening my sheets and put it back in the lock.

I walked over to the connecting door but the keyhole was empty. I could see straight into the room next door – and for the first time I realised that they could see straight back into mine.

TEN

When the traffic woke me the next morning I moved to the bathroom at the end of the corridor to get changed, feeling newly exposed by the line of sight the keyhole provided into my room.

Another search for the missing key yielded no results, so I sat down on the bed and ran through all the people who might have moved it. Although I wanted to believe it had been one of the maids, I couldn't think of a good reason why they would have done it. I could well imagine some of them fishing under mattresses in search of hidden banknotes, but surely they would have left a key alone?

The list of the other people who had access to my room was short; I locked myself in at night, and I'd never noticed any indication that the main door had been tampered with. That only left access through the adjoining door.

I wondered if Vivienne had looked for the key when she came in to drop off her clothes. I would have understood if she'd had a quick scan along the ledges or the table, but under my pillow? And if she'd found it, why wasn't it back in the lock?

I wrenched open the window and blew the smoke from my cigarette outside. Families paraded through the streets in their

Sunday best, and as I watched them I wondered for the first time what it would be like to go home.

I pictured the beech trees lining the paddock of the stables, their new leaves emerging at this time of year, but I had no doubt that everything else would have stayed the same. My father would get up this morning to go to church and then the pub, and because I wasn't there to cook for him, he would stay there all day before beginning the weekly cycle again.

How would he react if I returned home, bag in hand? Other parents might be angry at first, but ultimately their relief would weigh out. Not my father, though. He'd tell me I was no better than my runaway mother, and I could almost hear his drunken slurring as he accused me of trying to send him to an early grave. He'd seen red the day he threw his plate at me, and I didn't want to think about what else he might have done if Vivienne hadn't intervened.

The peel of the bells tumbled down the street and I stubbed my cigarette out on the ledge, watching stragglers running to church through the wisps of smoke.

No. I could never go back.

I shut the window, muffling the sound of the bells, and went downstairs to collect some fresh bread and fruit for our breakfast.

Turning around to call out a greeting to Nikos on my way past the reception I almost collided with Vivienne coming the other way.

'What are you doing?' I asked, confused to see her up so early. She was already decked out in slacks and a shirt, and she had a bag of groceries dangling from her arm.

Lie to Me

'I was just coming to find you. Robert's gone off on his own to motor about for a bit, so I've decided we're going on an adventure. Leave your room keys with Nikos and then let's go,' she said, turning away and striding towards the door.

'I should probably change if we're going out,' I said, gesturing down at the gingham shorts and sleeveless top she had left in my room. My outfit wasn't appropriate for anything more than a trip to the bakery, but Vivienne glanced back and assured me it would be fine.

'Hurry up,' she said, clicking her fingers when I hesitated. I'd been lulled into a false sense of security over the previous weeks, but I was suddenly acutely aware that she was still my boss.

Nikos looked at me expectantly and held out his hand. With a sigh, I tossed the keys over to him and followed Vivienne.

'Good luck,' he called after me, and I turned to give him a look of resignation before running to catch up with her.

I slid into the hot car and tucked in my top where it had come loose. 'I meant to say before, the outfits were a surprise,' I said, patting the shorts. 'Thank you, I'll just borrow them for a bit.'

'Don't be silly, they're for you to keep. They'll suit you much better than they do me.'

I knew she wanted me to disagree with her, but I couldn't think of anything convincing to say so I kept my mouth shut.

'They would have suited me when I was your age,' she mused. 'But not any more.'

She sounded strangely melancholy, and I was thankful when she revved the engine loudly, bringing our discussion to an end.

'Where are we going then?' I shouted when the traffic forced Vivienne to slow down, and she handed me a map with a great red cross marked over a deserted-looking area further inland.

'I was telling the woman in the bakery about our little drive up the mountain yesterday and she said we hadn't seen anything until we'd visited the monasteries in Thessaly. She marked them out for me so we could find them.'

'I didn't have you down as the religious type?' I said, bemused.

'Of course I'm not, but apparently these buildings are magical. Anyway, they're only about two hours away so I thought it would be decent navigation practice for you. And surely you'd rather do this than spend another morning with Marie and her sniping?'

I tried to look enthusiastic, but I was a bit ticked off. I'd have liked more time to study the map before we went across an unknown terrain, but mostly I didn't want to drive two hours inland to see a few old buildings on such a hot day.

The Saab was a piece of precision engineering that went like anything if you put your foot down, but it was no more than a workbench on wheels. Every small comfort had been stripped out to fit tools and spare parts, and the heat of the engine came back into the car so it felt like a furnace even on a normal day.

The only way to cool the interior was to open the side screens, but those sucked in so much dust that it got down our necks and coated our eyelashes until they were heavy, so we often sweated through drives without any fresh air.

The clock on the dashboard showed that it had only just gone nine. Hopefully we could get there and back before lunch – and then we could make our way to the beach.

'Somewhere you'd rather be?' she said when I failed to reply.

'No, not at all, it's just a bit hot for a drive, isn't it?' I found a wire hairgrip in my pocket and used it to clip back my fringe to stop it from getting sweaty.

'Oh, I see, you'd rather be frolicking with Robert,' she retorted.

I flushed, remembering the look on her face as she'd watched us from the riverbank. 'I promise it wasn't like that,' I stuttered.

'I was joking. I'm sure you wouldn't dream of such a thing,' she deadpanned. The corner of her mouth curled up in an almost imperceptible snarl, but when I blinked her gap-toothed grin was back in place.

It was after Maverick had escaped that I started to get tangled up in Vivienne and Robert's lives.

Tom was no longer welcome at the stables after the incident and Mr Grant asked me to take charge as Vivienne's groom. At first I felt a niggling sense of guilt every time I saw Tom's spotty friend around the stable, but I soon managed to absolve myself. It was clear that Maverick was receiving better care from me, and he seemed much more settled since I'd started taking him for more exercise around the yard.

When Vivienne came back to England for an extended period she seemed to be impressed with what I'd done as well. I made sure I was in Maverick's stall whenever she came to see him, and she chatted warmly with me. Soon I was invited to join her for rides, and then to a showjumping competition where I met Robert for the first time.

Vivienne had told me that her husband would be there, and I spent the days before the competition anxiously trying to think of things I could talk to him about. But I hadn't prepared myself for hours of being sat arm-to-arm with him in the stands. I tried to ignore the heat of his bulky frame beside me as I volleyed back answers to his polite questions, crossing and uncrossing my arms and legs for something to do.

Things became less strained when it was Vivienne's turn to compete. Robert's enthusiasm was infectious, and I found myself jumping out of my seat when it looked like Maverick might clip a pole, just missing to land with surprising grace. I held my breath as Vivienne led him around to the final jump and leant right forward in the saddle. He soared high over the bar, and when he landed Robert and I let out ecstatic yelps before turning to each other and bursting into laughter.

By the time we'd sent Vivienne off to thunderous applause and sat back down the tension had vanished, and Robert laughed as I asked him breathless questions about Vivienne and Maverick. 'Are you sure you want to hear all this? I don't want you to feel like I'm just talking at you,' he said, but when I protested he happily continued his tales.

We sat in the stalls long after most people had filed out, and eventually Vivienne had to climb up to call us back down. 'You two looked thick as thieves sat up there,' she said, and Robert grinned as he leant his arm around the back of my chair.

'I hope he hasn't bored you,' she said, giving him a playful dig in the ribs.

'Not in the slightest,' I replied.

'Are you sure?' Vivienne said sceptically.

'Definitely.'

'Jean, that is the right answer. Congratulations,' Robert said in a faux serious voice. 'You are very welcome to accompany us again.' He held out his hand and I shook it, pursing my lips to hide my glee.

The next weekend Vivienne asked if I'd like to keep her company while she practised her racing, and I accepted the offer immediately without a clue of quite how testing an excursion this would be.

She picked me up in a sporty red Austin Healey 3000, and even when she told me to strap in I didn't quite realise what she had in mind. The first part of the journey was easy enough, but when we'd cleared the slippery track leading to the farm she hit the accelerator.

The car roared into life and I clung to my seat. I thought my teeth might shake clean out of my gums as we bumped over the roads, but still the speedometer climbed higher. Vivienne took one bump so fast that my stomach lurched as the car left the ground, clipping the exhaust with a clang.

My silence only seemed to egg Vivienne on, and I had to focus on the spirals of heat pirouetting off the bonnet to keep my nausea at bay as we slid around corners and mounted grassy slopes.

Eventually Vivienne brought the car to a stop with a hair-raising squeal, and I flexed my fingers to get the blood back where they'd gone white from my tight grip on the seat.

'Your go.' I turned to her in disbelief, but she was already opening the door.

Not wanting to displease her, I moved gingerly over to the driver's seat. I nudged the accelerator and the car shot forward, my head thwacking into the leather headrest. The steering wheel was stiff and unwieldy and, struggling to retain control, I wrestled it with enormous effort around the first corner.

Sensing my discomfort, Vivienne talked me through the knack for turning the nose of the car around and guided me through some tight corners – coaching me to drive into them as deeply as I could so I didn't overheat the brakes. Although she had to strain above the sound of the engine, she spoke patiently and with the deeply impressive knowledge of a true expert.

When I was feeling a little more confident we ventured onto a quiet stretch of winding country roads. I'd learnt to drive on unpredictable farm tracks and I found I could quickly correct my steering once I'd got the hang of the heavy car.

Vivienne seemed pleased with my first attempt, and she took me on several more excursions after that.

She tried to convince me that rally drivers only ever have their foot fully down on the accelerator or on the brake and nowhere in-between, but at that point I was still too nervous – I couldn't imagine ever being able to throw around such a powerful car at those breakneck speeds.

The first part of the drive to the monastery was simple enough to navigate, with clear tracks and little opportunity to deviate from the main route. But as the clock rolled into the second hour of our journey and the tracks became less pronounced, I started to wonder whether I'd taken us the wrong way.

The landscape of Thessaly was dramatic – jutting rocks pierced the canopy of lush foliage, and as we drove higher into the mountains everything became shrouded in a thick blanket of fog. I wanted to look up and admire the scenery, but I was too busy scanning the sides of the roads for any sign of life that might suggest the monastery was near.

'Are you sure they marked the right place on the map?' I ventured when another thirty minutes had gone by.

'Yes. I did say it was in the middle of nowhere,' she said disparagingly.

'But this really is out in the sticks. I'm not even sure this track is meant to be a road,' I said, all confidence in my navigation skills gone.

'Be patient,' she retorted, and I sighed under my breath.

Turning the map around at a right angle, I compared it with the treeline in the hope of finding a clue as to where we were. All I wanted to do was give up and turn back, but as we came out of a clearing I looked up and did a double take – there was a tiny red-roofed building high up on the horizon, seemingly suspended in the air.

As we drove closer the fog cleared a little to reveal that the miniature building was in fact sat atop a towering rock. It seemed to move further away the closer we got, and it looked as if the rock must stretch up thousands of feet into the sky.

'Now do you see what I mean?' Vivienne said. I nodded, struck dumb. 'The view from the Parthenon is a fine thing, but this could give it a run for its money.'

'Does anyone live up there?' I managed eventually.

'Apparently there's a whole community of monks.'

'But how do they get up there?'

'You're about to find out.'

'But surely you can't drive the car all the way up?' I said, stupidly.

'No, of course not. We'll have to walk it.' I studied her face for any sign she was joking, but none was forthcoming.

'But when we arrived in Igoumenitsa you said you didn't want to go on a hike . . .' I trailed off as she pulled onto the verge, flattening the greenery as she went.

'Sure, but that was just up to the top of a hill. This is so much better.'

'I don't have the right shoes.' I looked over to see that she was wearing a pair of plain white lace-up tennis plimsolls, and I was surprised she owned such shoes. Except for when she was racing, she was practically attached to her heels.

'Those will be fine,' she said, glancing at my leather sandals.

Thankfully they were closed-toe and had a sturdy ankle strap, but they were hardly appropriate for hiking. 'The monks probably wear sandals just like that,' she said, pulling herself up and out of the car before I could reply.

I realised I wasn't going to get anywhere by arguing with her and peeled my bare legs from the hot leather seat. 'Do you know how to get up there then?'

'The woman from the bakery told me where to go, remember? Follow me.' She slung her bag over her shoulder and set off.

I followed her through the trees to a path sloping down to the rock. The route felt counter-intuitive if she wanted to climb up to the monastery, but Vivienne seemed to know where she was going so I followed silently.

The gentle gradient meant that we could let gravity pull us down with very little effort on our part, though I had to be careful with my sandals on the jagged surface. When we got to the bottom the trees cleared to reveal the wide base of the rock, but I still couldn't work out how we were going to climb it.

'Round here,' Vivienne said, and when we emerged from a clump of wizened trees I was surprised to see a steep winding staircase carved into the rock.

I looked up to see if I could spot the monastery, but all I could see was the hostile angle of the incline. Even with the steps I was doubtful we'd be able to climb high enough to see the monastery up close.

Vivienne set off at a steady pace and I followed behind, glad the staircase was at least in the shade.

My legs felt heavy for the first ten minutes, but I soon built up a rhythm and overtook Vivienne on a bend. The steps were smooth under the thin soles of my sandals, and I noticed that there was a very slight dent where the middle of the rock had been worn down over time.

I looked up hopefully as I climbed, but when the spiral staircase showed no signs of relenting I hung my head. A lizard ran in front of me and I spooked it with a swift flick of my sandal, sending it scuttling away.

Even in the shade the heat was oppressively sticky on my skin, but I could do nothing more than fan myself furiously with my hand.

The others were probably on the beach by now, splashing around in the tantalisingly cool water, but I knew I couldn't have refused Vivienne's request to accompany her. Especially not after her loaded comment about Robert.

I was jolted from my thoughts when I turned the corner and the wall dropped away on one side. The gap revealed a wide view of the thick canopy below, and the fog gave the scene an eerie half-light. As I turned to call to Vivienne over my shoulder I realised that she'd lagged behind. I shouted down to her, and when I heard her distant response I sat down and waited for her to catch up.

A few minutes later I heard the telltale clinking of her bag. When she came around the corner she looked a little pink in the face, and I could see the heaving of her chest through the close fit of her shirt.

'Don't look at me like that,' she said.

'Like what?' I turned my head away too quickly to look at the view.

'You're thinking how old and slow I am. Look at you, you're barely out of breath.'

'That's not at all what I was thinking.'

Lie to Me

'Make the most of it while you're still young,' she said, ignoring my protests. 'One day you'll be like this too.'

I took out my cigarette packet and handed it over to her as a distraction. She pulled one out with her mouth, and when she handed the packet back there was a bright red smudge of her lipstick on the corner.

We set off again a few minutes later, and this time I made sure to slow my pace. We had to stop several more times on the way up, but when we finally reached the top we sat down heavily on the final step and admired the view.

The fog was starting to burn off a little as the sun battled its way through, but I could feel my skin cooling in the high altitude as the heat from the climb wore off.

I turned my head to look at the monastery as Vivienne fished a bottle of lemonade out of her bag. The staircase had led us up to a pristine courtyard flanked by red-roofed buildings, and I was astounded by their scale. Staring up at them from the car they had looked like toy houses. But up close they were imposing structures with domed towers and ornate brick archways framing the windows.

'Shall we see what's over there?' Vivienne said when she'd finished her drink, and I squirmed as she abandoned the empty bottle on the pristine patio.

The buildings seemed completely deserted from the outside, and I indulged in the fantasy that we were the only people there. But when she pulled me towards the heavy doors of what looked like a chapel I felt a flutter of discomfort at the thought of what might happen if someone found us trespassing.

'I'm not sure about this,' I said, but Vivienne pushed the doors open with a hideous squeak of their hinges and ducked through the gap. She beckoned for me to follow, and after a quick glance over my shoulder I darted inside.

The cavernous space was illuminated briefly before Vivienne pushed the door closed behind us, but it was just long enough for me to see that we were in an ornate church with frescoes covering every inch of the walls and ceiling.

I couldn't see any movements from the shadows, but someone must have been there recently because candles had been lit and a cloying fug of incense filled the room.

Vivienne walked up to one of the golden candleholders and plucked two of the sticks from it. I felt the damp close around me as I followed her inside and hesitantly took one of the candlesticks she was holding out.

We drifted over to the closest wall and circled the chamber with our candles held up to the frescoes. Rows of saints and angels stared back, the gold paint of their haloes glimmering in the light of the flames. The sweat from the climb had turned cold on my neck and bare arms, and a shiver ran down my spine.

Thoughts of my God-fearing father took hold of me as I locked eyes with a grim painted face and I quickly looked away.

One Sunday he had beaten me for wearing a skirt that almost came up to my knees after I'd found it in a drawer. I came to suspect his fury had been unforgiving because it was one my mother had left behind, but I always took care in dressing for church after that.

Returning my gaze to the painted figure, I made an effort to draw my shoulders back and stand proudly. I had no intention of seeing my father and his religious zeal ever again, and if nothing else, his behaviour had taught me a profound mistrust of God.

While I'd been lost in my thoughts, Vivienne had covered the perimeter of the wall and was hovering by a doorway that led to another room.

'Do you want to explore?' she whispered loudly, and I had no choice but to nod.

The only source of light in the corridor was our candles, and the passageway blended into dark ahead of us as we walked.

We passed several rooms that seemed set up for prayers, but further down was one with a large pot hanging from the ceiling, its walls lined with shelves of bottles with woven covers.

We stepped inside and Vivienne pointed to a basket of grapes on the floor. 'It's wine,' she said, turning to pick up one of the smaller bottles. I tried to pull out the cork but it was stuck tight.

Vivienne put the bottle down and held it firmly while I tried again. Slowly the cork started to shift under my fingers and I grunted with the effort of one final tug – flying backwards as it came loose. I caught the side of a basket and grapes scattered across the floor, sending Vivienne into a fit of giggles.

I tried to shush her as I scrambled to pick up the grapes, but when one burst messily under my foot I had to cover my own mouth to muffle my high-pitched wheezing. We sank to the floor, cheeks aching and shoulders shuddering with the effort of trying to contain ourselves.

Vivienne dared me to take a sip and, emboldened by the thrill of sneaking around, I lifted the bottle to my lips. I tried to tip it slowly, but more of the ruby wine slopped onto my top than it had into my mouth. The sour taste of it flooded my mouth and I had to force myself to swallow.

'Not nice?'

I puckered my lips. 'It's even worse than Konstantin's,' I said, which set her off again. When I'd hidden the opened bottle in a corner we made our way back into the corridor and spotted one more door at the far end.

Vivienne went in first, and when she lingered I poked my head in after her. It took me a second to work out what I was looking at, but when I did I recoiled.

This room had shelves too, but they were lined with rows and rows of human skulls. Many were broken but some were complete, all the more unnerving for their recognisable humanity.

'What are they doing up here?' I whispered as we made our way back to the main chamber.

'I'd assume the monks don't have many graves up here. Once they've decomposed that's probably where they go.' I tried not to wonder where the rest of their bodies had ended up.

The light of the main chapel seemed bright now that our eyes had adjusted, and we went over to an ornate altar we hadn't noticed before.

There was a row of intricate paintings depicting holy figures propped up against the wall, and hanging off the edge of one of them was a necklace with a painted miniature on a gold chain, shimmering diamonds set into the metal around it. I had just picked it up to admire the heft of it in my hand when we heard the distinctive screech of the door.

Without a word, we both stubbed out our candles and dropped to the floor. We were hidden from the doorway in a dim corner, but if anyone walked past we would be spotted immediately. I held the necklace tight, pressing my back against the wall as I crouched so that the cold of the stone seeped through my thin top.

Whoever had come in was shuffling around, and after a few minutes we glimpsed a man in black robes and a cap with a large cross hanging from his neck.

He disappeared behind a large column, but when he next came into view he was carrying a long match. He muttered to himself as he made his way around the incense lamps hanging from the ceiling, lighting them one by one.

Vivienne pointed to the door and I held the necklace close to my chest as we shuffled along the wall, the raised pattern of it digging into my skin.

'When he reaches that last lamp we make a run for it,' she whispered. I nodded and put the necklace down in preparation, but she picked it up again and held it out to me. 'Take it with you. A trinket to remember our trip,' she said with a sly smile.

A tingling sensation spread across my skin as I wrapped my fingers around the cool metal, taking it from her grip. I heard my father's voice and thought of him bringing down his fist, but I gripped my hand harder around the chain and gritted my teeth.

'Go,' she whispered when the monk reached the last lamp, and he looked up in alarm as our feet slapped against the stone.

The door screeched and we were momentarily blinded by the midday sun, but the pristine courtyard soon came into focus. I heard a shout behind us but we were already hurtling down the stairs, the jewels of the necklace cutting into my palm.

ELEVEN

I was still on a high when we returned to the hotel, and I savoured the unfamiliar thrill of sneaking the stolen memento inside in Vivienne's shopping bag.

Rather than shrinking away, I walked with new purpose right through the middle of the lobby and called out a hearty greeting to Nikos as we passed.

'Wait,' he called after me when we'd almost reached the lift, and I turned slowly on my heels. 'Aren't you forgetting something?'

My confidence wavered and I shifted the bag so it was behind my back. 'I don't think so?'

'No?' He jangled a set of keys, and I remembered that I'd given them to him to look after. I walked over as slowly as I could manage to retrieve them, resisting the urge to hug the bag to my chest.

As I was walking back to Vivienne my stomach growled loudly and she laughed.

'You sound like you could do with some food. Get ready and I'll call for you in half an hour,' she said, leading the way to the lift.

When I got into my room I tried on the stolen necklace, and the surprising weight of it pressed against my chest.

I did a quick spin in the mirror to admire the jewels and then slumped back on the bed, using a pillow to elevate my swollen feet. My soles had chafed and blistered on the run back to the car, and I tried to focus on that rather than the guilty buzz of excitement I'd got from making a getaway with my new find.

The pipes whirred as Vivienne ran a bath, and when the room fell silent I got up and started getting ready. My new dress needed a wash, so I tucked a blouse into one of the skirts Vivienne had given me and combed my hair.

I looked in the mirror. Sun-bleached strands fell limply on either side of my face and the skirt clung to my newly filled-out frame; the sophisticated young woman who had drawn second glances gone, the stable girl back in her place. I scraped my hair back into a tight bun that made me look rather severe, but at least it hid the grease.

Vivienne knocked on the adjoining door and I called out for her to wait. I dug out the cheap lipstick I had bought in London and scraped off the cracked top layer before applying it.

I looked expectantly in the mirror. The pale shade made my lips disappear against my newly tanned skin, so I hastily rubbed it off and hunted around for something else I could put on.

'Hurry up,' Vivienne called. I admitted defeat, but just as I was about to open the adjoining door I heard footsteps coming down the corridor.

I stepped back, uncomfortable with the thought of Robert finding out we'd been using the door between the two rooms, but as the footsteps came closer I heard the distinctive clack of heels.

A few moments later there was a loud knock next door. 'Viv, it's Marie. Open up.'

I hoped Vivienne would ignore her, but after a few moments Marie called out again: 'I have an exciting surprise for you . . . *ah bon*, there you are,' and I heard the door click as she went inside.

I waited a few minutes, but when I realised she might interrupt our lunch plans I hastily made my way out into the corridor and knocked on Vivienne's door.

Marie must have been standing just inside because it swung open abruptly. She was wearing a low-cut dress and pumps, and the smell of sickly sweet perfume that had been lingering in the corridor enveloped me entirely. I looked over her shoulder to catch a glimpse of Vivienne, but she must have gone back into the bathroom to get ready.

'Jean, what are you wearing? You look like you're here to clean the room,' she said rather abruptly.

'Oh,' I stuttered, realising my mistake as soon as the words left her mouth. I hadn't noticed how much my outfit looked like the one the maids wore.

'And people wouldn't think twice about letting you into their rooms with hair like that. Imagine all the trouble you could get up to.' She was trying to make a joke of it, but my cheeks reddened as if I'd been slapped.

'Sorry, I didn't realise you were here,' I said, and then felt silly for the white lie. She must have known that I'd heard her from my room.

'Vivienne's just getting ready, do you want me to pass on a message?' She leant casually against the door frame, blocking my view.

'Oh no, don't worry. It's just . . . we'd made plans for lunch,' I said falteringly, my earlier bravado gone.

'That's rather a pity. I'm taking her to see one of Hugo's old friends so you'll have to go without her. He's only here for a day so we're pulling out all the stops.'

'Oh, how fun. Where are you taking him?' I was imagining a lavish restaurant spread like the ones Vivienne had told me about in London, with platters of lobster and champagne on ice. I thought she might extend an invite to me, but it wasn't forthcoming.

'Another of Hugo's friends has a villa along the coast so we're going to drive over there.'

'How fun,' I said again, and she frowned at me. 'Is Robert going as well?'

'He's going in our car with Hugo. They're already outside.'

'I suppose I'll go and find somewhere to have lunch in town then,' I said, but I lingered in the doorway. 'I'll just say goodbye to Vivienne first, seeing as we'd made plans.'

She looked like she might be about to tell me to go away, but at that moment I heard Vivienne fling open the bathroom door. 'Is that Jean?' she called out. 'Is she coming with us?'

'No, she's just about to go into town for some lunch,' Marie said, giving me a challenging look. I held her gaze stubbornly, convinced Vivienne would intervene and insist on taking me with them anyway.

'Surely not?' Vivienne stuck her head around the door and I could see the corner of one of the hotel's threadbare towels wrapped around her.

I looked away quickly, feeling Marie's eyes on me. I knew I wouldn't get much of a look-in with Vivienne if she was there, and no doubt I'd end up stuck next to some insufferable bore.

'My new dress needed a wash so I thought I'd throw this on to buy some food,' I said, turning to point in the direction of the shops to hide my disappointment.

'This is where your maid outfit comes in,' Marie said, giving me a wicked grin. 'I'm sure you could go to the kitchen and steal someone's room service. Nobody would notice.'

They caught each other's eyes and Vivienne quickly looked away, but the twitch of mirth at the corner of her lips made me want to cower as if I'd taken a blow.

At first I did a pretty good job of laughing along, but when my eyes started smarting I had to excuse myself.

'Are you sure you don't want to come?' Vivienne called after me half-heartedly, but I nodded vigorously and turned away.

The lift was painfully slow to arrive, and I didn't want to risk any of the others seeing me in a state, so I hurried downstairs and out the front door.

I pushed through the people idling along the tiny streets off the harbour to get to the restaurants on the seafront. The smell of meat slow-cooking in preparation for the evening was torturous, but I suddenly realised I didn't have enough money to pay for a meal.

Avoiding the gaze of the waiters trying to tempt me towards their tables, I returned to the backstreets and found a man selling fruit from his van. I bought a brown bag of flat peaches and sat down in the first doorway I came across to eat them undisturbed. They were beautifully sweet, and I didn't even care when the juice dribbled down my chin and onto my top.

Sated, I tried to distract myself by wandering around the market. I spotted a man in police uniform who could have been Konstantin, so I turned around and ducked out of sight.

He waved enthusiastically whenever he spotted our car around town, but I kept my distance. It wasn't that I didn't want to see him again – quite the opposite, in fact – but I was scared to get involved with a policeman. I'd already got too close to telling him my secrets before.

I managed to push my way to the middle of the market and admire a few trinkets, but the shouting and jostling was overwhelming without Vivienne to guide me and I soon gave up.

When I got back to the hotel I retrieved a magazine from my room and curled up on a sofa in the corner of the lobby. The furniture might have been faded, but I felt quite content there once I'd settled in. It was cool and quiet in the lazy afternoon lull, and it was reassuring to see Nikos's friendly face. Though the calm didn't last as long as I'd hoped.

'What's up with you?' David's nasal voice filled the hushed lobby. The sofa sighed as he lowered himself down opposite me.

'I thought I'd take a breather.' I tried to look as though I was absorbed in my magazine, but he didn't get the hint.

'But we're in Greece.' I winced as he spread his arms wide and raised his voice, drawing curious looks from an older English couple on the other side of the room.

'It's a bit hot out there for me at the moment,' I mumbled. I knew it was a limp excuse, but I didn't have the energy to think of anything more persuasive.

Anne joined David on the arm of the sofa as he started telling me that a decent hat was the thing to get me through the heat. She smelt of soap, and her wet hair looked dark ginger from where she'd washed it.

'What are you two doing over here?'

'I was reading and David came over to join me,' I said, trying not to sound bothered by the interruption.

'Where's Vivienne, I thought you two were attached at the hip?' Her tone was jovial, but I felt a pang of regret.

'She's gone out with Marie to see one of Hugo's friends.'

'You didn't fancy going with them?'

'I didn't get the invite.' This time I didn't succeed in concealing my bitterness.

'Oh, Jean, I'm sorry, don't take it personally. You'll start to learn that Viv's just like that.' She leant over to give my shoulder a reassuring squeeze.

'What ever do you mean?' I asked, my curiosity piqued.

She slid down the sofa to nestle in the crook of David's arm, and I felt suddenly exposed.

'Well, Vivienne's very all or nothing.'

'All or nothing?'

'One moment you're her favourite, and the next you're not. She'll take a wild dislike to something completely irrational like your clothes or the way you talk, then you'll have to wait for her to come around. It's silly really, but we've learnt to put up with it.' She looked to David and he nodded his agreement.

'Oh,' I said, wanting to tell her that it was Marie, not Vivienne, who had refused to offer me the invite.

'How long have you been navigating for her now?'

'Five months.' I tried not to stare as David absent-mindedly fanned her wet hair out across the arm of his shirt.

'You've done well, the old navigator only lasted a few months,' David said, and I realised that I'd never thought about the women who had taken my seat before.

'The old navigator?' I said, my throat tightening. 'What happened to her?'

'Vivienne never told us why, but they must have fallen out because the two of them parted ways pretty suddenly. Though I did see her a few months ago at the Express and Star Rally.'

'David.' Anne shot him a sharp look and he shrugged.

'What? We're bound to see her eventually. She had a sporty Mini and a young navigator with her, so I assumed she was going to try her luck as a driver.'

'Do you think she'll be at the Acropolis?' I butted in.

'No, I flagged her down when I saw her in Wales and she said she wasn't going.'

'Why? What was her name?'

'Gosh, I can't remember,' David chuckled. 'Young girls are always dropping out to get married or have kids. Do you have plans for when the season's over? No man at home?'

I thought back to the stable – to my father and the boys, and how I'd left without saying goodbye or even telling them where I was going. 'No, I'm not sure what I'll do,' I admitted.

'Don't worry, we still have a few more rallies after the Acropolis before the season's over,' Anne said kindly. 'You know how competitive Vivienne is. She really thinks you're in with a shot of winning the Ladies' Championship and she's not going to let you leave until you do.'

I gave her a stiff smile, refusing to contemplate the idea of being let go by Vivienne.

'You know what, it would be swell if you came to stay with us in Lake Garda after the races. We'll be there until October,' David said, and Anne nodded enthusiastically.

I let myself imagine for a moment what it would be like to tear myself away from Vivienne and embrace a few uncomplicated weeks of easy company and bountiful food.

'Please do, we'd have a blast,' Anne chipped in. 'And anyway, the end of the summer is ages away. You're far too young to be worrying about the future. We shouldn't have asked.'

'Exactly,' David said. 'I think the more important question is, what are you doing for lunch?'

'I'm not sure,' I said, but I didn't really feel like eating any more.

'That's sorted then, come with us,' Anne said, clapping her hands together as she finished David's train of thought.

'I've already eaten.'

'Why not come for a drink?' David countered.

My cheeks were starting to ache with the effort of returning their encouraging smiles and I didn't think I could face another few hours of polite chat.

'That really is very kind, but I'm feeling rather hot so I might just go back to my room.'

Anne tilted her head to look at me. 'You are looking a little peaky. Cold flannel over your face, that will sort it. I can lend you mine if you don't have one?'

'You're terribly kind. Don't worry though, I've never been very good with the heat.'

'You're so English.' David shook his head, but he was smiling. 'Well, we'll call for you later to see how you're doing,' and with that they headed off, David's light shirt now dark where the moisture from Anne's hair had soaked the fabric.

When I reached the safety of my room I collapsed onto the bed without taking my sandals off.

I wondered what the other navigators looked like. I imagined them riding with Vivienne in her car, their headscarves trailing out behind them. I wondered how old they were, and how she'd met them, and where they were now. I thought this must be what it's like to be married and hear a tantalising detail about your spouse's former flame.

I hadn't thought to ask Vivienne about any of the women she'd raced with before taking the job and I felt suddenly stupid at my naivety. When I'd finally got her attention all those months ago I'd been too elated to think of anything else.

As I'd started to spend more time with Vivienne I felt the confines of my narrow life at the stable begin to lift. Some days we motored about in the countryside on our own, but if Robert was around the three of us went out for picnics or to a country show, and they even bought me the occasional present from one of the stalls.

I squirrelled the gifts away under my bed but my new confidence was plain to see, and it didn't take long for my father to react. He hauled me out of bed early to complete menial tasks around the yard, and one day he took my key for the cottage so I had to wait shivering on the step for him to let me back in.

Things came to a head one Sunday when he got wind of my plans for an afternoon out with Vivienne and Robert. He had been out all morning at church and then an inevitable trip to the pub, and I had prepared a lunch of roast chicken and a crumble for him to eat when he came back.

He stumbled in later than I had expected, the sour smell of beer lingering on him. I knew he hated cold food so I offered to reheat his lunch, but when he snapped back at me I realised he was angling for a fight.

After glugging back a whole pint of water, he sat down to eat his lunch. 'I've got a lot of jobs for you this afternoon,' he said between mouthfuls, sending a spray of gravy droplets across the table. My heart sank as he listed off a string of gruelling tasks, and I knew I'd have to tell Vivienne and Robert to go without me.

I looked up at his drawn face and the gravy dribbling down his chin and my resolve hardened. I set the water jug down more forcefully than I'd intended and his head snapped up.

'I've already made plans. I'm not doing any jobs this afternoon.'

I was thinking on my feet, already scrambling around for what I'd say when he challenged me. But he was so shocked he didn't reply immediately.

Making the most of his stunned silence, I reached out to open the door, but just as I was about to clasp the handle something exploded next to my head.

Jumping back, I looked up to see globs of gravy dripping down the wall; potatoes and chicken strewn across the floor. I pressed my hand against a sharp pain in my cheek, and when I brought it away it was spotted with beads of blood.

'Don't you dare turn away from me,' he slurred. My heart was racing, and I put a hand on the door in case I needed to fling it open and run.

'Clean it up,' he said, but I didn't move. We locked eyes, and then he banged his fist on the table and repeated more loudly: 'Clean it up.'

A sharp rap on the wood behind my head made me jump, and my father's mouth hung open in confusion at the unfamiliar sound.

I froze but he lumbered across the room and pushed me aside to wrench open the door himself.

Vivienne was standing outside wearing her jodhpurs and a riding jacket.

'Hello,' she said frostily, not offering out her hand. 'Is Jean ready?' She craned her head around my father's thick neck, but if she was surprised to see me standing there with the debris from the roast scattered around she didn't let on.

'She's not coming,' my father growled. 'She's got work to do.'

'This is work, I can't go out without my groom. Mr Grant said she was mine for the day.'

Although Vivienne said this confidently and without pause, it seemed like an obvious lie. It was unlikely that she had spoken to Mr Grant about taking me out, but my father wouldn't want to run the risk of displeasing him. He'd seen how our boss fawned over Vivienne, and everything we had was dependent on his goodwill.

He clenched his fists. 'Fine. But she'll clean this mess up first,' he said, slamming the door in Vivienne's face.

Cheeks burning, I ran to the other side of the room to pick up the brush – partially to sweep the floor, but mostly to protect me from my father's swinging fists if he decided to have another go at me.

Much to my relief he stormed upstairs without causing any more of a scene. I tidied away the lunch, vowing with each sweep that this would be the last time I cleaned up his mess, and without stopping to change my outfit I grabbed my coat and fled down the steps.

Vivienne must have already told Robert what had happened because when I got to the car he had vacated the passenger seat for me, though he still looked shocked by my face.

'Bloody hell, take this,' he said, handing me a pristine monogrammed handkerchief.

'I couldn't possibly.' I tried to push it back towards him.

'For God's sake, take it. You're bleeding,' he insisted.

I could hear his unasked question in the air, but we were forced into silence by the roar of the engine as Vivienne tore out of the drive. She motored along the straight country roads for some time, but when we joined a windier route she slowed and the din mellowed to a purr.

'Say, do you live only with your father?' she asked, turning to assess me before fixing her eyes back on the road.

'Yes,' I said simply, wondering where the conversation was going.

'No other family?'

'No.'

'Friends?'

'No. The only people I've really spent time with here are the other stable boys. And I wouldn't really call them friends.'

'Surely there must be someone looking out for you?'

I thought about it for a moment. When I was a child the ruddy women who kept their horses at the stables had made a point of cooing over me, but when I became a teenager they turned their backs – either through apathy or jealousy at my youth. Mr Grant was nice enough, although he barely seemed to notice me even when I was right under his nose.

'I could disappear into thin air and nobody would care,' I said after some consideration.

'We would notice if you disappeared,' Robert said from the back, and I turned around to give him a grateful smile.

'How would you feel if you never had to see the stable again?' Vivienne asked.

'I'd like that very much. When can I leave?' I quipped, not even daring to hope that she might be offering to take me away.

'I'm assuming you wouldn't miss your father?'

'Not in the slightest,' I said, sadly but truthfully.

'That's sorted then. Pack your bags when we get back and then come with us. I need a navigator for my next tour, and you've just won yourself the job.'

TWELVE

The next day the others were full of tales from their party, which they told with unbound enthusiasm despite their somewhat croaky voices and bleary eyes.

I'd been invited by Anne and David to share what turned out to be a long, leisurely lunch of Greek salad and keftedes at our usual seafront taverna, and the afternoon breeze was whipping across the cove by the time the others ambled down from the hotel to join us.

After some particularly inventive swearing, Robert and Marie managed to light their cigarettes and launched into a string of crude anecdotes that made Anne squirm, and the more her mouth puckered the more provocative their tales became.

Anne's warning about Vivienne taking a sudden dislike to people had echoed around my head as I got ready that morning, and I'd tried to make myself presentable in my new dress. I even attempted to coax my hair into a style, but when that failed I had to tie it back in a simple headscarf.

While everyone else's focus was on Robert and Marie, I studied Vivienne. She sat up straight with her feet planted firmly on the ground, and her composure made me realise how much I fidgeted. Whenever she chimed in to the conversation everyone stopped to listen, and when she leant forward conspiratorially we all followed suit.

Eventually she caught my eye and called across the table to ask where I'd gone to lunch the day before. The chatter around the table lapsed momentarily, and I felt my face redden.

'Just a small taverna, I can't remember what it was called,' I replied, acutely aware of how hesitantly I was stumbling over my words.

'Aliotiko? Stani?' Vivienne suggested. Everyone was still listening so I made an effort to reply steadily, matching my pace and volume with hers and controlling my hands by sitting on them under the tablecloth.

She threw out a few more names, but chatter resumed when I maintained my ignorance, and inevitably moved on to the topic of the upcoming race in Athens.

The Acropolis was notoriously one of the hardest rallies in Europe. The tracks were rough and dangerous, and where the route intersected open roads there were horses, sheep, goats, snakes and even tortoises to make a nuisance of themselves.

Most of the group were old hands at the Acropolis, and Robert and Mark had once won it outright. It was only Anne, David and I who were novices, so Robert laid out a map he'd brought with him and walked us through the rough spots.

When he reached a particularly hairy turn he became more animated. He demonstrated the best way to steer into the bend, but when Marie tried to chip in to describe the perilous drop he continued to talk over her.

Marie shot him a look, and when he traced his finger along the map to move on to the next turn she stopped him.

'Say, aren't you going to tell the story?' she demanded, but he shrugged and repeated that the corner was one to watch before carrying on.

'What story?' Anne asked, oblivious to the strange hush that had descended over the group.

'Considering Vivienne almost killed someone there, she might like to explain it,' Marie said, and I snapped my head around in shock to look at Vivienne.

'You're so dramatic. It wasn't anything like that – and besides, you weren't even there,' she said, rolling her eyes at Marie.

'If you say so,' Marie said.

Anne looked alarmed. 'Nobody got hurt, though? Did they?'

'No, Anne,' David said reassuringly, placing his hand on her arm. 'This course is quite safe.'

This wasn't strictly true, and not for the first time I wondered if Anne and David were really cut out for this kind of event.

'Has anyone ever died on this course?' she asked the rest of the group, clearly unsatisfied with David's answer.

'Not quite,' Mark said quietly. He opened his mouth as if he was going to say something else, but Robert gave him a stern look and he shut it again.

'So what happened with this accident?' Anne persisted.

When nobody spoke Vivienne took charge. 'You see this turn?' She tugged the map towards her to point at a hairpin bend. Anne and I both nodded. 'When you drive around here the road narrows so that only one car can drive through – and as you can see it's a pretty steep drop on either side.' She slid her finger along the map and I saw how close together the contour lines were. 'I was ahead of another car and the driver decided he was going to overtake, so of course we collided. It was a miracle the cars didn't tumble into the abyss, though we both had a terrific dent.'

Her voice remained low and detached as though she was recounting an anecdote that had been told to her by somebody else, and it set me on edge.

'That sounds like it wasn't your fault though?' Anne said, winding her hair tightly around her fingers.

'It wasn't,' Vivienne said with finality, throwing her cigarette on the ground.

'That's not quite what the other driver had to say about it, though,' Marie added, a sly smile betraying her delight.

'Yes, but he's an idiot. He would rather accuse me of trying to force him off the road than own up to his mistakes,' Vivienne said, pre-empting further questions from Anne.

Mark gave Vivienne a searching look across the table, and when she didn't return his gaze he downed the dregs of his drink.

'Why would he do a thing like that?' Anne asked. Vivienne sighed and busied herself with lighting a new cigarette. It was clear she was ready to move on from the subject.

'Simple. He couldn't stand a woman coming in ahead of him so he lied.'

Anne went to ask another question, but Robert wrestled back control of the conversation. 'Anyway, that was a long time ago now and thankfully he doesn't race any more. Can I continue?'

He smoothed the map out with his palm, and without giving anyone a chance to answer he barrelled on with his run-through.

I found myself next to Mark when it was time to make our way back to the hotel, and as we walked in companionable silence I watched Vivienne out of the corner of my eye. She walked with long, deliberate strides – drawing sideways glances from the men she passed in her tight racing overalls.

When I turned back Mark was watching me, a strange look on his face.

'You should be careful.' His voice was so quiet I wasn't sure I'd heard him right.

'Sorry?'

'Sometimes I wonder how far she'd go to win.'

'What do you mean?' I started, but Robert stopped still in front of us and swung around, patting his pockets.

'Do you have the car keys?'

Mark fished the keys out of his pocket and tossed them over to him. The three of us fell into step, with Robert keeping up a jovial monologue until we reached the hotel. He accompanied us to the lift, and when it reached my floor I stole one last glance at Mark before I got out. The pinched look on his face had gone, and I wondered if I'd imagined it.

When I got back to my room I stripped off my dress and surveyed the contents of the wardrobe. I didn't have any choice but to wear one of the outfits Vivienne had left me, so I picked out one that looked cool and went down to join the others in the lobby.

Lie to Me

I watched Vivienne's face closely as I stepped out of the lift. She was sitting on one of the misshapen lobby sofas talking animatedly to Marie, and I didn't want to disturb them so I hung back and flicked through a discarded guidebook until they noticed me.

Eventually they looked up to give me a wave but they didn't break off their conversation. I thought I caught a satisfied smile play across Vivienne's lips, but I was glad Marie didn't seem to have noticed I was wearing one of her outfits. I didn't want to encourage any more of her jibes.

The clothes were unremarkable enough – a pair of cropped cigarette trousers in pale blue gingham with a white blouse – but the material was wonderfully light, and the sleeveless top showed off my toned arms. I'd used an ornate silk scarf Vivienne had left me to accessorise my bag, and I fancied the whole outfit looked rather Audrey Hepburn.

I was glad for the short cut of the trousers. Even in the lobby the heat was stifling, and as I fanned myself with the guidebook and watched some guests checking in my mind wandered back to the missing key. I had turned over everything in my room several times now, but it was still nowhere to be found. Maybe the maid had swept it up when she changed the sheets and it had got lost in the washing room – at least that way I would no longer have to grapple with the lingering guilt of hiding the key.

The sensation of my hair sticking to the nape of my neck was starting to irritate me, so I unravelled the scarf from the bag and tied it back.

Even with my hair off my neck I was still restless from the heat, so I opened the guidebook to distract me. My stomach lurched when it fell open on a page about Corfu, and I looked around the lobby instinctively to see if anybody was watching. When I realised how foolish I was being, I quickly flicked through the rest of the sections until I got to one about Athens. It was illustrated with a photo that made the Parthenon look like it was glowing gold in the early evening light, and I imagined what it would be like when we finally made the sweaty climb up the rocky outcrop to reach that view.

I was surprised to find that the text was all in English, and I soon became absorbed in the history of the old city and its cuisine. The writing was richly descriptive, and I could almost taste the sun-drenched tomatoes and delicate honeyed sweets the writer had taken a liking to.

Halfway through a section about the different neighbourhoods I became aware of a set of brisk footsteps ringing out across the lobby, followed by a familiar whiff of woody aftershave. I put my thumb over the passage to hold my place, but before I could turn to greet Robert a pair of hands gripped tightly around my waist.

I let out a yelp of surprise and wriggled loose, and when I turned around he was holding his hands up as if he'd been burnt.

'Jesus Christ, Jean. I thought you were Vivienne,' he said, and we both laughed a little too loudly.

Marie spun around to see what was happening. 'What's up with you two?' she called across the lobby, but we just shook our heads.

I stole a look at Vivienne, but I couldn't be sure if she'd seen the incident play out. She was smiling too, but tightly – unnaturally.

When Vivienne and Marie had resumed their chat, Robert leant forward and whispered to me under his breath. 'Your outfit threw me. Why are you wearing Vivienne's trousers? And her headscarf for that matter?' He seemed intrigued rather than accusatory, and the proximity of his lips to my ear sent chills up my neck.

'Vivienne . . . lent them to me.'

He puffed out his lip in surprise but didn't pry. 'Well, I'd be a little more careful if I were you,' he said quietly, and I thought I caught him wink as he turned on his heels and stalked away from me.

'I'm heading to the car,' he called out to Vivienne and Marie. 'We're all waiting for Hugo, so come and find us when he's ready.'

I turned back to the guidebook, but my eyes scanned over the pages without taking anything in.

Robert's words had left me giddy – part of me was uncomfortable with his suggestive tone, but the rest of me was intrigued to see how much closer to the line he would dare to go if Vivienne wasn't there.

I wondered if she'd seen him lean in to speak to me. There was no way she could have heard what he'd said from that distance, but I didn't want to look up and see her steely gaze boring into me.

A few minutes later Hugo finally appeared in a creased outfit that nonetheless looked like it had cost more than the rest of ours put together, and the four of us walked down to the garage. I purposefully lagged behind, stopping to pet a scruffy dog to give myself time to regain my composure before being sealed in the car with Vivienne.

I'd lost track of how long we'd been in Igoumenitsa by that point, but as we were driving away from the garage Vivienne told me that our leisurely days would soon be over. There were plans for us to pack up soon and head out to a hotel in Athens, and from there we'd start the final preparations for the race.

Now that the Acropolis Rally was within her sights Vivienne was impatient to get on and win, and she rattled through tactics as we skidded along the mountain passes. She eased off the accelerator a little as we approached a meandering stretch of road surrounded by trees, and the pattern of sunlight passing through the trunks was dazzling.

Even in this partial shade the car was overheating. The warm air gushing in from outside did nothing to help, and I could feel a damp patch spreading across the small of my back.

Vivienne's frantic monologue was hard to follow over the roar of the engine, and I had to keep reminding myself to tune in to what she was saying rather than dwell on Robert's words.

As the road straightened out again she resumed racing speed, rendering the flickering of the light through the trunks so fast that it made me feel dizzy. I blinked, trying to concentrate on the road, and when I opened my eyes I saw something bulky jump out from the trees in front of us.

I shouted but Vivienne was already wrenching the wheel around. Bracing for the impact, I squeezed my eyes together and my hands flew up to clasp onto my lucky necklace as I was thrown against the door – but instead of the sickening crunch of metal I heard Vivienne let out a whoop of triumph.

My eyes flew open. We were still moving at speed. Whatever had run in front of us hadn't even dented the car.

'What are you doing?' I yelled.

'It's fine,' she shouted, pumped up by the near miss.

'What was it?' I said breathlessly.

'A boar.'

'Was it big?'

'Huge. I dread to think what would have happened if we'd hit it,' she said gleefully.

Unsettled, I studied her face in the rear-view mirror and saw that her pupils had grown, making her eyes seem almost black.

'For God's sake. Slow down,' I shouted.

'Relax.' She seemed to be almost enjoying my distress. 'I know what I'm doing.' I realised that she hadn't thought for even a second that we were going to crash. She was in complete control.

I opened my mouth to counter that she'd got it wrong before, but the words died in my mouth.

I tried to swerve but I clipped him.

Taking a deep breath, I tried to think back to what Vivienne had drunk on the beach that night. Although there had been plenty of bottles spilling across the sand, I couldn't remember her drinking that much.

I lost control.

But Vivienne had never lost control – even in the dark and under the influence of drink. A violent shiver ran down my spine despite the stifling temperature in the car.

Vivienne was still driving fast, but at a steadier speed now, and all the while she chatted along as if nothing had happened. I tried to murmur some coherent replies to stop her from noticing how rattled I was, but my mind was whirring. Vivienne was an imperious driver, and it seemed almost unbelievable that she had lost control that night.

I thought back to the wild fear in her eyes when she had come to wake me up. I wondered now if those wide, dark pools that had stared back at me, imploring me to help, had indicated something entirely other than fear.

I tried to rearrange my face in the mirror, but a ghostly image stared back at me.

'Are you OK?' Vivienne caught my eye. 'You've gone very white.'

'I'm fine,' I said, but a waver in my voice betrayed me.

'Must be the shock,' she decided. 'I don't have anything substantial, but there are some mints in my bag. It's just behind the seat so you should be able to fish them out?'

'No, don't worry, I'm fine.'

She shrugged, but she did seem to slow down a little, taking care to manoeuvre the car around smoothly with her slender wrists.

Eventually we caught up with the others, and when we got out Vivienne took great pleasure in recounting the details of our close shave with the boar, and in particular her expert handling.

'It was more likely to have been a bear, *non?*' Hugo said, but Vivienne was adamant she'd seen a boar. When I was asked to weigh in I told them it had been moving so fast that I couldn't be sure, and I felt embarrassed that I'd lost my nerve.

'It would definitely have been a boar,' Robert said dismissively. 'Vivienne has the eyes of a hawk.'

I stood rooted to the spot as he sauntered off.

The rest of the day went by in a blur, with everyone going about their usual routine.

When we got to the beach I was desperate to lie down and hide my face, but Hugo found a ball in the sand and wanted me and David to join in with a boisterous game he'd invented. He exuded wealth even on the beach with his tailored, belted trunks and neat watch, and when I tried to decline he pestered me until I gave in.

The game involved nothing more than tossing the ball to each other and seeing how many times we could clap while it was in the air. We started with one and then worked our way up, with whoever managed the highest number claiming victory.

Normally I would have enjoyed this chance to mess around, but I couldn't muster the energy to plaster over my distress. My mind kept wandering back to Vivienne, and I soon lost track of how many claps we were aiming for.

'Try again. Where's that racing driver instinct?' David teased when I fumbled the ball. He counted down loudly and then tossed it back to me in a ludicrous arc to give me more time to clap.

'*Tricheuse*. Cheat!' Hugo wailed in mock reproach. I forced a tight laugh, but when my poor performance continued they eventually let me bow out.

I must have looked as peaky as I felt because Anne asked me if I was feeling OK when I went to lie next to the others, and I ended up going for a long swim around the bay just to get away from their scrutiny.

Even as my hands wrinkled from exposure to the water and my limbs began to ache, I waited until everyone had lain down for a nap before coming back to shore. I studied Vivienne's sleeping form as I straightened my towel and wondered whether I was just being paranoid.

She was reckless and callous, but surely she would never have tried to hurt someone on purpose?

THIRTEEN

It was a huge relief when we finally got back to the hotel and gathered in the lobby to discuss our plans for the evening. It was decided that we should trek out to one of the better restaurants before we left for Athens, and we settled on a small taverna in the hills for dinner that night. Vivienne decreed that everyone should wear their finery, so we agreed to meet back in the lobby in two hours and went our separate ways to get ready.

Somehow I'd managed to hold it together as I walked with Vivienne and Robert down the corridor, but once my door was locked I slumped against it and slid down until I was kneeling on the floor.

Vivienne hadn't driven any slower on the way home, and I was on high alert as we raced through the forest. In my distressed state the stumps of wood by the roadside kept taking on the shapes of boars, and I had to dig my nails into my thighs to stop myself from shouting out.

The nervous energy had left me now I was back in the safety of my room, and I stayed crumpled against the door for so long that I lost the feeling in my leg.

As I sat there I went over the night of the crash. On solid ground it was easier to convince myself that I was overthinking things, but there was a niggling unease that I couldn't put my finger on. I wished I'd asked more questions before helping Vivienne hide what she'd done, but what could I possibly have asked?

Eventually the sound of the pipes gurgling behind my head jolted me from my stupor and I clambered up, telling myself to get a grip. Vivienne was right, I needed to push the whole thing out of my mind.

I dug out the halter neck dress she had given me and laid it in an emerald green pool on my bed.

I sluiced off the day's dust in a shallow bath, and when I returned to my room I found that Vivienne had left a pair of heeled sandals just inside our adjoining door.

Repressing an urge to get changed in a corner, I stripped off in the middle of the room and carefully slipped the silky material of the dress over my head. I adjusted the ends of the ribbons so they draped elegantly down my bare back and then pinned my hair up using a tortoiseshell clip I'd haggled for at the market.

As an afterthought I put on the necklace we'd stolen from the monastery for good luck and tucked the solid bulk of it under the neck of my dress.

I bent down to slip on the sandals Vivienne had left me and froze. They were the ones I'd tried on in her room, but there was no way she could have known. She must have seen that I'd laid out this green dress and decided they matched the outfit.

The pipes gurgled next door, and I wished I'd waited a bit longer to get ready. If Vivienne was only just running a bath, I'd work up a sweat in my room before they were ready to go. There was no point getting undressed, though, and I didn't want to sit in the lobby looking all trussed up on my own.

I tied a scarf around my wrist to give the outfit a final flourish, and when I spun around to look at the effect, my reflection made me catch my breath. The emerald green of the dress brought out the golden strands where the sun had bleached my hair, and the cut made the most of my new curves.

If I squinted I could almost have passed for Vivienne, but when I walked around the room the illusion crumbled. The sound of the heels on the floor was too loud, and the voluminous fabric billowed out awkwardly with every unsteady step.

The click of Vivienne and Robert's door stopped me in my tracks, and I listened as the unmistakable rhythm of Vivienne's heels clipped down the corridor. It must have been Robert running a bath.

When the sound had almost faded away I opened the door to take a peek at her outfit. She seemed almost to glide along in a froth of polka dot taffeta, and when she disappeared around the corner something compelled me to follow her.

I slipped off my sandals and tiptoed down the corridor as quietly as I could, and when I reached the end I pressed myself against the wall. A clunking sound announced the arrival of the lift and I took a furtive glance around the corner – but it wasn't Vivienne standing there.

The porter jumped when I leant out further, but he quickly regained his composure and gestured for me to enter the lift first. I hastily declined, and he gave my bare feet a sidelong glance before pressing the button.

Vivienne's disappearance threw me. She couldn't have got to the lift that quickly, especially wearing those heels.

A door creaked and then slammed shut, and my head jerked around as I heard the muffled clack of her heels somewhere over to my right. I followed the sound and emerged onto a landing with an ornate banister.

The clacking of heels echoed up loudly around the bare walls, and I tiptoed across the wooden floor to steal a glance at Vivienne.

She glittered below me in the dimly lit stairwell, her throat and slender wrists encircled with jewels, and although there was nobody else there to admire her, she walked slowly with her chin up and her shoulders back as if she were already in view. I could see her lacquered nails where she was resting one hand lightly on the banister, and I noted how she was using the other to waft the train of her dress.

Because our rooms were a few floors up we mostly used the lift, and I'd stopped noticing the sweeping staircase in the lobby when we walked past. But clearly Vivienne had kept it in mind for when she wanted to make a grand entrance.

Fixated on her graceful descent, I watched until she disappeared from view and then slipped back to my room. I smoothed down my dress and waited until I heard the clomp of Robert's shoes. I peeked my head out to see him disappearing around the corner with his hair still wet and made my way back to the staircase. I didn't want him to miss my entrance.

My steps were hesitant at first, and I gripped inelegantly to the banister. But as I relaxed into the movement I lifted my chin up and pulled my shoulders back, trailing my fingers lightly along the grooves on the cold marble surface.

As I made my way carefully down through the deserted floors with their grand columns and faded curtains, I imagined what the hotel would have been like in its prime. I could picture movie stars and diplomats' wives making this very same descent, and raucous dance parties in the ballroom that now seemed to do little more than house abandoned chairs.

I stopped to steel myself when I reached the first floor. From the sound of the chatter the others were standing directly below the stairs, so I fixed my gaze on the middle distance and lowered myself onto the top step.

My eye was drawn to Anne as the group came into sight. Her fuchsia dress and its loud zigzag pattern stood out against the men's pastel suits and looked practically garish next to the monochrome outfits the women had opted for. Vivienne's dress was terribly elegant now I could see it in full, and Marie was sporting a floaty white trouser suit that would have swamped anyone else but made her look powerful.

I was a little overdressed, but not outrageously so.

Nobody had noticed me yet, so I slowed my steps and scanned the group again. Robert and Mark were nowhere to be seen, and I suspected they might have planned to stop in Mark's room for a drink before coming down.

Anne spotted me first and let out a squeal of delight, prompting the others to turn around. Heat rose in my cheeks, but I tried to maintain my composure, wafting the hem of my dress around as Vivienne had done until I reached the bottom of the stairs.

I was engulfed by a wave of enthusiastic compliments, but I was listening out for Vivienne to say something. I couldn't read the look on her face, and when David leant across her to tell me how charming I looked she pursed her lips.

'I knew it would suit you,' she said finally, making her way over to me when the hubbub had died down.

I wasn't sure whether to acknowledge the oblique compliment or give her one of my own, but she quickly cut me back down to size.

'You could do with some lipstick, though,' she said, leaning in. 'You don't have the complexion to get away with not wearing colour.'

I fought the urge to press my fingers up to my mouth, my new-found stature shrinking.

'Here, try this.' She took out her lipstick and wiped off the top layer of coral paste on her wrist. 'It's the perfect colour to bring out your tan.'

I shook my head. 'Come here,' she insisted, and when I'd made sure that none of the others were watching I tilted my head back reluctantly and let her paint my mouth.

When she'd finished she leant back to admire her work, and I noticed that a smattering of freckles had appeared on the bridge of her nose during our afternoon out in the sun.

'Press your lips together.'

Like a child I followed her instructions, and the creamy texture of the lipstick felt strange on my mouth.

'It looks good. You should keep it,' she said, pressing the warm container into my hand. I felt like I should decline her offer, but instead I thanked her and slipped the tiny bullet of colour into my bag.

I wondered if I had time to find a mirror to inspect my new look, but when I glanced over at the lift Robert and Mark were already striding towards us. Turning back to face the group, I felt a hum of anticipation running through me.

'Sorry we're late,' Mark slurred apologetically, and I was surprised by just how drunk he was.

'You're not fooling me this time.' Robert's voice rang out beside my ear and I jumped, staggering to keep my balance as my heel clipped his shoes. He caught hold of my waist to steady me, his hand lingering.

'Got her,' he said, letting go as Vivienne and Marie looked over.

He leant in and I could smell the whisky on his breath. 'You look delightful.' He didn't bother to lower his voice and I cringed. I could see the others watching us, perfectly within earshot.

'This is Vivienne's outfit,' I said loudly, gesturing towards her. 'Oh, I do like your shirt, though.'

My words had been no more than an attempt to change the subject, but now I looked more closely it was quite distinctive. It was red, short-sleeved and wide-collared, and he'd tucked it into his trousers with a belt; it suited him greatly, but it was quite the departure from his usual style.

'I wasn't sure, but I got it on a whim.' He tugged at the material and gave me a wide grin. 'Did you hear that Viv? Jean likes my shirt,' he called over to her.

'Shall we go now our guests of honour are here?' she said, ignoring his remark, and everyone followed as she sauntered towards the door.

I hung back to let the others go first, and I couldn't help but notice that Robert stuck rather closely to my side.

FOURTEEN

We took a few wrong turns before we finally found the tiny taverna tucked up on the hillside. As we parked under the broad yellow light thrown from the restaurant some of the diners left their tables to admire our cars, and I felt self-conscious as I slid out. We'd climbed so high that the air was cool on my skin, and I could taste the pine of the surrounding forest on the tip of my tongue.

Enjoying the attention, Vivienne took the lead as we picked our way across the rough path and up the stairs to the open-air decking. When we reached the top I couldn't help but think we looked like animals escaped from the zoo in our chirpy colours and patterns next to the modest black outfits of the locals sat around the bar.

Our bohemian appearance didn't seem to have put off the rotund waiter, who introduced himself with much theatrical grace as Andreas. I found it difficult to understand his thick accent, but he seemed delighted that we'd travelled up to his taverna in such a large group – an attitude no doubt helped along by the expensive cars we'd parked outside.

Andreas led us over to a long table at the edge of the decking with a vertigo-inducing drop to the trees below. I took the seat closest to the edge, and during the lulls in conversation I could hear the whisper of the early evening breeze stirring the leaves.

Robert took the seat to my right, and I was acutely aware of the heat of his thighs spread too close to mine. I tried to distract myself by craning my neck to watch the swallows dipping and darting over the other diners.

Everything about the taverna was unapologetically Greek. The twang of traditional music blasted out from the radio, and the menus were handwritten with amendments all over the pages. It soon transpired that even with these modifications they weren't up to date – almost every time we pointed to something Andreas shook his head regretfully and explained that the kitchen had run out.

Robert had been jovial up until that point, but his tapping on the table betrayed a growing impatience and it made me feel tense. We almost managed to get through everyone's orders, but when Anne's dithering became too much he finally snapped. 'What's the point of giving us these if you don't have anything listed on them?' he challenged Andreas, waving his menu at him. I recoiled, but Andreas didn't seem concerned.

'You like wine? Meat? Fish?' he asked, and we all nodded. 'I will bring you our best selection.' He plucked the menu out of Robert's hand and marched off before he had the chance to reply.

Two large carafes of wine arrived quickly, followed by some generous bowls of fava bean dip and a selection of freshly baked breads. Robert's irritation mellowed after he'd had something to eat and drink, and I made sure that I was quick to top up his wine. The locals watched curiously as we ate, but nobody else on our table seemed to care so I tried to shake off the feeling of being watched.

More trays arrived carrying Andreas's promised selection, though this seemed to include dishes that weren't even on the menu. There were plates of salted fish, capers, aubergines, wilted greens, corn, lamb, rabbit and chicken, as well as a few I didn't recognise.

We fell upon the food, anxious to sample the full spread before it disappeared. I'd never tasted so many different flavours in my life, and the fresh ingredients made even the simple salads taste divine; the swollen tomatoes were intensely sweet, and the olive oil had an almost peppery taste.

Anne normally liked to maintain a sense of British decorum at dinner, but even she was so overcome that she ended up leaning far out over the others to prong the items that were out of reach on her fork.

When all the plates had been scraped clean we sat back, cupping our stomachs in our hands. The sun had sunk low in the sky, and when it touched the horizon everything turned a pale shade of red.

One of the other waiters brought us shots with the bill, including one for Andreas. I steeled myself before throwing mine back, but I was pleasantly surprised by its sweetness and the warmth that spread across my stomach.

Andreas didn't seem to be in any hurry to kick us out so we sat there a bit longer, chatting until the sun dipped out of sight.

Vivienne dragged her chair over to sit between me and Robert, and the three of us shuffled around so we could admire the afterglow that hung on the horizon. My earlier unease seemed ridiculous here on the hillside sandwiched between them, and as we chatted away my niggling anxiety faded to the back of my mind.

It was getting late by the time we left the taverna. The drive seemed to take much longer on the way down, and the warmth of the car lulled me into a stupor until we reached the garage and Vivienne jolted to a halt.

The copious amounts of food and wine seemed to have had the opposite effect on everyone else, and when we reconvened the mood was one of restless energy rather than doziness.

Vivienne proposed another drink, and this was met with hearty agreement from the others. She led the way to the centre of town and I followed resignedly, Robert still lingering by my side.

The first bar we found was a bit of a dump with some wooden benches outside, but nobody seemed to care. As we were all squashing up to fit on the seats Anne slipped in between me and Robert, and I thought I saw a look of irritation flit across his face.

I felt drowsy and all I wanted was a cool glass of water, but Hugo emerged from the bar carrying a tray of shots. David insisted on us all linking arms to drink them so I couldn't back out, and I coughed as the alcohol hit the back of my throat. I was hoping for the sweet drink we'd had at the taverna, but this cheap imitation was chemical in its strength. It burnt rather than warmed as it trickled its way down to my stomach.

Vivienne batted away my excuses when another round of shots appeared. I looked around desperately for somewhere I might be able to discreetly pour it out, but she tipped the glass up so that I had to swallow the liquid to stop it dribbling down my chin.

Eventually the waitress came out to pack up the tables and shooed us away. Old women tutted at us as we swayed past, and on the way back Anne tripped over a loose cobblestone. She took a graceful tumble and lay on her side giggling and waving her arms around like an upturned beetle until David knelt down and peeled her off the floor.

As we passed the harbour Vivienne came to an abrupt stop. 'I know what we should do.' The rest of us carried on walking but she called out to us again. 'Wait, I have an idea.'

'What now?' David said, turning around with Anne swinging limply from his arm.

'I want to go swimming,' Vivienne said, and we followed her gaze to the bit of concrete where the local boys jumped into the sea to cool down in the afternoons.

David groaned. 'Absolutely not. I'm taking this one home.' He marched up the hill with Anne clinging to his arm, and I was surprised by the strength hiding underneath all his excess mass.

'*Bonne idée*,' Marie said gamely, tugging at Hugo's sleeve until he agreed to join them.

They turned to Mark next, but he shook his head. 'Too drunk,' he said simply before following David and Anne up the road with unsteady steps. At least we had someone in the group who was able to take themselves off to bed when they needed to.

'Come on then, don't just stand there,' Vivienne shouted towards me and Robert. We hesitated, and the next thing we knew Vivienne was running with surprising agility towards the sea.

Hugo and Marie followed, whooping and laughing as they went, but we stayed behind to watch. The three of them stripped off hastily when they got to the edge, and the pale skin where their swimming costumes had blocked out the sun was just visible.

I laughed nervously but Robert stayed silent, the only sound their screams carrying on the air as they adjusted to the cold.

Now that we'd stopped walking I realised how unsteady I felt. 'I think I'd better get some sleep . . .' I said, trailing off. I held my breath and avoided looking at Robert's face.

'That sounds like an excellent idea, I'll come with you.'

We set off steadily up the hill, neither of us talking, but when Robert sped up I found it difficult to keep up with his long strides.

My whole body hummed with anticipation as we passed a row of cramped flats, the muffled conversations of the inhabitants floating down to us from behind net curtains. Robert's strong jaw was illuminated in the soft glow from the windows, but when we turned onto a dark side street it was the blond waves of his hair that picked up the moonlight.

The residential patter faded quickly as we climbed, and soon the only sounds were my laboured breath and Robert's heavy footsteps.

Lie to Me

My foot caught on the uneven stone and Robert's hand flew out to steady me. He held on a moment too long, and when he let go my hair stood on end as he traced his fingers along the sensitive skin on the inside of my wrist.

I felt a jolt of relief as we re-emerged onto the well lit road running up to the hotel, but I took a step away when I saw his shadow hulking over mine.

When we finally reached the hotel I stopped at the entrance to catch my breath but he beckoned for me to follow him to the lift. I saw Nikos at his desk out of the corner of my eye, but an overriding sense of shame stopped me from calling out.

We made the rest of the journey up to the room in silence, the only sounds the click of the lift and the anxious tapping of my shoes against the floor. The walk down the corridor was just as awkward, and over far too quickly. When we reached our doors I drew out the process of locating my keys, unsure what to do next.

'Maybe I can come in for a drink?' Robert leant against the door frame, towering over me.

His proximity was unbearable, but there was nowhere for me to go. I'd been waiting for the opportunity to see if his perceived flirtation was real, but I'd never thought anything would come of it.

Robert misread my hesitation. 'The others won't be back for a while.'

'I'm quite tired . . .' I said feebly and he gave an unkind laugh.

'Don't be like that. I only want to come in for a drink.'

'I don't have anything interesting in here, but you can come in if you want.' I didn't think he'd follow up on my offer, but when I held the door open he stepped inside.

He did a lap of the room, his gaze flicking from corner to corner.

'Do you want a tea?' I picked up the kettle and walked over to the door.

I was eager to have a few moments in the kitchenette at the end of the corridor to compose myself, but Robert shook his head. 'I have a bottle of something a bit stronger stashed away.'

'I think I've probably had enough to drink for one night,' I said, but he sidestepped me and disappeared back out through the main door.

I wandered over to my bed. My legs felt tired and achy now that we'd stopped walking, so I perched myself on the bed and let my torso slump against the headboard.

'Here we go.' Robert made me start as he clattered back in with two glasses and a bottle of amber liquid. Everything was silent around us, and I strained my ears for the sound of any footsteps in the corridor.

He perched himself next to me and I held up my hands in refusal when he tried to pass me a glass. 'I think I could probably do with getting some sleep,' I said, but he just shrugged and poured a generous measure for himself. Clutching the glass, he made a show of looking around for a chair that he knew wasn't there and then perched beside me on the bed.

'Cheers.' He threw his drink back and the glass made a dull clunk as he set it down on the bedside table.

He looked on in amusement as I picked it up for something to do with my hands, and in the silence I became unbearably conscious of the fact that he was sitting on my bed.

Unable to think of anything intelligent to say, I sat there counting the ticking of the clock. I thought that if enough seconds passed, Vivienne might return.

'I don't think you're going to find anything in there,' Robert said, and I realised I was staring intently at the bottom of the empty glass. He tapped his fingers against the bedframe, and the sound put my hair on edge.

Summoning all my resolve, I looked up and met his gaze.

His eyes were a little bloodshot, but my attention was drawn to his lips. I'd never noticed them before, but they were thin and mean, curled up at one end in a smirk. Not like Vivienne's, with her creamy lipstick and her perfect cupid's bow. Her smile often quivering on the verge of laughter.

Trying not to look away too quickly, I placed the glass back on the bedside table. Robert moved his thigh over so it was touching mine and I felt the atmosphere shift. A buzzing started up in my ears, drowning out the sound of the clock.

'How's your cut doing?' he took my hand in his, gently turning it over to inspect the puckered skin where I'd sliced my finger chopping tomatoes on the beach.

'It's fine,' I managed to stutter as he ran his fingers higher up my arm.

He shifted my hand so it was resting on the inside of his leg, and as I opened my mouth to protest he leant forward to kiss me.

I froze as he wrapped his hands around the back of my head and drew me closer. For a second I stopped thinking and let him kiss me, shocked by the feeling of his lips against mine. But then I came to my senses.

I tried to wriggle away from him, but he only tightened his grip.

'Don't.' He ran his hand down my leg, tugging up the hem of my skirt. 'I know you want this.'

He shifted so that he was pressed against me, his bulky frame trapping me against the headboard.

'I'm sorry.' This time I shoved him hard in the chest, and he looked bewildered.

'What's wrong?' he said, and I had to avert my eyes from the sight of Vivienne's coral lipstick smudged around his mouth and on his teeth.

'Vivienne,' I blurted out. Shame flooded through me and I pulled the duvet covers over my bare legs.

At the sound of his wife's name Robert grew angry, and I thought too late about how much he'd had to drink.

'Now you think about Vivienne, you little tease.'

'I'm sorry,' I repeated dumbly.

'You were never interested in me, were you?'

I shook my head vigorously, realising too late it was the wrong thing to do.

'You're obsessed with her, aren't you?' he sneered, and I felt like I'd been punched in the gut. 'I see the way you look at her, the way you copy her every move.'

I shook my head again, flinching as he leered over me. 'Answer me when I'm talking to you.' His voice was raised and a spray of spittle landed on my face. 'I should have known, you're sick in the head.'

Repulsed, I turned my head away and he gave a cruel laugh.

'Well, you're not going to last very long around here. Vivienne doesn't like to hang on to her protégés, and she'll be particularly keen to get rid of you when I tell her about your little infatuation.'

The springs of the bed squealed as he stood up abruptly. I had thought his departure would fill me with relief, but panic gripped tight around my stomach.

'Robert,' I begged, and he snarled. 'This was all a terrible misunderstanding. Please can we just forget about it?'

He wrenched the door open, but without warning he swivelled on his heels and stormed back towards me. I shied away as he got closer, but he veered away just before he reached the bed.

'Give me those.' He snatched the whisky glasses off the bedside table and they made a terrible clinking as he took them to the door.

When the door slammed shut I sank back onto the pillows, wiping the rest of the lipstick away until it became a gash of colour on the back of my wrist.

I hoped he would have enough time to cool off before Vivienne got back. If he didn't, who knew what he might say.

FIFTEEN

Vivienne got back from her swim later than I'd expected, and I could hear her careening around the room as she got ready for bed. I pressed my eye to the keyhole and watched her pacing up and down in her nightdress, narrating a steady stream of information to Robert. I thought about what he'd said – *You're obsessed . . . I see the way you look at her* – and a shudder rolled down my spine.

The only sound I could hear from him was an occasional grunt of dissatisfaction, so I could only assume he was already half asleep. I kept my ear pressed against the door for as long as I could bear to kneel on the floor, and when I could stand the shooting pain no longer I pulled the pillows off my bed and wedged them underneath my knees.

I must have drifted off shortly afterwards because I woke up on the floor with a stiff back.

I rolled over to stretch my spine out and pressed my ear to the door. Nothing.

Pulling myself up by the door frame, I looked through the keyhole and was relieved to see that everything was still.

A sudden light-headedness washed over me, and I clasped onto the door frame for support. I had drunk far too much the night before, and my body was crying out for something sweet and greasy from the bakery.

I rearranged my sheet and pillows back on the bed and sat down. I was anxious to hear what Robert would say when he woke up, but if I left now I could pick up a pastry and make it back again before they woke up.

As I was getting ready I noticed that the bin in my room was almost overflowing. The observation stuck out to me, but it wasn't until I came back from the bathroom that I realised why.

Reaching for a towel, I saw that it still had the makeup stains from a few days before. The maids normally changed the towels when they came to clean, and I wondered if they'd somehow forgotten my room.

A sense of dread took hold of me, and I tried to stay calm as I walked over to check the bed. I was relieved to see that the sheets seemed fresh, but when I lifted up the pillow something caught my eye. Leaning closer, I saw that it was the stain from the tea Konstantin had made me. I did the maths and my hair stood on end. That had been almost a week ago, and I had definitely felt the key under my pillow since then. If the maid hadn't moved it, who had?

Dressing hastily, I cursed as the heavy door slammed shut behind me and scurried down the street to the bakery just in time for opening. There was no queue, so I managed to pick up a pastry almost straight from the oven. I hastily counted out my coins and rushed back up the road, my tight grip making the butter leak through the brown paper onto my hand.

When I got back I tiptoed down the corridor and shut the door quietly. I placed the pastry on the side and froze as a muffled sound caught my attention.

Holding my breath, I turned to face the adjoining door and strained my ears until I heard the sound again. I hadn't imagined it. There was a murmur of voices coming from next door.

I crept over to the door and knelt down so I could see in. The curtain had been opened to let in a chink of light, and I could see the outline of the desk with a rumpled dress hanging over it, but Vivienne and Robert were out of sight.

Vivienne's languid yawn stretched across the room.

'Please don't do that right next to my ear,' Robert grumbled.

'You should have come swimming with us, I feel absolutely fine.'

'Good for you,' Robert said, and I pictured him pulling the sheets up tighter around himself and rolling over.

'Well, I thought you were right behind us. Where did you go?'

'I wanted to come back for an early night,' he said, and I was almost impressed by how unruffled he sounded.

'With Jean?' she said bitterly, and my stomach lurched.

I heard the rustling of the covers and the mattress squeaked, as if Robert was heaving himself up to a seated position. 'You've got some nerve.'

'What ever do you mean?'

'In Corfu. I woke up in the middle of the night and you were gone.'

'I couldn't sleep so I went for a walk,' Vivienne said defiantly.

Lie to Me

'Liar. Your keys were gone.'

'And then I went for a drive.'

'Fine. But what I'd like to know is who you were with?'

'No one,' she said, drawing out the gap between the words.

'How am I meant to believe that?' he spat. 'Who did you find? Some local Adonis who works on the fishing boats? A melancholy barman?'

'You're being ridiculous. Anyway, I saw the way you were watching Jean last night,' Vivienne said venomously. 'A younger model. I thought you were better than a sad cliché, Robert.'

'Ha, I was watching Jean to keep her away from you.'

There was a pause, and I heard the sheets rustle again. 'What do you mean?'

'I felt odd about her standing there watching you strip off so I made her come with me. Don't you find it unsettling how she stares at you? She didn't take her eyes off you last night.'

Vivienne let out a short, sharp laugh. 'Don't be ridiculous.'

'I'm telling you, there's something odd about her.'

'Shh, you do know how thin the walls are?' she hissed, her voice lowered.

'Jean won't be able to hear us, she's gone out,' Robert said confidently. 'She always goes to get breakfast at this time in the morning, and I heard her door shut earlier.'

My skin crawled with the thought that he'd been listening to me coming and going, and I pressed my ear to the keyhole so it was flush with the door.

'Do you not find it at all strange that she's started dressing like you? I swear she's even starting to pick up on some of your mannerisms.'

'Have you noticed that you're starting to come off a bit mad?' Vivienne retorted, but I thought she sounded rather pleased.

'I'm not the one that's mad. The others were saying how charming she is yesterday and I almost had to ask if they were talking about the same person. She's fashioned herself as your shadow, and I don't even think she knows she's doing it.'

I could feel a headache coming on, as if someone was slowly tightening a band around my temple. I tried to tell myself that this was just Robert lashing out after he'd been rejected, but some of it rang far too true.

'What's she ever done to you? She's completely harmless – most of the time I forget she's even there,' Vivienne laughed, and I felt a stab of shame.

'Whatever you say, I think it's time for a changing of the guard.'

'Robert, we're just about to race. Where am I going to rustle up a new navigator in Greece?'

'There are loads of other teams to poach from, or you could just pick someone off the street like you normally do,' he jibed, and I thought I heard the thwack of her hitting him lightly with her magazine.

'Stop it. I'm not ready to part with her yet, and I won't have another word said on the subject.'

She steered the conversation onto other things, and when I was sure the topic was closed I staggered as quietly as I could over to the main door. I opened it wide and then let it swing shut with a crash.

Vivienne and Robert fell silent as I crossed the room and flopped back onto my bed.

My stomach rumbled loudly, so I sat up and pulled the pastry towards me.

The custard filling had gone cold since I'd picked it up and been smeared around the brown paper on our walk, but I needed to gorge. Tearing off thick strips I pushed the pastry into my mouth and chewed angrily, wondering how I was ever going to face Robert again.

SIXTEEN

The owner greeted us brightly when we arrived at the garage later that morning, but much to Marie's disappointment his son wasn't with him.

'Too hot,' was his only explanation when she gestured to indicate the height of the small boy. 'You're crazy going out in this,' he said, waving his arms around to emphasise his point. We nodded along to appease him, but we had no intention of turning back.

Marie and Hugo had blocked our car in when they parked the Ferrari the day before, and they purred out of the garage first before we made our way to the Saab. I had avoided eye contact with Robert all morning and feigned a cough as I walked past him, flinching at the memory of his stubble against my skin.

We got in and Vivienne turned the key, but the car made a feeble clicking sound before the vibrations stilled.

'Oh, for God's sake,' Vivienne said as Robert and Mark roared out of sight in their Saab.

She turned the key again, and I could see the sweat beading on her forehead in the close air of the garage. We called over to the owner to see if he had some cables we could use to jump-start the car, but he didn't make any moves to help us.

'Too hot,' he repeated with a shrug of his shoulders, as if to suggest we should have listened to him before.

Vivienne sighed and pulled at the navy pedal pushers she was wearing. They looked tight against her skin, and I was glad for my looser gingham ones. She tried to start the car a few more times and let out a growl of frustration when it stayed still.

'We could give it a push start?' I suggested, and Vivienne frowned at me.

'How? The others are long gone, and he can hardly help us to push it, can he?' She nodded her head towards the mechanic as he limped across the room.

'I can push it,' I said defiantly, my ears burning as I remembered how quick she'd been to dismiss me to Robert that morning. I was sure I'd pushed heavier vehicles at the stable.

'Come off it.' She gave my girlish outfit a dismissive up and down. 'I think even Robert would find it difficult to push this alone, so you most definitely couldn't,' she said, and I sat up straighter.

'Watch me.' I jumped out and lined myself up at the back of the car. Planting my feet firmly on the floor, I was glad I'd decided to wear plimsolls rather than my leather sandals.

Vivienne sighed loudly, but I was undeterred. 'Ready?' I called out and waited for her to give the go-ahead.

'Ready,' she said reluctantly, and I pushed.

Nothing happened at first, and Vivienne turned to gloat. Taking a deep breath, I squatted down further and braced my torso before throwing my weight forward against the bumper.

The muscles in my back screamed and my thighs burnt, but the pain eased up as the wheels started to turn.

The car began to inch along the concrete, and when the engine kicked in I gave it a final push. Vivienne did a few tight circles before stopping to let the engine run while I got back in.

She gave me an appraising nod and I pulled my lips into a strained smile.

It was market day, and the pungent smell of livestock hung in the air as the farmers jollied goats along with sticks while small children ran around cradling watermelons bigger than babies in their arms.

As we rounded a corner the sight of a large group of policemen in navy uniforms made me stiffen, and I tried to remind myself that we were quite safe inside the car. I was confident they wouldn't be able to identify us from that distance through the glass, but one of the men lifted his gaze to meet mine as if he'd heard my thoughts.

I quickly turned my head so the policeman was out of my line of sight and stared through the opposite window until I was sure we'd left them far behind in the winding streets. I was tempted to tell Vivienne to put her foot down, but I knew she'd tell me to stop worrying. The officers had probably just been admiring the car, after all.

The buildings became less frequent and more derelict as we continued beyond the suburbs. Vivienne sped up instinctively, and I tightened my scarf to secure it against the breeze.

We'd taken several long journeys after the incident with the boar and I'd settled back into the pace of it now I'd shaken off the shock and realised I was being paranoid.

We took a few tight corners with the tyres throwing up dust, but when the road straightened out Vivienne told me to hang on.

I knew not to wait around, and as soon as I caught hold of the grip on the door Vivienne put her foot down and my head banged back painfully.

At first I had wondered how Vivienne would ever race again after the accident in Corfu, but I'd failed to factor in her addiction to speed – one I was starting to share.

My driving had improved in the past couple of weeks, and where I had once been cautious, Vivienne's goading tuition had taught me to relish the rush of taking a bend at speed. I started to imagine that I was racing in my own car, and I dared to wonder if Vivienne might one day put in a good word for me with Saab if she no longer needed me to navigate.

But even when I wasn't behind the wheel I shared in the excitement of riding shotgun. I watched the road carefully and tried to anticipate how Vivienne would take every bend, leaning into each turn as time slowed down until it became a series of freeze frames.

It didn't take Vivienne long to catch up with the others, and we spent the morning practising on tough mountain passes so hairy that I instinctively sucked my breath in every time a drop came into sight. The narrow dust tracks had loose gravel that made the car slide perilously every time we took a corner, and despite being almost 8,000 feet up there was not a single wall or parapet.

You wouldn't want to meet someone coming the other way on these tracks when you were in a hurry, so we had all bundled a few bottles of wine into our cars and took it in turns to race while everyone else sat at the top of the track and flagged down approaching drivers. With the help of much hand-waving we managed to explain that there was going to be someone belting it down the road and invited them to have a drink, and by the end of the morning we'd collected a small huddle of balding farmers who gestured excitedly every time one of the cars slid past in a terrific cloud of dust.

By the time it was my turn to race with Vivienne I'd had a few glasses of wine to calm my nerves, and I regretted it as soon as I got in the car. We'd drawn the short straw to race Marie and Hugo, and as soon as Mark waved the shirt we were using as a temporary flag Marie cut in front of us and we had to swerve dramatically.

Vivienne snarled and gunned after her, making the car skid menacingly around the dusty corner. It didn't take her long to get back on Marie's tail, but it was too narrow for us to pass.

The roads we'd already encountered in Greece had been pretty poor, but these were something else. The rutted, pitted surfaces made the car tilt so much that the paint was scratched from the sides with an ear-splitting squeal. And the sharp-topped hills sent us shooting into the air – my stomach lurching every time the wheels left the ground.

Landing heavily after one of these jumps, Vivienne threw all caution to the wind. We had a straight run-up to the designated finishing line where the others were waiting, and it was our last chance to win.

She floored the Saab and we edged alongside Marie and Hugo bumper-to-bumper.

The swirling clouds of dirt made it difficult to see who was out in front, but Marie wasn't taking any chances. She rammed into us, and we were flung sideways.

'What the hell is she doing?' Vivienne shouted. She wrenched the wheel to the left to get away from them, but the cars were wedged together.

'The bumpers are locked,' I screeched.

Vivienne banged her fist against the window and shouted at Marie. 'Brake. Now.'

I looked over to their car and saw Hugo's face pale against the window, his mouth hanging agape. Vivienne slammed her foot down on the brake but the Ferrari dragged us along, the static wheels scraping along the ground beneath us.

Marie's horn blared out, and I looked up to see that we were hurtling towards the others.

'Vivienne!' I shouted, but we were already too close. So close I could see the whites of the farmers' eyes as they stared at us in horror.

'Get out the way!' Vivienne screamed, and Mark snapped into action, shouting and pulling the farmers up by the scruff of the collar. They jumped out of the way and I heard the crunch of glass as we flattened the impromptu picnic. The car began to slow as the road climbed uphill again, and when we bumped into the cliff face the cars popped apart. As soon as she was able to, Vivienne pulled on the handbrake and forced the door open.

She marched over to the driver's side of the Ferrari and I hurriedly followed. She looked like she might punch Marie's window in, but Mark got there first and held up a calming hand.

'I think we can call that a draw,' he said dryly, and Vivienne threw her hands up in exasperation. Marie flung open her door and launched a volley of French expletives at Vivienne, who just turned her back and marched down the hill.

I slumped against the car and Mark joined me, lighting a cigarette.

'Sorry, it's my last one,' he said, and we passed it between us, taking long drags.

We watched Vivienne and Marie square up to one another again at the bottom of the hill, and Mark sighed. 'Definitely a draw. Equal points for idiocy.'

We called it a day there, but after the rush of the mountain passes Vivienne quickly became frustrated when we arrived back in Igoumenitsa and got stuck in the dying throes of the market. Many of the stallholders had laden up their donkeys with unsold wares and were making slow progress down the road while the more persistent of them braved the motorbikes, whizzing around the sad animals to hawk their goods from car to car.

'That's it,' Vivienne huffed when a trader knocked loudly on our window. 'Drive the car back to the garage, will you?'

She flung her door back so quickly that she almost hit him, and she was out of the car before I had the chance to agree. 'Meet you back at the hotel,' she called behind her, but the end of her sentence was dampened as the door slammed shut.

I shimmied over to the driver's seat and watched Vivienne's progress through the rear-view mirror. She pushed her way past a man trying to sell her trinkets, but when she reached the road that led to the hotel she turned in the wrong direction and strode off. I blinked, and then she was gone.

While I'd been distracted, a fruit seller had pulled in front of me and then stopped in the middle of the road to have a chat. He shouted and gestured at me to squeeze around him but there wasn't enough room, so by the time I got back to the garage the others had already been and gone.

I spun the car around and reversed it smoothly into the tight gap, and I was thrilled when I realised the mechanic had witnessed the whole manoeuvre. He nodded his approval and I beamed – maybe it wasn't so silly harbouring driving ambitions of my own.

My elation was dampened by the indignity of trying to cover the car with the heavy dust sheet on my own. It was hard enough on a normal day, but after the terrific effort I'd put into pushing the car that morning my arms were shaking. I almost managed to secure it but at the last moment I lost my grip, and the material slid off and lay in a heap on the floor.

Leaning against the bonnet to give myself some respite before a second attempt, an image of the car as I had found it on the night of Vivienne's crash jumped unbidden into my mind.

I tried to push it away, but my focus snagged on something.

Vivienne had left it in a garage at the edge of town, covered with a dust sheet. I had approached it cautiously and grabbed hold of the material, pausing in this position while I worked up the courage to lift it. After several moments I steeled myself and pulled, all the muscles in my arms straining until the dent slowly came into view.

My stomach flipped and I clasped the bonnet for support.

The dent. It was in the wrong place.

I was quite sure Vivienne had told me she'd clipped the man with the side of her car. No, I was certain – I remember thinking what a cruel near miss it must have been. But the dent I had fixed that night was deep and squarely in the middle of the bonnet.

I tried to swerve but I clipped him.

A shiver ran through me and I gripped the car tighter, willing myself to remember some detail that would account for this inconsistency in Vivienne's story.

I stayed there for a while, my breath coming in short, sharp gasps as I racked my brain and came up with blanks. What had I got myself mixed up in?

When the mechanic came back to check on me I abandoned the dust sheet on the floor and left as fast as I could, my legs dragging beneath me like lead as I considered my options. In-between hideous stabs of guilt I tried to think clearly, but even in my terrified state one thing was clear: I knew I had to leave. I had to get away from these people.

SEVENTEEN

We were planning to drive to Athens the following day, and once we got there I reasoned it would be easier to slip away. I'd already decided I couldn't go back to the stables and my father's wrath, but maybe I could catch the ferry to another country and start afresh – Italy or Spain maybe. God knows what I would do there, but even as I considered this I felt an instinctive attraction to the raw and careless freedom of absconding alone to a new country.

The main problem was money. Because Vivienne had insisted there was no point paying me until we got back to England, I had little more than the petty change she'd given me to spend while we were away. She'd offered to pay for all my food and board, so I hadn't seen any reason to grumble about this proposal at the time, but now I cursed myself. I'd been foolish, and it would raise too much attention if I asked for any funds at this stage.

I continued to pace around my hotel room, my clammy feet leaving a trail of prints along the floor.

Could I make it to Spain with the loose change I had? Probably not. Without the language or any contacts it would be hard to find a job, and I didn't want to test my chances on the streets.

I had visions of traipsing around under the harsh sun, the heat of the ground burning through the worn soles of my shoes.

No, I would have to find a way to sneak on to a ferry back to England and move as far away from the stables as I could. There would be something that I could turn my hand to, especially if I moved to a city.

My gaze slid over to the cabinet where I kept my passport, the practicalities of what I was planning now settling in. I pulled the drawer out and a pencil rattled across the dusty wood. The drawer was empty.

Disorientated, I pulled the whole thing out and tipped its contents onto the bed. Old ticket stumps and a handkerchief that had been wedged in one corner fell out, but there was no sign of the blue passport. I stuck my head inside the cabinet to make sure it hadn't slipped down the back but there was nothing apart from cobwebs.

I cast my mind back. I was almost certain I'd last seen my passport when I showed *The Times* clipping of me and Vivienne at the Tulip Rally to the others. I remembered carefully sliding the thin paper between the pages of my passport to keep it safe and putting them both back in the drawer, but now they were gone.

A rap on the door made me jump. 'Are you ready?' It was Vivienne.

'Be right there.' I pushed the drawer back into place, a heavy weight settling in my stomach.

Pausing for a moment to organise my face into what I hoped was an easy smile, I took a deep breath and opened the door to find Vivienne in a billowing silk dress with an intricate purple pattern.

The sight of her threw me for a moment. She looked just as surprised to see me still in my dusty clothes, and then I remembered we'd agreed to make a last visit to our favourite taverna that night.

A cough made me aware of Robert lurking further down the corridor, and I was thankful he hadn't come to the door.

'You look like you've seen a ghost,' Vivienne said, taking a step back to get a better look at me.

'I'm so sorry, I sat on my bed for a moment and fell right asleep,' I said, studying her face carefully while I talked. Her forehead was creased, though whether in mock concern or the real thing I wasn't sure. 'I think the heat wore me out,' I added for good measure.

'Poor you,' she said a little too emphatically, and I could almost hear the whirring as she did the calculations in her head. The race was just over a week away, and she needed me in peak health if I was going to be any help on the gruelling course. 'Can we get you anything?'

'Don't worry. Go without me and I'll catch you up,' I said firmly, desperate for them to be gone. Robert had remained out of sight further down the corridor, and I wondered whether Vivienne had become at all suspicious of the sudden end to the volley of jokes between us.

When she continued to linger, I leant heavily against the door frame and let my mouth gape into a wide yawn.

'OK, we'll be at that bar with all the flags down the road. Don't you dare fall asleep again or I'll come back and find you.'

I waved them off, and it took all my remaining strength not to slam the door behind them.

When the sound of their footsteps had receded I lay back on the bed. I stared up at the flaky paint on the ceiling until the beating of my heart had dropped closer to its ordinary rhythm and I could start to think straight again.

As little as a week ago it would have seemed outlandish to suspect that Vivienne or Robert could have taken my passport, but now I wasn't so sure.

I could well imagine Robert trying to get back at me after I'd snubbed his advances, but taking my passport? He'd made it clear that he wanted me gone, so it didn't seem likely he'd force me to stay.

Vivienne, on the other hand, was another matter entirely. She needed me to stick around if she wanted to win the race, and I'd seen enough to know that she wouldn't have a problem taking exactly what she wanted. But what reason did she have for fearing I would try to leave?

Sweat pooled under my armpits, and I sat up to eye the connecting door. Now that this suspicion about the passport had wormed its way into my mind, I knew I wouldn't be able to rest until I'd searched for it next door. Steeling myself, I gripped the door handle and let myself in.

I'd avoided going into their room since the incident with Robert and it took me a moment to orientate myself. The curtains had been pulled across carelessly, and the light filtering in from the gap between them caught on the buckles and buttons of the clothes strewn across the room.

The worn tread of my sandals skimmed across the polished floor as I twisted around to get my bearings. Their bedroom seemed much larger than it had before, and there was no shortage of potential hiding places for a stolen passport.

I started with the desk, but there was nothing there or in the small drawer under the wardrobe, so I moved on to the chest of drawers. I opened the first drawer then hastily slammed it shut, a flush of shame rising up my neck as I spotted a lacy bra poking out from underneath a pile of socks.

I took a deep breath and opened the rest of the compartments in turn, glancing briefly at the clothes, bags, boxes of makeup and perfume before jiggling them back into place.

When I'd shut the last one I slumped down to rest my head against the cool wood. There must be something here.

I tried again, lifting out piles of clothes and accessories before carefully placing them back. I felt right to the back of each drawer to make sure there wasn't anything stashed away, but my fingertips were met with the rough grain of wood.

I spun around to scan the room again. If I was going to hide something, where would I put it?

Although my instincts hadn't worked out, I had assumed the safest place to hide the key for the adjoining door would be under my pillow. The thought of searching their sheets was uncomfortable, but I was unlikely to get this chance again so I knew I had to try.

The messy piles of magazines and toiletries made it obvious which side was Vivienne's, and as I drew closer I could smell her rose scent clinging to the fabric.

Careful to make sure I didn't leave any of my own longer hairs on the white sheet, I slipped my hand under the pillow. The bobbly material was cool against my skin, but there was no passport hiding there.

I walked over to try Robert's side, but there was nothing there either so I moved on to the mattress. Sliding my fingers under the edge, I worked my way around until I was sure I hadn't missed anything.

Disappointed, I stood back and thought about how I'd hidden my own holdall where nobody could spot it. Lowering myself down, I peered under the bed and waited for my eyes to adjust.

The first piece of luggage I pulled out was heavy, resisting my efforts to pull it along the floor, and inside I was bemused to find a neatly packed collection of medals Vivienne had won. The next one felt empty, but when I pulled it out I realised it was locked. I cursed. Who would lock an empty suitcase?

When the clasp wouldn't budge I gave it a punch of frustration, catching my knuckle so that the sharp edge of the metal sliced through it. I sucked at the cut until it had stopped bleeding and sat back on my heels.

I surveyed the cheery red suitcase – I hadn't seen any small keys that would fit the lock, and it looked too sturdy for me to use brute force.

Remembering I had used a wire hairgrip to hold back my fringe during the morning's practice, I tugged it out, wrenching some dark strands with it, and bent it into a V-shape. I'd never tried to pick a lock before, and as soon as I tried to push the pin into the keyhole I realised I needed to remove the rubber stoppers from either end. I prised them off with my teeth, and then tried to get a purchase on something inside the lock. I jiggled the pin back and forth until I heard an encouraging click, but still the clasp would not budge. After a few more tries I gave up and pushed the suitcase back under the bed, throwing the mangled pin in after it.

A profound chill had settled in my bones, and I hugged my arms around me as my eyes scanned the room desperately for somewhere I might not have looked. Vivienne and Robert's passports weren't here either, so all three of the documents must be in that locked suitcase.

Once I'd checked the seats of the chairs and the underside of the drawers there was nowhere else I could think to look, and I realised it was time for me to get out.

Casting my eyes over the bed one more time to make sure I hadn't left any of my hair on the pristine white sheets, I rushed back to my room and shut the door.

As an afterthought, I picked up the full water glass I had put on my bedside table earlier and placed it on the floor by the door. It wasn't a particularly sophisticated trap, but it would at least wake me up if somebody tried to get into my room during the night.

I stalked over to the window and threw it open wide. The wind had died down since the afternoon, and I was able to light my cigarette easily. The light had faded to a pale pink, and down below the lamps lit up the faces of the people passing by.

When I'd finished I ground my cigarette down to a smoking stump, but I couldn't face getting dressed yet so I stayed at the window to watch the long shadows following people down the street.

The pattern of the movements below lulled me into such a daze that I got a shock when Vivienne and Robert stepped into the light. I ducked instinctively, and then realised they were unlikely to be able to see me from the street.

They ambled along until they were right outside the hotel and then paused to look in the window of a shop. They were facing away from me, but Vivienne's bag caught my eye. I'd never really thought about it before, but I knew she took it everywhere, and it was certainly big enough to carry a few passports.

There had to be a way for me to get to it.

I slammed the window and tugged on a deep red dress with a gathered waist that Vivienne had left me. I smeared on some lipstick and scraped my hair back into a bun, taking a fleeting glance in the mirror before rushing down to join the commotion on the street.

EIGHTEEN

When I woke the next morning the brightest stars were still hanging in the sky, but I pulled the curtains wider and flicked on my lamp for fear of my twisted nightmares returning if I dozed off again.

When the light grew stronger I began packing for Athens, but as I folded and smoothed my clothes all I could think about was outlandish ideas for escaping without my passport.

The temperature had reached an unbearable level by the time I'd finished, and when Nikos came upstairs to help me carry my bag even he had sweat patches blooming across the back of his shirt.

Downstairs the others were sprawled around on the sofas fanning themselves with magazines, their feet propped up on their luggage. The only space left was next to Vivienne so I reluctantly lowered myself down, careful not to disturb her. She was lying back with her eyes closed, and I was relieved when she stayed that way.

We'd been asked to clear out our bedrooms by noon so they could be cleaned for the next guests, but we were in no rush to leave the hotel. The plan was to pile everything up in the lobby and wait until the afternoon sun had died down a little before starting the drive over to Athens.

Mark had bought some cheese breads from the bakery for our lunch, but nobody could contemplate eating in that heat. Flies had settled on the greasy patches seeping through the brown paper bags and he took a few lacklustre swipes at them. They buzzed around noisily in the still air before settling again, and nobody else could be bothered to shoo them away.

I flapped the linen skirt of my dress to get some relief, but as soon as I stopped the fabric clung to my thighs again. The dress was a little formal for a day of driving, but it was the lightest outfit I had.

We remained inert on the sofas until Marie heaved herself up and rummaged through her bag to check she'd packed her passport. Vivienne still had her eyes closed and I was loath to disturb her, but it seemed as good a moment as any to mention that mine was missing and gauge her reaction.

'Say, Vivienne, have you seen my passport anywhere? I couldn't find it this morning and I'm getting a bit worried I've lost it.' My concern sounded wooden even to my ears, and I could barely breathe as she opened one eye lazily to look at me.

'Jean, you gave it to me to look after. Remember?'

'Oh.' Her tone was edging towards condescension, and my instinct told me to play stupid and go along with whatever she said. 'Did I? Sorry, I'm going mad.' I rifled around in my bag to give me an excuse to look down.

'It's here.' Vivienne sat up and pulled her bag onto her lap. Her demeanour was so relaxed that I almost began to doubt myself, but I was sure I would have remembered handing it over to her.

Lie to Me

She pulled out three passports and held the least faded one up to show me the photo page. My pale complexion was unmistakable, and I tried to rearrange my face into an expression of relief.

'Phew.' I placed my hand on my chest and tried to ignore my racing heartbeat.

'See, just as I said, you gave it to me.' My passport was so close that I could have reached out and plucked it from her grip, and my heart sank as she tucked it back out of sight in her bag.

'The heat is melting my brain.' I tapped my head a little harder than I had intended and let out a brittle laugh.

We lapsed back into silence. The drone of the buzzing flies made it even harder to get a hold on my spiralling thoughts, and I was glad when Anne and David appeared. She was trying to hide her discomfort by leaning heavily on him, but it wasn't hard to spot that she was walking with a slight limp.

'What's wrong with you?' Vivienne asked without preamble.

'I hurt my leg when I fell over last night,' Anne said, cringing as she sat down. 'I should never have had the shots.'

'Well, at least you didn't strip off in public,' David said jovially, prompting Vivienne to roll her eyes.

'You're making it sound like we flashed the locals. We only went swimming.'

'Gosh, I don't even remember you doing that. Sounds like I missed all the fun,' Anne said as she flopped down next to me, though she was clearly relieved to have missed that particular activity. She propped her leg up on the coffee table and I caught a flash of deep purple bruising as her skirt rose up before she quickly tugged it back down.

Niceties had gone out of the window in the stifling heat, and the round of mumbled sympathy quickly petered out. I could feel the pressure building behind my eyes, and I leafed through the magazine I'd picked up and pretended to look at the pictures – anything to avoid looking in Vivienne's direction.

A few minutes later the slap of a magazine on the coffee table made Anne and I jump and sent the flies whirring back into the air.

'I can't take this any more. I'm going swimming,' Vivienne said, pushing herself up from the sofa.

'That's a fine idea,' Mark agreed, hauling himself out of the chair. There were murmurs of assent as Robert, Marie and Hugo stood up to join them. 'David, are you coming?' Mark said, turning to him.

He was sweating profusely, and he looked torn. 'I think I'd better stay here.' He gestured apologetically towards Anne and the big pile of luggage at her feet.

'You go. I'll be fine here by myself,' Anne insisted.

'I don't want to leave you when you're in pain,' David said, tenderly placing his hand on her arm.

'You should go, David. I was going to stay here anyway,' I cut in quickly, sensing a chance to pick Anne's brains while I had her to myself.

'But you love swimming?' he said doubtfully.

'I can't think of anything worse than going outside right now. Even for a swim,' I said firmly.

'There you go, David. Jean can keep me company. Are sure you don't mind?' she said, turning to me.

'Of course.'

'Whoever is staying here should keep an eye on our luggage,' Vivienne commanded as she put down the bag containing our passports and unlocked her red suitcase to pull out a towel. I nodded, hardly daring to believe my luck, but my hopes were dashed when she put the bag in the suitcase and locked it. I tried to make out the code from where I was sitting, but Vivienne's hand was in the way.

I eyed Vivienne's suitcase and wondered if I could force it open. Shuffling forward until I was perched on the edge of the sofa, I watched Marie and Hugo brace themselves and step out into the searing heat. Mark and Robert followed, but Vivienne hung back to talk to the doorman. She pointed towards us, and I cursed inwardly as I realised that she had asked him to watch the bags.

I slumped back and Anne looked at me quizzically.

'How long have you known Vivienne and Robert?' I asked, resolving to cut to the chase.

'Gosh, about a year now. David has known them for ages, but I only met them when I started racing,' she said, and I wanted to cry out in frustration. 'What about you? I never asked how you got into rallying?'

'I looked after Vivienne's horse at a stable back home before I started racing,' I said, hesitating before spilling out my story. I didn't like talking about life with my father, but if I wanted her to speak freely with me I would have to open up a bit.

After giving her a censored version of my life at the stables I tried to turn the conversation back to Vivienne. 'I got the call-up when her last navigator left. It was about five months ago now . . .' I trailed off, hoping Anne would fill the gap.

'Oh yes, I can't for the life of me think what her name was.' She wrinkled her nose and I willed for her to remember, wondering how this girl had managed to escape Vivienne's grip.

'How annoying, but I suppose it doesn't matter now. She came from a farm somewhere on the south coast,' she said, distractedly turning down the corners of the magazine she was holding.

'The south coast is quite near to where I'm from,' I said, surprised at the coincidence. 'David thought she was probably racing for another team now?'

'Maybe. Like David said it was all quite odd really, she left very abruptly. It must have been some months before Vivienne signed you up because they parted ways at the end of last season.'

'How did she leave?' I asked as casually as I could, my body suddenly tense.

'You know Vivienne won the women's cup at the Liège-Sofia-Liège?' She looked at me for confirmation and I nodded – it was one of the high points of Vivienne's career. 'Well, the week after they won that together she left without even saying goodbye.'

'That is odd. You don't have any idea why?'

'Not really. She told Vivienne she had an emergency at home, but I have no idea what it was. It was rather a pity for her not to carry on racing – although it is fabulous to have you with us, of course,' she added tactfully. 'But from what she told me she loved navigating, and I never got the sense that she was particularly close with her family.'

'Oh.' I was running out of questions, but thankfully Anne had latched on to the topic.

'I probably shouldn't be telling you this.' She leant forward and lowered her voice even though there was no one around to overhear. 'I saw Vivienne having a terrific shouting match with her the morning after the Liège-Sofia-Liège. Apparently Vivienne has a bit of a habit of going through her navigators, but you seem to be holding your own.'

'I'm tougher than I look,' I said lightly, lining up the magazines on the table in front of me in the absence of anything else to say. It didn't take much creativity to imagine how unpleasant a shouting match with Vivienne would be.

I thought this was probably as much information as I was going to glean without drawing attention to myself, so I picked up a brochure for something to talk about.

I flipped it over and studied the jarring scene – a close-up of an ancient statue next to a tanned couple wading through impossibly blue water. I read the catchline. *A holiday in Greece isn't a myth!*

'Which areas have you been to before?' I said, handing it to her.

As she flicked through the rest of the gaudy spreads my eyes were drawn to the suitcases, and I nodded along to what she was saying without taking anything in. I wondered what had happened to Vivienne's previous navigator – and how I was going to make my own escape.

It was still sweltering when the others got back from their swim, but Robert was anxious to press on and get to Athens in time for dinner.

Even in our lethargic state the process of ferrying our bags from the hotel to the garage was over too quickly, and before long I was trapped in the car with Vivienne again. The garage owner and his son waved enthusiastically as we pulled out, and I watched them in the wing mirror until their reflection slid out of sight.

The hustle and bustle of the town helped to diffuse the intensity of my confinement at first, but as the buildings became sparser and eventually petered out I felt more uncomfortable, not trusting myself to attempt small talk after everything I'd learnt.

The car became airless as the long silence continued, and I fanned myself to keep my fidgeting at bay. Beside me Vivienne was focused on the road, her assured hand shunting the gearstick from second to third with ruthless efficiency.

When I glanced over I noticed that she looked tired, an effect exacerbated by her lack of makeup, and without thick liner her eyes looked narrower and mean. Her clothes were odd too – she was wearing an unflatteringly loose shift dress and flat pumps I'd never seen before.

Vivienne never normally went out anywhere without being fully made-up, but I supposed she hadn't been able to go back to the room after her swim so she'd decided to go without.

After about half an hour I couldn't take the tension any more. 'Do you know your way on this first bit? I'm feeling a bit sleepy so I might need to shut my eyes for a few moments.' My voice sounded odd even to my ears, and Vivienne looked over at me with some alarm.

'Are you ill? Do you need water?'

'No, no, I'm fine. I'm not thirsty, I think it's just the heat again.' I tucked the map under her seat where she'd be able to reach it if she needed.

Rummaging around behind me, I caught hold of a beach towel and scrunched it up into a makeshift pillow to wedge against the side of the car. It felt like the vibrations of the metal were rattling my brain, but that was better than the silent intensity of sitting still and staring ahead.

I stayed in that position for what felt like at least an hour, but as sleep continued to elude me I slowed my breath and let my body go slack to make it seem as if I'd nodded off.

Even when the car ground to a halt and Vivienne cursed under her breath at whatever animal was blocking the road I tried not to react. But it was hard to remain unresponsive when I was so alive to every bump and the shifting of my bodyweight as we zipped along.

The journey turned out to be frightfully long and took us through winding country roads, and as time wore on I began to second-guess my attempts to feign sleep. I wondered if I should be breathing more deeply, or whether my head would have lolled forward and woken me up. To make matters worse the mosquito bites on my ankles were throbbing in the heat, and it took all my willpower not to reach down and scratch them.

I faked a yawn and turned with my eyes still shut so I was angled further away from Vivienne's beady gaze. I tried to cover as much of my face with my arm as I could, allowing myself to scratch my ankles against each other once before settling back into stillness.

We carried on like this for some time, but just as the journey began to feel interminable the sound of the traffic built up around us. The car juddered in fits and starts as the congestion slowed our progress, and the flickering of the sun between the trees stopped as buildings blocked out the skyline.

'Jean, can you help me with this last bit of navigating?' When I stayed still Vivienne raised her voice and gently shook my arm. Unable to fake sleep any longer, I innocently fluttered my eyelashes open.

The sun was already dipping, but even in the waning light I was struck by the riot of colour. We'd come to a stop at a small road leading off from a square, and the traffic system was straining to contain the pedestrians weaving in all directions between blue buses and yellow tramcars. Everywhere I looked there were clamouring children, glamorous women walking with purposeful strides, traders hawking impossibly large vines of ruby red grapes and dogs snapping at their heels.

'Which turn from here?' Vivienne said impatiently as I stared around me. I fumbled under the seats until I got a purchase on the map and tried to get my bearings. When we came to a stop at a traffic light Vivienne snatched the map from me and pointed to our location before handing it back.

Chastened, I focused on providing directions for the next few minutes, pushing down the urge to swivel around in my seat to take everything in. As we pressed further into the city centre Vivienne opened the window and the car was flooded with a wall of sound – honking cars, men shouting, the revving of motorbikes – and a heady hit of diesel.

Vivienne scowled at the noise.

'Are the others in front of us?' I asked, trying to distract her from her mood.

'No, I lost them in the first ten minutes. They're way behind.'

The car turned a corner, and when I glanced up to check the street sign I did a double take. A gap between two buildings revealed a lush hill topped with the gleaming white stone of the Parthenon.

'It's quite something, isn't it?' Vivienne interrupted my thoughts, and I quickly bowed my head to check where we were going. I was half expecting her to snatch the map from me again, but when we stopped I looked up to see her gazing at the ancient structure in awe.

As we weaved in and out of the densely packed streets I caught glimpses of the ancient citadel. It loomed out from the hill like a mirage, getting seemingly no closer or further away.

'I'd forgotten how the sun sets differently in Athens,' Vivienne said wistfully, and when we next slowed I took her words as permission to lean out of the window and study the sky.

She was right. It was cloudless, humming with a vibrant violet hue. Everyone had told me Athens was magical and I had assumed their reverence to be an exaggeration, but now I understood why.

'I know the way from here,' Vivienne said, dismissing me from my navigating duties. Her irritation seemed to have passed and I was taken aback by the excitement in her voice. 'We stay at this hotel every year.'

'What's it like?' I said, trying to match her enthusiasm. After pretending to be asleep for most of the journey, I knew I needed to convince her everything was normal until we got to the hotel so I could plan my getaway.

'I think it might be one of my favourite places on earth. The service is impeccable – I've known the concierge forever – and the food is divine.'

'Are the rooms nice?'

'Let's just say you're going to get a shock, especially after the dumps we've been staying in. And you won't believe the view from the rooftop.'

'Ah, here we are.' We rounded the corner and an imposing cream building came into sight.

I gazed in silence as Vivienne circled around until she was in front of the entrance. The arched balconies were bathed in a soft glow of light from the windows, and the words Hotel Grande Bretagne were etched in large lettering on the stone. Despite everything, a frisson of excitement ran through me at the opulence of it all.

When we pulled up I was startled by a man knocking loudly on my window. Vivienne signalled for me to open the door so we could hear what he was saying, and the large camera strapped around his neck came into sight.

'Rally Acropolis?' he said, and Vivienne nodded.

'Yes, we're with Saab.'

'Photo?' he asked, waving the camera cheerily.

'Of course, one second,' she said before I could shoo him away, reaching down to grab her handbag.

'What are you doing?' I hissed.

'Stop being so nervous, we'll be fine. It's been more than a month now, are you planning on hiding for the rest of your life?'

'No, but we can't be photographed. Have you gone completely mad?'

'Shush, lean forward a bit. You could do with some of this,' she said, waving a tube of lipstick in the air. She reached over to cup my jaw in her hands, and I pursed my lips in disgust. The colour felt horribly gummy on my mouth, and I tried not to breathe in the sickly scent as she snapped the lid back on without applying any herself.

She took off her headscarf and wrapped it around my hair, securing it too tightly under my chin. 'Much better,' she said, sliding gracefully out of the car. I glanced unsurely at the gash of red lipstick in the mirror before stumbling out of the passenger seat.

'I can't do this,' I said, edging around the car to escape.

'Don't be silly.' She held me by her side in a vice-like grip.

The man waved us into position, and when the flash went off I was left with lines floating around my vision.

The photographer ambled off and a tall valet in a fern-green uniform came down the steps to take Vivienne's car keys. Another man took our luggage, and I felt a stab of panic as he carried them easily up the steps and through the entrance, my passport disappearing with him.

'Go on then,' Vivienne said, shooing me up the steep marble steps. I handed her back the headscarf then followed in his wake, hastily wiping off the lipstick.

Yet another man with a green suit and a small white hat was waiting at the top, and the gold buttons on his jacket caught the light as he pulled the door open for us. I hesitated, letting Vivienne go first, and when the door swung shut behind us the chaotic sounds of the street were sealed off, replaced with a pleasant hum of chatter and the click of heels on the marble floor of the lobby. Vivienne let out the satisfied sigh of a woman returning from a long day at work and turned to beam at me. 'Wait here one second,' she said, and I perched on a chair and looked around me.

The lobby was vast, its high ceilings supported by grand marble columns, and gold leaf detailing winked out at me from all corners. There was a plum-coloured sofa astride an ornate Greek key mosaic in the middle of the room, and around the edges heavy velvet drapes separated off the various adjoining areas.

When Vivienne came back she had applied some lipstick and tied her hair up in a yellow scarf, bringing some warmth back into her face.

'Let's go.' I followed as she sashayed across the lobby, acutely aware of the heavy crystal chandeliers suspended above me.

I hung back as she greeted the concierge enthusiastically. She didn't introduce me, so I looked down at my shoes and noticed that the tongue was peeling loose.

At the sound of my name I looked up to see Vivienne handing our passports across the desk. The concierge had been pulled away momentarily to help another guest, and a girl who seemed even younger than me had taken his place. She spoke English falteringly and I could tell she was becoming increasingly frantic as Vivienne fired off demands. When I gave her a shy smile she didn't notice.

'Are you sure nothing has arrived for me?' Vivienne asked, and the girl turned a deeper shade of puce as she shook her head. 'I was expecting a letter. Have another look.'

'Of course,' the girl said, nodding her head respectfully. She hurried off, and Vivienne drummed her fingers against the desk until she returned. 'I'm sure there's no post madam,' she said, and only then did Vivienne relent. It was odd, but despite all the fuss she'd made she seemed relieved the letter hadn't arrived.

As Vivienne signed the paperwork a woman in a yellow dress slipped past me and put a hand on her shoulder, making her cry out.

'It's just me.' She held her hands up to pacify Vivienne and I realised it was Anne.

'You almost gave me a heart attack,' Vivienne snapped.

'Sorry, sorry, I didn't mean to sneak up on you,' she said, almost cowering in the face of Vivienne's anger.

I used the distraction to edge towards the desk, where the girl was diligently copying out the details from our passports.

'How did you catch up with us?' Vivienne demanded.

'I don't know, David was driving. We were right behind you most of the way,' Anne said. 'Didn't you see us?'

'No,' Vivienne said coolly, and I could tell she was ticked off at being caught out by her own complacency.

'All ready,' the girl behind the reception desk announced. Vivienne scooped up my passport before I could reach it and I let my hand fall loosely by my side.

A bellboy wheeled our luggage around the desk and gestured for us to follow him to the lift. He was carrying two leather key holders and I made a mental note of the room numbers.

'Oh, wait, Jean,' Anne called out. I slowed my pace, but Vivienne marched ahead. 'Wait, if I don't tell you now I'll forget again,' she repeated and I stopped.

I caught sight of my reflection in an ornate mirror as I turned, and what I saw made me flinch – there was still a smudge of colour in the corner of my lips, and my dress had rumpled where I'd slept on it in the car.

'The navigator. I remembered her name,' Anne called over. My gaze darted to Vivienne, but she was already disappearing around the corner and there was no way she'd be able to hear.

'I knew you would, what was it?' I said, feigning indifference.

'Angela,' she said triumphantly.

NINETEEN

Coming to with a start in the morning light, I looked down to find my clothes rucked up around me.

I'd slumped on my bed as soon as I had shut the door behind me, and I stayed there tossing and turning all night trying to piece together the scant information at my disposal.

Vivienne's old navigator was called Angela.

Was she the *A* whose passport I'd found in Vivienne's room? Going by the remaining stamps, that woman had certainly been to some of the countries where Vivienne went to race.

The only innocent explanation I could think of was that Vivienne had taken Angela's passport for safekeeping because she'd left it behind, but that didn't explain why she would have hidden it under the bed.

I heaved myself up and walked to the window, the cool of the tiles a welcome relief under my swollen feet. I threw back the curtains and leant against the windowsill to survey my new room, taking in the details I'd barely registered the night before.

Vivienne had warned me that my room was the smallest so I was expecting something poky, but what it lacked in floor space it more than made up for in trimmings. A generously proportioned bed with plumped-up pillows was bathed in the warm glow of a tasselled lamp, and the high ceilings gave the space a roomy feel.

I made my way across the tiled floor in a daze, the geometric pattern adding to my disorientation. There was a door next to a dressing table, and when I pushed it open I was pleasantly surprised to find a marble en suite with a deep bath.

I perched on the edge of the tub and turned the cold tap to full, sending water gushing and spurting out.

A prickly heat spread across my body as I thought back to Anne's revelation and I had a sudden urge to submerge myself in icy water. I needed to think about my next move.

When the bath was nearly full I turned the tap off and stripped. My clothes smelt strongly of diesel and I could almost picture the fumes rising off them, so I opened the bathroom door and threw them out into the bedroom. There was a bottle of bath foam on the side and I poured in a generous glug. Although it didn't bubble up in the cold water, the sweet lavender smell was a balm.

I held my body over the water and slowly lowered myself in, gasping when my legs broke the surface. I eased myself down, and even when the water lapped up over my chin I didn't stop. Taking a deep breath, I put my head under and scrunched up my eyes against the sting of the cold.

At first the sensation of being submerged was uncomfortable and I had to fight an instinct to push myself back up. But soon the prickling heat of my body began to seep away and I felt as if I was at one with the water – no separation between the liquid and my skin.

Letting my head drop back against the bottom of the bath, I relished the feeling of weightlessness as the water swayed to and fro around me.

I stayed like that until my lungs burnt and then pushed myself back up, gasping for air. The hotel had provided a large block of embossed soap, and I used it to scrub every inch of my skin and scalp until I finally felt clean.

I let the water out and stared at the whirlpool that formed around the plug, lying there long after the final suds had washed away. When I got out, I swaddled myself in a fluffy towel and padded back to the bedroom, feeling a determined calm descend as I thought ahead to my escape from Vivienne and her ruthless, threatening world.

Breakfast was served in an airy room with patterned tiles and a stained-glass roof that let in the light, and I spotted the others sprawled across a selection of high-backed chairs and a sofa off to one side.

They were either chatting away or absorbed in the imported English newspapers, and they barely looked my way when I pulled out a chair to join them.

I reached over and poured some coffee from an elegant silver pot, desperate for some caffeine after my sleepless night. The whole breakfast set-up felt imposing for that time in the morning, but everyone else seemed much more relaxed than they had in the previous hotel. The men had loaded their plates up with sausages and eggs, and Marie and Anne were picking at dainty pastries while they chatted.

I sipped the bitter coffee, taking the opportunity to scan Vivienne's face as she flicked through a stack of newspapers. She looked up suddenly and I was too slow to look away so I panicked and pointed to the fruit next to her. She held up the platter for me and I reluctantly speared a few pieces with my fork.

'The colour of that top suits you.' She studied my face as I placed the glistening segments on my plate, and despite everything I felt a flush creep up my neck.

I popped a piece of fruit into my mouth, but when I got a hint of the sharp taste of grapefruit I swallowed it uncomfortably, not wanting to bite down and release the rest of the acidic juice into my mouth.

Vivienne returned to the newspapers, working her way efficiently through the pile and setting them aside one by one.

'Aha,' she said eventually, spreading one out excitedly on the table. The writing was all in Greek and it took a moment for me to work out why she was showing it to us. Then I spotted the photo of me and Vivienne outside the hotel the night before.

All at once I could picture the potential ripple effects: What if there was a witness to the car accident? What if the photo jogged their memory?

I stared at Vivienne in horror, but she pretended not to notice.

'I can't believe it. You managed to get another photograph in the paper,' Anne said. Her tone was bright, but her slight frown betrayed her disappointment. 'When did this happen?'

'Yesterday when we arrived at the hotel. You just missed him,' Vivienne said, smiling cheerfully.

The others leant over to get a better look, and I had to stand up to get a glimpse. Though I quickly wished I hadn't.

The flash of the camera had caught the grimace of my bright red lips in horrible definition, the headscarf wrapped tightly around my face. Vivienne slouched next to me in her loose shift dress, the creases from our long car ride evident.

I turned and scanned the people sat in the breakfast room, half expecting a group of policemen to barge through the door and disturb the peaceful clink of cutlery at any moment.

'If I were you, I'd track that photographer down. He's done a bit of a job on both of you,' Robert sneered. 'Jean, you look like you're in pain.'

'No she does not,' Anne said, swatting Robert with one of the other papers.

She laid a reassuring hand on my arm, but it only made me feel more trapped. I didn't care what I looked like. I just wanted to run, and I didn't understand why Vivienne wasn't more scared the picture might expose us.

'So, what are we going to do today then?' Mark said, diplomatically moving the conversation on. 'These are our last few days before the rallying starts in earnest, so I think we should take it easy for a bit.'

'It has to be the Acropolis,' David said, and he seemed affronted when his suggestion was met with some head shaking. 'Why the hell not?'

'It's meant to be scorching today,' Mark said. 'I definitely want to go, but maybe we should make the trek up there tomorrow when we can set off early.'

'Plenty of neighbouring islands by the looks of it. Why don't I find a boat to sail us somewhere?' Hugo suggested. 'It will be cool out on the water, and I'm sure we can find one with some shade.'

The prospect of cooling down in the sea was an inviting one, and in a rare show of agreement the others all nodded their assent.

Hugo said he'd spotted a boat at the port that looked like it was available to rent, so when we'd finished picking at our breakfasts we set our napkins down and followed his lead.

I hung back as we walked through the lobby, scanning the low coffee tables until I spotted another copy of the newspaper carrying our photo and snatched it up. The paper felt too thick between my fingers to be a cheap regional one, and the thought of our faces being reproduced across the country made me squirm.

I checked to make sure I was alone and ripped out the page, not quite knowing why, and tucked it in my pocket.

The band of pressure across my forehead was closing in again, and I didn't think I could face a day out on the water so I made my way back to the lift. By the time the others noticed I was missing they would probably be on the boat, and they wouldn't come all the way back up the hill to find me. That way I could try to retrieve my passport while they were gone and make my escape.

I could already imagine myself sinking into an intercity bus seat with the hotel disappearing behind me, but then Vivienne's voice cut across the lobby.

Lie to Me

'Jean? Where are you going?'

I wondered if I could pretend not to have heard, but she was already clopping across the lobby towards me.

'You can't get away that easily.' Her gaze bore into me, and I felt as if she could see my intentions to escape.

'Where are you going?' she repeated.

'Up to my room. I've got a headache and I'm not sure I'm feeling up to a day on the water.'

'Don't be like that, the boat trip will be a hoot. And anyway, it will probably make you feel better – all you have to do is sit there.'

'I don't think I can face it. The main thing is the race, I want to make sure I'm rested and well for it.' I was convinced she wouldn't put her chances of winning in jeopardy, but to my surprise she brushed off my excuses and took my arm in a tight grip.

'Don't be silly, you're coming with us,' she said, and I clasped the corner of the newspaper clipping in my pocket as she led me away.

TWENTY

Vivienne was wrong about the restorative qualities of the sea. I could feel the salty air filling my lungs as the sails billowed out, but I felt more trapped than ever as we aimed towards the shimmering heat haze on the horizon.

The boat Hugo had found was sleek, with cream sails, a mahogany saloon and ample cushions strapped to the deck for sunbathing. It was owned by an Englishman who was more than happy for us to take it out when he realised we were racing the Acropolis, and in exchange Hugo said he'd be glad to take him for a spin in the Ferrari.

Anne and Mark made us a simple meal with barbecued fish and salads, washed down with a copious amount of wine. After lunch the others took it in turns to throw scraps overboard and dive in after them, sending shoals of fish into a glimmering frenzy as they broke the surface of the water.

When the wind picked up Hugo steered us over to a sheltered cove and I allowed the wine and exhaustion of the past few weeks to wash over me, dozing as the sun beat down and the waves slapped rhythmically against the hull.

I was dazed when I came to and spent the rest of the journey staring out into the distance as the others exclaimed over false dolphin sightings.

All day I had expected a row of policemen to be waiting for us when we got back to the port, but when we neared the dock and there were no uniformed men in sight I wondered if Vivienne was right. Maybe I was overreacting to the photo.

After another cool bath back in the room I sat down at the dressing table to get ready for dinner. I still felt as if the world was swaying gently after the constant motion of the boat, but it wasn't an altogether unpleasant feeling.

I looked at my reflection. The sun had brought out the pretty highlights in my hair, but my face was blotchy and a little red from the exposure to the wind.

When Vivienne caught sight of my skin under the unforgiving lights of the hotel lobby she had insisted on giving me a selection of her makeup. She had offered to come to my room to apply it herself, but I fended her off by allowing her to do a short demonstration for me.

Laying everything out on the dressing table, I went through the unfamiliar process of making myself up as Vivienne had taught me – with eyeshadow, eyeliner, blush and a slick of lipstick.

As I plucked and tamed and rubbed my options came into focus. My half-formed plan to sneak off in the dead of night had been misguided. It would be foolish to leave with no passport or money to my name just because Vivienne and Robert had put me in a difficult situation.

No. They might not recognise it, but I was stronger than that.

When I'd finished coating my lashes with the sticky black solution from Vivienne's mascara block, I tied up my flyaway strands of hair in a headscarf and surveyed myself impassively in the mirror.

I turned my head to one side and then angled it the other way, and I was pleased with the result. My eyes seemed wider and my lips more pronounced, and the blusher had softened the edges of my face. For the final act of transformation I took a deep breath and lowered my shoulders, baring my teeth at myself in the mirror the way Vivienne did.

That was more like it. Now people would pay attention to me.

I zipped up my dress, and this time I felt like I belonged as I walked through the opulent corridor. When I got into the lift with another couple I didn't feel the need to look down at my shoes, and they murmured a polite good evening in my direction.

The lift shuddered to a halt on the ground floor and I got out first, feeling like a completely different person to the one I had arrived as earlier that evening. I walked confidently past the underlit paintings and the smartly dressed guests sipping elaborate drinks, and I felt myself unfurl like one of the ferns placed in tasteful pots along the corridors.

I had only planned to see if any of the others were in the lobby, but when I got downstairs I decided to take a short walk. Maybe the movement would help me to decide on a new plan.

As I swept past the reception desk a voice called out. 'Excuse me!'

I didn't recognise the woman's voice so I assumed she was calling for someone else and continued to stride forward.

After a few moments I heard footsteps behind me and she called out again, her voice shrill. 'Stop!'

I spun around to see the young woman from the desk hurrying after me.

She came to an abrupt halt and held out a letter. I took it, and the paper felt thin and flimsy in my hand.

'I'm sorry for earlier.' Her words came out in a rush, and she avoided making eye contact. 'I was wrong, there was a letter waiting for you. It must have come in a few weeks ago because it was tucked right at the bottom of the mailbag.'

My mind raced as I tried to work out what she was talking about. I hadn't spoken to her earlier and I wasn't even sure how anyone would have found this address – let alone why they would want to write to me in the first place. I wondered whether someone had tracked me down to pass on the news that my father was dead, and the possibility of it filled me with a strange mix of hope and fear.

I flipped the envelope over to see if I recognised the handwriting and froze. Vivienne's name was spelt out in curly lettering on the front, and there was something familiar about the handwriting that I couldn't place.

Looking up to tell the receptionist that she'd made a mistake, I saw that she was still avoiding my gaze as if she was scared about how I might react.

I was thrown for a second, but then the truth dawned on me.

'Thank you,' I said, channelling Vivienne's curt tone.

'You're welcome,' she said, half turning to rush back to the desk. 'Please tell me if there's anything else you need.'

'I will.' I stashed the letter in my bag and strode over to the doorman.

When I stepped outside the vacuum of the lobby I felt as if I'd rejoined the world after a long sleep. There was the usual cacophony of car horns, barking dogs and motorbikes whizzing up and down the roads, but when I listened more closely there was much more to hear: I could make out the tolling of church bells, the mournful whine of a street musician and the occasional laugh rising above the hum of chatter from the rows of tables in the square opposite the hotel.

I held my bag close to my body, wondering what was inside the letter. The envelope didn't feel as if it had anything concealed inside, but Vivienne had seemed anxious to know whether it had arrived.

Turning onto a tree-lined street, I was hit by a peculiar floral smell. The narrow passage was illuminated with the warm glow of flickering lamps, and as I left the main road behind I noticed that the trees were covered in small oranges and tiny white flowers.

My fingers itched to prise Vivienne's letter open and read it under one of the lamps, but I felt exposed with only the spindly trees for cover. If I did decide to open it, I'd be better waiting until I was back in the safety of my room.

I stopped at one of the trees and reached up to pluck an orange. A few of them were too soft and felt as if they were on the turn, but when I found a firm one I yanked it off the stubborn branch. It was an effort to peel the skin away, but when I finally managed to get to the tiny fruit I tore off two segments and popped them in my mouth.

I bit down and gagged as a sour taste flooded my mouth. I spat the pulpy mess into my hand and wiped my lips on the back of my arm.

I'd been picturing an idyllic scene with the residents hanging out of their windows to pluck the oranges off the trees, but the shock of the rancid fruit brought me back to reality. The grime and the dust of the city came back to the fore as I looked around me, and I felt, childishly, that the mood of my walk had been spoiled.

The last of the sun dipped from sight on the way back to the hotel, and I was grateful for the cover of darkness as I spat on the floor and tried to wipe the aftertaste from my tongue.

As I turned onto the road leading to the hotel, I thought I saw Vivienne, walking alone, turning off onto a side street. I wondered if my mind was playing tricks on me in protest at the day's heat, but I turned instinctively and walked after the woman regardless.

After a few minutes I was certain it was Vivienne – her brisk stride gave her away even if I hadn't recognised her clothes and shoes.

I followed her all the way to a park with manicured hedges and a wide fountain. She hovered on the pavement for a few moments before suddenly setting off across the square and I followed again, making sure to stay low behind the greenery.

Vivienne waved to someone as she broke away from the path and I craned my head to see who it was.

She walked over to a petite brunette and shook her rather formally by the hand. The woman's hair was tied back in a high ponytail and she was dressed smartly but with minimal fuss.

In the moments before I'd spotted her companion I'd expected this mysterious evening rendezvous to be with a man, and I couldn't think of any reason for a clandestine meeting with this woman, whoever she was.

They wandered away from me into the open part of the park and sat down on the lip of the fountain. The sky was clear and full of stars, and I watched the moonlight play across the water as they talked.

I racked my brains, trying to remember if Vivienne had mentioned any friends in Athens, but I couldn't come up with anything.

Squinting, I studied the woman's outfit more carefully. She wasn't decked out in the floaty socialite attire of palazzo pants or long dresses preferred by Anne and Marie. Instead, she had opted for a sporty pleated miniskirt and a simple cream polo shirt.

I shifted position and tried to work out the dynamic between the pair. The woman seemed to be saying very little, looking intently up at Vivienne as she gestured freely.

There was no way I could hear what they were saying from this far away, but it would be almost impossible to get any closer without being seen.

With little to go on, I decided to give up before they saw me skulking there.

I set off on a long walk and tried to work out what I'd just seen. I didn't really know where I was going, but I used the looming outline of the Acropolis as my guide.

Lie to Me

Passing feral children and street performers and countless stray dogs, I moved mindlessly until the pinch of my sandals told me it was probably time to turn back.

By the time I reached the hotel I still hadn't come up with any reasonable theories for Vivienne's meeting, and I was still horribly aware of the powdery texture of the bitter orange lingering between my teeth.

I was so distracted by the aftertaste that I barely registered the concierge's grim expression when I stepped inside.

'Come with me.' He rushed out from behind the reception desk to steer me away from the other guests sat in the lobby.

'What's going on?' I asked uncertainly, but he said nothing, leading me through a swinging door to a long corridor. We had to stop and press ourselves against the wall to let a group of women with clinking trollies pass, but when a man with a steaming tray of food appeared the concierge ordered him to wait as we brushed past.

We emerged in a deserted kitchen with an open door leading out to the street. Feeling like a trap was closing in on me, I considered making a dash to get outside, but he blocked my way and ushered me into another room.

Vivienne and Robert were there sat behind a table, but I barely noticed them. Instead, my gaze was drawn to the two stony-faced policemen opposite them. They had the nut-brown skin of men who were used to patrolling the streets, but their crisp suits and polished shoes gave me pause.

'Jean?' the tallest man said in barely accented English, pulling out a chair for me. I nodded, and as I sat down the door slammed behind me.

TWENTY-ONE

There was a buzzing in my ears as I wobbled to and fro on the rickety wooden chair.

The silence was excruciating – the only sound a fly careening around the room trying to find a way out – and when I finally plucked up the courage to speak my voice came out hoarse.

'What's happened?'

When nobody answered I turned to Vivienne and asked again, but my question was met with a shrug.

After a few more uncomfortable moments the shorter man leant forward. He was handsome, with close-cropped wavy hair and dark, watchful brown eyes.

'I'm Detective Spyros Doukas and this is Detective Antonis Papadimitriou. We're from the police station and we'd like to ask you a few questions.'

He handed me a newspaper clipping, but I already knew with a dreadful certainty what it would be. My bold lipstick jumped out at me from the page when I dipped my head to look, and the words Hotel Grande Bretagne were just visible behind the car.

'Is this you?' When I nodded he took the clipping back. 'Someone recognised you – and the car. They called us.'

I tried not to squirm as he drew out a dramatic pause, eventually leaning forward and placing his hands on his knees.

'You were in Corfu last month,' he said, and I gripped the chair. It was a statement rather than a question, but he waited for me to confirm before carrying on.

I looked to Vivienne for a sign as to what I should say, and she gave an almost imperceptible nod. 'Yes, we all were. What's this about?' I hoped they hadn't heard the wobble in my voice.

'You surely don't need this lady to remind you where you were a month ago,' he said with a gesture towards Vivienne, and I pursed my lips. He had his shirt unbuttoned to his chest, and I could see dark hair curling around the gold chain peeping out at the neck.

'Please can you tell me what's going on?' I implored, and this time the taller man answered.

'Someone was killed in Corfu, and you were on the island at the time,' he said, and I felt like time had stopped.

'That's terrible, what happened?' I asked after too much of a gap. Every twitching muscle in my body was telling me to run, but I knew I'd draw attention to myself if I fidgeted so I kept my fingers clamped firmly around the seat of my chair.

'There was a car crash,' he said, but I barely had time to react because the handsome policeman quickly chipped in.

'A young woman was killed,' he said, and my emotions flipped to soaring relief.

Too late I remembered to control my expression, but the policeman must have seen something he didn't like flick across my face.

He frowned and pulled his chair closer until our knees were almost touching, leaning forward to fix me with a cold look. 'She was young. Your age,' he said, and I was hit by a gut punch of guilt.

'God, how awful.' My voice quivered, and this time it wasn't an act.

'I believe you caught the ferry the day after this girl had been found dead, do you remember seeing or hearing anything odd before you left Corfu?'

I jumped in and started speaking the second he stopped. 'I didn't see anything. I'm so sorry I can't do more to help.' He gave a sideways look to the second policeman and I wondered if I'd been too quick with my denial.

'Well, we would like to ask you a few questions anyway,' the tall man said. 'OK?'

Out of habit I turned to Vivienne for her approval again, but quickly snapped my head back when I remembered his jibe about answering questions on my own.

'Of course.'

'They've already answered them,' the policeman said, jerking his head towards where Vivienne and Robert were sitting. My eyes followed the movement, and I was surprised when I took in Vivienne properly for the first time.

Her face was bare again, and her clothes were out of character too – a prim blouse tucked into a loose skirt. It wasn't that she looked bad. In fact, her skin was glowing from weeks of exposure to the sun. But it made her look younger and more vulnerable in a way that made me feel disorientated.

I wondered if the policemen had gone up to their room and caught them unawares.

'Would you mind if I had a chat with this young lady by myself?' the tall man said to Vivienne and Robert. They stood up obligingly and Vivienne gave my shoulder a squeeze on the way out. 'We'll be waiting for you outside.' Before I could reply the door slammed shut and I was alone with the two policemen.

'First, what are you doing in Athens?'

Knowing now that this was all to do with an unrelated case about an unfortunate young woman, it was easier to speak freely about why we were in Greece and the different islands we had travelled to, though I still felt on edge under their beady gaze.

They seemed happy enough with my answers and nodded along, scribbling a few things down in a notebook here and there. When my responses petered out they readjusted themselves on their chairs and crossed their arms. Now the real questioning begins, they seemed to be telling me.

'Our colleagues spoke to your friends on the island shortly after the accident,' the handsome policeman said, flicking back in his notebook to find the names. 'Hugo and Maric Boucher, David and Anne Jackson and Mark Reid. But you three left the next day and they didn't have time to question you.'

I nodded, and the tall policeman took over.

'What were you doing the night of the crash?'

I took a deep breath and recited the alibi Vivienne and I had created weeks ago, hoping never to use it. I'd practised this speech almost every day, but under the scrutiny of their gaze I faltered as I told them that we went out for dinner, driven to and from by a taxi, and then stayed at the hotel until the next day.

They nodded and scribbled more notes, and I wondered if this much attention was being put into finding justice for the man Vivienne had hit – I could hardly bring myself to think that he'd been killed.

'Why did you leave so early the next day?' the tall policeman asked.

'We got bored. We wanted a change of scenery,' I said limply.

'Bored of Corfu? How?' he challenged.

'There aren't many places to drive,' I said, clutching at straws.

'Because you want to speed with your expensive cars?' he countered.

'No, not at all.' I shook my head emphatically, trying to remind myself that this accident had nothing to do with us.

'But you went on a cargo ship. Why?' I hadn't expected this level of research and I felt a lump forming in my throat. I wondered how he could know that, but I supposed Robert and Vivienne had stood out among the traders.

Thinking back, there had been an awful lot of policemen at the dock. Maybe one of them had been watching us the whole time.

'Your friend Robert said it was your idea not to wait for the passenger ferry. Why would that be?' the handsome one chipped in, and I cursed inwardly.

'It was the only one going that early,' I explained, but they didn't look convinced. The fly buzzed close to my face and I was grateful for the excuse to shift from my rigid position to swat it away.

'You weren't fleeing the scene of the crime?' the tall one said, reaching up to wipe some sweat from his forehead.

'No,' I said, trying to keep my voice in check. I couldn't imagine them being this difficult with Vivienne and Robert.

'Fine,' his partner said. He held his palms up in resignation, but his tone did nothing to put me at ease.

I flinched as he stood up abruptly, scraping the legs of his chair along the rough floor.

'No need to jump,' he sneered. I looked down at the floor, and he swaggered slowly across the room to pick up a metal briefcase before bringing it back and placing it down forcefully on the table in front of me.

'OK then,' the tall one said, taking over. 'Let's try this.' He undid the clasps of the case noisily and pulled open the lid. I braced myself for what I might see inside, but whatever they wanted to show me was wrapped up tightly in a brown paper bag.

The handsome policeman took the bag out and waved it at me. 'Do you want to know the strangest thing about the young woman who was killed?' I didn't bother giving a reply. 'Nobody knows who she was, she certainly wasn't Greek. She had no documents, and none of the locals had seen her before – it's almost as if she appeared out of thin air.' A shiver rippled down my spine.

'Or at least that's what everyone is telling us,' his partner added. 'So that's why we would like you to do a simple task for us. Can you please look at this picture and tell us if you have seen this girl before?'

I shook my head before I could even think about what I was doing.

'No?' he asked incredulously. I didn't want to rub them up the wrong way, but I didn't think I could take the sight of this poor woman's body. I was already haunted by nightmares of the man Vivienne had hit, and my brain didn't even have an image of him to conjure up. 'What do you mean no?' he repeated.

'I really struggle with blood.' It was a lie, but I was feeling decidedly faint in the hot, airless room.

'There's barely any blood.'

'I'm really not very good with it.'

'Let me put this another way,' the tall man said, snatching the paper bag out of his colleague's hand and standing up to intimidate me with his full, towering height. 'We're not going to let you out of here until you look at it. It's a simple yes or no answer. Understood?' There was a swollen vein throbbing under his leathery skin, betraying his waning patience.

Before I had the chance to reply he reached inside the bag and pulled out the photo.

In the silence the ticking of the clock got louder, and I realised the fly had stopped buzzing. I wondered if it had died.

He flipped the photo over with a flourish and I found myself looking at a woman of about my age. There was no blood, as promised, but her skin was an unnatural white and her hair was matted.

Lie to Me

The walls closed in on me as I took in the familiar blonde hair and watchful, almond eyes – the ones from the passport I'd found hidden in Vivienne's room – and then everything went black.

'Jean, Jean,' Vivienne's voice was loud in my ear and I felt her shaking me awake. 'Jean, can you hear me?' Vivienne said more urgently this time, and I managed to croak out a reply.

'Yes, I can hear you.'

'Sit up and I'll give you some water. Stop sulking and come and help me, Robert,' she commanded over my shoulder.

Soon after I felt myself being tugged up by the armpits from where I'd slumped onto the table, and the room swam as I was pulled into a sitting position.

When my vision cleared up Vivienne strode across the room with a glass of water and held it out for me. I managed to raise my arms and take hold of it with shaking hands, but when I tried to take a sip some of it slopped down the front of my top.

'What happened?' Vivienne asked when I'd managed a few more sips.

'I fainted,' I said, and she looked at me like I was an idiot.

'Obviously. Why?' She directed her question at the policemen that time, but they shrugged.

I looked around for the photograph of the young woman but they must have already packed it away.

'We're leaving now,' Vivienne said. She turned to glare at the policemen, and I saw that even she had beads of sweat forming on her upper lip in the heat.

'Fine,' the taller policeman said. 'But you must stay in the hotel until we say you can go.'

'I don't see why that's necessary, but we'll be here for a while anyway because we're competing in the Acropolis Rally next week.'

They nodded, uninterested in her grandstanding.

We made our way to the door but they called out after us.

'Where is your car being kept? We want to see it.'

Vivienne told them the address and the name of the valet, and they shut their notebooks with an air of finality – though it was obvious from the looks on their faces that the interrogation wasn't over yet.

The lobby felt even bigger when we emerged from the side door and Vivienne guided me over to the lift while she sent Robert to get drinks at the bar.

'What happened in there?' Vivienne tried again when the doors started to shut, and I checked to make sure Robert wasn't about to force his way in behind us.

'Did they show you that picture of the woman who died?' I said, lowering my voice out of a perverse respect. I was expecting Vivienne to recoil, but she nodded while keeping her impassive expression completely intact.

'What does that have to do with anything?' she hissed impatiently, and I struggled to swallow as a sour taste filled my mouth.

Not only was Vivienne a killer, but she had no remorse.

'It reminded me of the . . . you know, the accident,' I said falteringly. It took all my strength to maintain my composure, but still her face hardened against me.

The lift announced its arrival at our floor with a jarring chime. 'Did you say anything?' she challenged.

'No, of course not. I just stuck to our story,' I said, and her expression softened a little as my voice cracked.

We reached the end of the corridor and she turned to face me. 'I'm sorry for snapping. I'm as stressed as you are, but they clearly don't have a clue so you should put the whole incident out of your mind.'

I leant heavily against the door frame as I fumbled with my key. Vivienne could see that I was struggling so she prised it out of my hand and opened the door for me. 'Get a good night's sleep,' she said, and I nodded miserably. 'We'll visit the Acropolis tomorrow. It's a new day, we'll put this all behind us.'

I hung up my bag, but when I put my hand in to retrieve my handkerchief I heard an odd rustling sound. Rummaging around, my fingers brushed against the small envelope the receptionist had given me. I'd forgotten it was there, but I didn't have the energy to go up a few floors to the room Vivienne was sharing with Robert to give it to her now.

Reaching out to put it on my bedside table to give to her later, the handwriting caught my eye. I lowered my arm and angled the envelope towards the light.

There was something about the swirly lettering of Vivienne's name that didn't sit right. I looked more closely, and when I realised why I dropped the flimsy envelope to the floor.

There was a neat circle carefully printed for the dot of the *i*.

The same as on the signature in the passport under Vivienne's bed.

TWENTY-TWO

I spent the rest of the evening pacing up and down my room.

The temptation to abandon my possessions and flee from the hotel was compelling, but now the policemen had told us to stay put I knew I'd look guilty if I disappeared without a trace. I doubted I'd be able to find somewhere to shelter in the hostile streets of Athens, but the thought of being trapped with Vivienne and Robert any longer made my skin crawl.

Every now and then I picked up the unopened letter and started to ease away the seal, before changing my mind and placing it carefully back on the bedside table.

As soon as I recognised the handwriting I knew I wasn't going to pass it on to Vivienne. But the possibility of opening the dead woman's correspondence myself seemed almost too awful to contemplate.

I propped myself up in bed with the plush hotel pillows and tried to work out what to do next, but after the shock of that evening I could barely resist the heaviness tugging at my eyelids. Eventually I gave up and looked around for somewhere to hide the letter so I could revisit it in the morning with a clearer head.

A wave of relief washed over me when I realised Vivienne and Robert no longer had access to my room through a connecting door, but this quickly gave way to a cold chill of horror when I realised Vivienne had kept hold of my key when she helped me get into my room. I got up and dragged a chair in front of the door, placing my half-empty holdall on top.

Casting my mind around for the safest place to keep the letter, I decided that the only option was to sleep with it under my pillow.

I drifted off quickly but woke up several times in the night, convinced I could feel the cool skin of Vivienne's wrist grazing my cheek as she slid the envelope out from under me. I clawed out in the dark every time expecting to hear a scream, but there was nothing there.

Eventually I gave up on sleep and threw back the curtains so I could see the dull blue light creeping across the sky. I watched its progress until the swallows began their dawn chorus and I gave in to the morbid lure of the letter.

I pulled the envelope from under my pillow and sat on the cold floor with my back against the door – ready to hold my ground if anyone tried to force entry.

Carefully, I ripped along the edges and pulled out the paper inside. I could see the ink outline of a few lines printed neatly on the other side, and with trembling hands I flipped it over.

The page was almost empty, with just a few figures and dates written in curly handwriting. There was no greeting or sign-off, or any pleasantries. It simply read:

Payments to Yannis. I have proof.
355 on 27 March.
355 on 2 April.
355 on 12 April.
Meet me at Amalia on 27 April with 5,000.

I read the cryptic lines several times but I still couldn't work them out. Feeling foolish, I held the paper up to the light to see if there were any secret messages, or even indentations from another letter underneath, but there was nothing.

Unsure where I could hide it, I slipped it into my holdall and lay back on the bed. I wanted nothing more than to give in to my fatigue and stay there all day, but I knew I would draw attention to myself by refusing to join the planned trip to the Acropolis.

When it was finally time to get ready I begrudgingly pulled myself up and threw an outfit together.

I assessed myself in the mirror. Even with the armour of Vivienne's clothes my emotions felt perilously close to the surface, so I put on the makeup she had given me as a defence. I buffed and slathered until I could barely recognise the reflection in the mirror, then I made my way downstairs.

I had expected hysteria when the others found out about the police interview, but the civilised atmosphere at breakfast suggested Vivienne and Robert hadn't told them.

'Orange juice?' one of the waiters asked, pulling me out of my thoughts. I gladly put my glass on his tray so he could pour me some, hoping it would provide some relief from my dry mouth.

Gossip about our visit from the police didn't even seem to have spread between the hotel staff. After the waiter had finished pouring my juice his disinterested gaze slid to Anne without another look back. It seemed the concierge was more loyal to Vivienne than I had thought, though I supposed having the police troop in to question guests wasn't exactly something he wanted to shout about.

The only person who looked a little off was Vivienne, who seemed to have come downstairs without any makeup again. I took a piece of toast and nibbled at it, taking the opportunity to scan her drawn face whenever she looked down to spear another piece of fruit. Nobody else had commented on it, but after my weeks of watching her this departure from her normal form was jarring.

Weaving our way through the plants and tables after breakfast, I saw several racing drivers I recognised from the circuit. David and Hugo stopped for a back-slapping greeting with two men I'd seen at the Tulip Rally, and when they called for the others to join them I slipped outside.

There was a thickset man sat with a newspaper by the exit, and I thought I saw his head turn slightly to follow me as I walked past. I wondered if he had been stationed at the hotel by the police, or if my nerves were getting the better of me.

I sat on a bench and squinted into the sun to watch a group of soldiers directing traffic. They were decked out in traditional dress with black waistcoats and white kilts, but they moved with remarkable authority for men wearing pointy shoes topped with pompoms. The spectacle would have been almost amusing if it weren't for the bayonets they were carrying.

When everyone had made it outside Vivienne led the way through the palm-lined streets until we came to a residential area with houses festooned in bright pink bougainvillea.

I could feel a prickly heat on the back of my neck as if someone was watching us, but whenever I snapped my head around all I could see was the ordinary flow of Athenians going about their day before the heat took hold.

When we were slowed down by a boisterous group of children I saw Vivienne look at her reflection in a shop window and frown, tugging at the unflattering skirt before returning her gaze to the road.

The imposing columns of the Parthenon were just visible when we arrived at the bottom of the hill where the Acropolis was suspended and wordlessly started to climb.

The higher we got the more the crowds thinned out, but I still felt as if someone was watching me. Nobody reacted when I spun around, but the feeling was so strong that I made a note of the remaining people in my sight: a smartly dressed younger couple; a group of middle-aged women; two men with a map and an ostentatious camera; and a couple taking it in turns to carry their young child.

The sun had become fiercer as we climbed, and I was glad to have one of Vivienne's old headscarves with me. I stopped to tie it around my hot hair and then hurried to catch up with the others.

The dusty path turned into a steep marble staircase as we neared the crest of the hill. The steps had been worn down to a glassy smoothness by thousands of years of use, and I tried to hop my way up them as fast as I could without slipping.

I was so busy focusing on my feet that when I finally looked up I was taken aback to find the sun-bleached ribcage of the Parthenon towering above me. My hair stood on end as I approached the pallid stone, and when I was close enough I ran my hand across the cool surface, my chest still heaving from the climb.

Anne jolted me out of my trance when she called me over to the viewpoint where the rest of them were standing, and I reluctantly drew myself away from the Acropolis to admire the view over the urban sprawl of Athens.

True to form, Hugo had lugged an expensive-looking cherry wood camera up the hill and was busy fiddling with the stand, but the view behind him was so astonishing that it seemed unlikely he'd be able to capture it with even his professional kit.

Beyond the gnarled cypress, pine and olive trees clinging to the side of the hill, there were more ancient ruins and grand columns tucked in between cramped buildings – a dizzying display of human progress fringed by the deep blue of the sparkling Mediterranean Sea.

I stood silently with the others for a few minutes, but it wasn't long before I was drawn back to the Parthenon. As I neared the west side of the building I noticed that the columns had been replaced by a line of ethereal female statues proudly supporting the roof.

The six women looked identical from afar, but as I drew closer I noticed that they each had slight differences carved into the drape of their outfits and hair, their jutting stances an echo of one another. The overall effect was eerie, and I almost expected to see the rise and fall of their milky skin under the folds of their robes.

I turned back to see where the others were and froze. They were still standing at the edge of the Parthenon, but the two men with the map and the camera I'd noticed on the climb were staring at them from behind a rock.

Ducking down, I edged back until I was in the shadow of the columns. I kept my sights trained on the men for a few minutes, and eventually the one with the camera started taking pictures. I watched as he shifted his position and seemed to point his camera at Vivienne before moving on to each person in the group in turn. Walking as slowly as I could, I skirted around the rocks until I had a good view of the men and pretended to look at one of the sculpted figures.

When the man had lowered his camera he turned to his companion and started a heated discussion. I knew that Athens was a hotspot for crime, and I wondered if they were part of a gang that trailed wealthy tourists from the Grande Bretagne to fish around in their pockets while they were distracted by the sights. I decided to stay and watch so I could shout to the others if they approached.

It was nearing midday, and the temperature had risen sharply. I badly wanted to take off my headscarf and mop the sweat I could feel gathering at the back of my neck but I didn't want to risk drawing attention to myself.

One of the men with the map must have had a similar thought because at that moment he took off his hat and pulled out a handkerchief to wipe his head.

My breath caught in my throat. It was the handsome policeman who had interviewed us the day before. His companion was the other policeman – I now recognised his distinctive, towering stature.

I wanted to warn Vivienne but I knew they would spot me if I approached from this angle, so I was forced to hang back.

Without warning, they turned to face directly towards where I was half crouching behind a rock and the three of us stopped still.

The stone figures towering around us made the moment feel like a tableau – but the spell was broken when the policeman lifted his camera towards me and the flash went off.

I turned and ran, and as soon as my feet hit the smooth rock of the steps I knew I'd made a mistake. There was nowhere to hide on the exposed mountain, and the two men would catch up with me easily if I tried to outpace them in my flimsy sandals and tight-fitting dress.

I heard the clatter of loose stone behind me – I didn't turn for fear of falling flat on my face, but I was sure they were catching up.

As I emerged from the shadow I was momentarily dazzled by the force of the sun bouncing off the white rock. When my eyes adjusted I saw Vivienne and Robert standing with their back to me admiring the view and scrambled towards them.

They spun around as I skidded to a stop, gasping for air. I tried to tell them to move, but by the time they'd deciphered my garbled sentences our two interrogators had arrived, kicking up dirt from their heavy shoes.

The handsome policeman had lost his hat in the chase and I saw a look of recognition contort Robert's face, though Vivienne was unmoved.

'Why are you running away?' the taller policeman said breathlessly, doubling over to place his hands on his knees.

'I didn't recognise you. I thought you were journalists wanting to get some photos before the rally so I ran over to let Vivienne know,' I stammered, gesturing to the camera. 'Why were you taking pictures of us?'

'We weren't.'

'But I saw you,' I said indignantly.

'We were taking pictures of our wonderful landmarks,' the handsome policeman said, gesturing around at the towering columns. 'Do you have a problem with that?'

I waited for Vivienne to jump to my rescue with some witty remark, but she stood mute.

'Is there anything you want to tell us?' The tall policeman fixed me with a cold look.

I shook my head.

'Are you sure?' his partner prompted. They were trying to disconcert me, but I held my ground.

'No, is there anything you want to tell me?' I countered, but they just stared me down with a steely gaze.

'Make sure you stay at your hotel. We'll be in touch,' the tall man said, and I watched them walk away.

'What was all that about?' Vivienne asked crossly when they were out of earshot. 'What did he mean about having something to tell him?'

Lie to Me

'Nothing, it was a misunderstanding.'

'Well, try not to draw any more attention to yourself,' she hissed.

I walked back to the Parthenon to watch the policemen descend the hill, and as they scrambled down the dusty path the beginnings of an idea stirred in my mind.

TWENTY-THREE

I spent the precarious walk down Acropolis Hill mulling over my options, and by the time the path had levelled out to join the city I'd decided on a plan. I wasn't yet sure of how I'd go about it, but my best hope seemed to be tracking down the Yannis mentioned in the cryptic note to find out what he knew.

We turned off the path and wandered through the narrow streets of Plaka, pressing ourselves up against the walls as waiters rushed past to place ashtrays on rickety wooden tables and shoo away cats.

I looked intently into the men's faces as they went about their jobs, but none of them took any notice of me. Over the course of our time in Greece we must have met dozens of men named Yannis, but I had no recollection of Vivienne showing any interest in them.

She had a leather-bound address book that she always kept in her handbag, and I wondered if his details were in there. It wouldn't be easy to get hold of, but the slim notebook might be my only lead.

While I'd been lost in thought, the others had been engaged in an increasingly heated debate about their plans for the afternoon. Vivienne claimed she was famished and demanded we stop at the next taverna we found, but some of the others wanted to see the Agora, an ancient marketplace that apparently used to be the heart and soul of the city.

In the end we decided to split up, and I stayed with Vivienne and Anne to look for somewhere to eat while the others carried on their tour. The streets of Plaka were becoming crowded, so we turned our backs on the towering view of the Acropolis and made our way to the edge of town.

Anne and Vivienne seemed oblivious to the locals watching us as we left the main roads and marched through the sleepy residential backstreets, but after the encounter with the policemen my senses were heightened to the twitching of net curtains all around us.

The only thing Vivienne had any thought for was the tantalising smell of freshly baked bread and stewing meats coming from the houses, and her grumbling became more insistent as we walked. Just as I thought she might actually force entry into a Greek family's front room, we emerged into a courtyard with cloth-covered tables dotted around under a canopy of vines.

Most of the tables were occupied, but compared with Plaka the atmosphere was tranquil. There, the noise of people talking had ricocheted off the whitewashed walls, but here it was absorbed by the greenery – the light shafting in from between the vines adding to the impression of a lush oasis hidden away from the rest of the world.

Vivienne marched over to an empty table in the corner and I followed. She sat down and pulled the menu towards her, and

I positioned myself on the side where she'd slung her handbag over the back of the chair.

Anne joined us and Vivienne beckoned a waiter over. She rattled off a list of traditional mezedes for us to share and added a carafe of wine as an afterthought.

I eyed her darkly, my mind flicking back to my time at the stables when pickpocketing was par for the course. The boys never really took any notice of me, so I got good at relieving them of their tuck shop buys and then watching them sling the blame among one another. At first I went for the easy targets – open bags or items left unattended. But soon I got good enough to take things straight out of their pockets.

The trick was to cause a distraction or wait until lunchtime on a rainy day when we were packed together in the barn. I'd wait until someone turned around to talk to their neighbour and then make my move, a jumper or coat draped over my arm to disguise my roving hand.

When the wine arrived I stood up to pour a glass for us all, hooking my chair in with the back of my leg and shifting it over so I was right next to Vivienne's handbag.

I sipped the tart liquid, and my attention was drawn to two cats circling each other in the corner of the courtyard. A ginger cat with half an ear reared back onto its haunches and took a swipe at a tatty black one, which hissed and flattened its ears back. I kept my eyes trained on them, and eventually the ginger one lunged.

The yelp of pain that followed pierced the quiet of the square, making Anne jump so much that her wine slopped over her front. I shifted so that Vivienne's bag fell on the floor with a dull thud, and as Vivienne helped Anne to mop up her drink I knelt to the floor to search the bag.

I rummaged around, feeling the frustrating bulk of what felt like passports zipped securely into a pocket, until the back of my hand grazed a soft leather cover. I pulled a slim notebook out, slipping it into the folds of my skirt without looking down.

'I'll get you another napkin,' I announced, hooking the bag over the chair and striding across the cobbles to the taverna.

When I'd shut myself in the bathroom I shook out my skirt, and the red leather address book dropped to the floor.

I flipped straight to the entries for Y in the blind hope that Vivienne would have written Yannis's details there, but there were no matches. I turned back to the beginning and read my way through every single name one by one, but as I neared the end I lost my bravado.

Painfully aware that this might be my only chance to look through the address book, I tried again – this time scanning the whole page rather than looking at just the names. I still couldn't find any entries for Yannis, or even a cryptic Y, but towards the end I did find a number scrawled in the margin with an area code I guessed was Greek.

I tore the thinnest sliver of paper I could manage from the back of the book and used the gold pen attached by a piece of ribbon to scrawl down the number.

Suddenly aware of how long I'd been away from the table, I fumbled the latch open and snatched up a cloth to give to Anne on my way out.

I emerged from the dark interior to find the waiter walking over to our table with a tray piled with food. I sped up until I was tailing him and waited until he caught Vivienne's attention. I slipped the address book back into her bag and handed the cloth to Anne with a flourish.

The others tucked into various dips and fragrant rice-stuffed vegetables while I pushed some Greek salad around with my fork, unable to think of anything other than the scrap of paper with the telephone number tucked into my waistband and where it might lead me.

When Anne got up to go to the bathroom Vivienne leant towards me and lowered her voice. 'Are you OK?'

I looked up at her dark brown eyes and the concerned crease of her forehead, and I had to remind myself that this was all for show.

'I'm just feeling a bit jumpy about the police,' I said, squashing a piece of feta with the back of my fork. 'Why were they following us?'

'Don't worry about it,' she assured me. 'Eat up, we need you to be strong for the race.'

I nodded, scooping a stuffed pepper onto my plate and managing to force down some of the herbed rice inside.

I could feel Vivienne's eyes on me throughout the rest of the meal, but when she was distracted by the arrival of the bill I took my headscarf off. I ran it through my fingers absent-mindedly, ready to drop it on the floor when we stood up.

We paid up and wandered off, and when I felt like we'd put enough distance between us and the taverna I reached up with both hands to clasp my hair. 'My headscarf,' I cried, hoping I didn't sound as rehearsed as I feared.

They offered to walk me back but I politely declined, saying I would catch up with them later.

Taking a detour past the restaurant, I threaded my way through tourists and young boys trying to sell offcuts of gaudy material until I found the route back to the hotel.

Making my way up the front steps and through the lobby as fast as I could without running, I decided I couldn't face waiting for the lift. I veered over to the stairs and took them two at a time. My legs began to feel heavy from the morning climb to the Parthenon, but I didn't stop until I reached my room and slumped back against the door.

I pulled out the crumpled piece of paper and unfurled it carefully. I knew I should probably compose myself before calling the number, but my desire for answers overwhelmed my common sense and I took it straight over to the bedside telephone.

There was a printed note to one side warning that guests would be charged for calls, but I didn't have time to worry about that now. Hopefully it would only show up as a domestic call, and I'd think of some excuse before Vivienne was given the bill at the end of our stay.

I dialled the number and the handpiece emitted a long, flat ringing tone.

For some reason I hadn't really expected anyone to pick up on my first attempt, so I almost dropped the handset when a gruff male voice answered after only a few rings.

'Yassou?'

All the things I'd planned to say flew out of my head and I considered hanging up to give me some time to think, but there was no guarantee he would pick up a second time.

The man spoke again. He had a thick accent, and I pressed the handpiece hard against my ear to make out what he was saying. '*Yassou? Pios einai?*' he said impatiently, and I hoped desperately that he spoke some English.

'Hello.'

'Yes, hello?' I grasped the bedside table to steady myself, but he pressed me before I could even form my next sentence. 'I don't have all day. What do you want?'

'It's Vivienne,' I said. I'd had so much exposure to her clipped tones over the past few months that her accent had almost become second nature, and even to my critical ears this imitation sounded convincing.

'Oh,' he said, his discomfort palpable. This was all the confirmation I needed that my hunch about the number had been correct. I'd found Yannis.

Vivienne wasn't one for pleasantries, so I got straight to the point. 'Is that all you've got to say to me?'

'Why are you calling me here? What do you want me to say?' He lowered his voice so it was hard to make out his words.

'You've been avoiding my calls,' I stalled.

'I didn't know you'd called – but I don't want to be involved, whatever it is,' he added quickly.

'Why not?'

He didn't answer straight away but I held my ground in the hope that he would fill the silence with some answers.

Lie to Me

'Why not?' he said eventually. 'I mean, God. You said you were going to stop Angela threatening us, but I didn't think you'd kill her,' he hissed.

My breath caught in my throat, but Yannis seemed so relieved to get this information off his chest that he barely paused enough to notice my silence.

'When Angela's letters stopped I thought you'd paid her, but then I heard about the accident and I knew what you'd done. They were asking for people to help identify the body, but I didn't want to get involved.' He was speaking fast now, and I was struggling to keep up. 'I was checking the news every day to see if the police would find out what I did for you.'

There was a staticky silence, and I realised I needed to say something. 'Relax,' I said, echoing the patronising reassurances Vivienne had used on me. 'It was an accident, it was nobody's fault. And there's certainly nothing to link it back to you.'

'Accident?' he said, a wrangled laugh of horror escaping from his mouth. He seemed to want to say more but he held back.

'Does anyone else know what I did for you? Messing with your opponents' cars so you could win is one thing, but I'd never have agreed if I thought this was going to happen.'

'It's fine,' I said as firmly as I could. 'Calm down. Nobody knows.'

'I never wanted anyone to get hurt, you understand me? I'll be there for the race, but if you see me, pretend you don't know me.'

'Wait—' I started, but he cut in over me.

'We're done.' There was a dull buzz as he hung up.

Setting the handpiece back in the cradle, I lowered myself down until I was lying on the bed and stared up at the decorative criss-cross pattern on the ceiling.

I'd wanted answers from Yannis, and God knows I'd had my suspicions about Vivienne, but I wasn't prepared to process these revelations.

I sifted through the details of my conversation with Yannis, and all the things that had been bothering me over the past week fell into place.

Poor Angela must have got wind of Vivienne's scheme while she was navigating and tried to use the evidence as blackmail, but she had underestimated her old boss.

She must have sent the letter to the Grande Bretagne knowing it was where Vivienne always stayed, but when she heard Vivienne was in Corfu she thought she'd try her luck there first.

She'd travelled to the island to threaten Vivienne, but instead she had been lured to a secluded spot and run down. By the time the police found the body, Vivienne had disappeared without a trace – and she already had me with her as a replacement.

I pulled the sheet up and pressed it against my watering eyes, allowing the tears to flow until my panicky breaths had slowed and I was able to sit up again.

The news that Vivienne had cheated was less shocking once I'd had a moment to process it. She was obsessed with going faster and harder – but only in relation to everyone else. She didn't care about improving. She only cared about winning.

It also explained why she hadn't told Robert about the crash. Now I knew the truth I could hardly believe I'd bought into her explanation that he would push her to confess.

No, she'd kept Robert in the dark because her pride couldn't handle him knowing she'd cheated to win.

I thought about the way Yannis had spoken on the phone, and the echo of it chilled me. He was burly at first. But once I'd uttered Vivienne's name all of that had disappeared, replaced with an unmistakable shiver of fear.

TWENTY-FOUR

Athens was overtaken by a frenzy of activity as the rally approached. Ramps were assembled and flags were strung up at the foothills of the Acropolis, and the local newspapers featured grainy photos of racers emerging bleary-eyed from their flights at Ellinikon International Airport to join the fray. Every now and then I spotted another rally car on the crowded roads, its sleek lines and polished metal glinting conspicuously as it weaved between dented cars and boxy buses.

I watched all of this from the confines of the car, wishing I could throw back the door and disappear into the chaos of the city. I knew I needed to get away from Vivienne after speaking to Yannis, but the arrival of the policemen meant I couldn't leave just yet without them tracking me down.

Charged up by the appearance of our rivals, Vivienne wanted to take preparations for the race to the next level. She rapped on my bedroom door earlier and earlier each day, insisting we leave first thing so we'd be belting along the deserted country roads by lunchtime to get used to the sweltering heat.

Several times I thought I'd spotted the policemen among the early morning chaos as we drove through the city – watching us over the brim of a newspaper or sipping a small muddy coffee. I whipped my head around to get a better look as the figures slid out of sight, but I could never be sure.

An urge to come clean to the police overtook me some nights when I had nothing but the background noise of the road for company, but I quickly pushed it away. The two detectives I'd spoken to were suspicious of me, and I knew there would be no sympathetic treatment, no immunity bargain, no new life if I went to them and explained how I'd helped Vivienne cover up what she'd done.

If Vivienne had any fears about her actions catching up with her, they didn't show. Everything else paled in comparison to her focus on winning the race, and the intensity of her drive scared me.

Where once I'd found the closeness of her arm grazing mine as she went to change gear exhilarating, I now pulled away – every sharp turn and skid making me flinch with the thought of what she'd done to Angela.

Vivienne quickly caught on to my skittishness and started swerving tightly around corners and slamming on the brakes to see if I'd react. She hammered home the message that my job was to be unflappable, and in time I learnt to set my face into a grimace.

Even when we were back in the hotel her focus unnerved me. She made me run through the course endlessly so she could study the sticking points and memorise the route, and I feared her resolve to beat Robert and Marie could turn this into a first class free-for-all. I tried to calm her down with gentle reminders that I'd be there to do all this for her on the day, but she just ignored me.

Since arriving in Athens we'd started most evenings meandering through the streets to find somewhere for dinner, but with five days to go until the race we lost our appetite for exploring. The heat had been particularly close that day, and even when we were hurtling through the countryside with the side screens open it felt like we were being bombarded with warm, stale air.

Instead, it was decided we would eat in the hotel restaurant that night. This required a more refined outfit, and I rifled through my wardrobe a few times before I spotted a pale blue skirt suit of Vivienne's that might be suitable. It was beautiful, like something Jackie Kennedy might own, but there hadn't been an appropriate occasion for me to wear it until now.

The woven fabric looked too heavy for the heat, but when I pulled it out of the wardrobe I was pleasantly surprised to find it was remarkably light. Sliding it off the hanger, I shrugged it on carefully so I didn't catch any of the threads.

The boxy shape and cropped arms of the jacket meant it was comfortably loose despite my curvier frame, and the skirt fell at a flattering point just above my knees. I had a vague memory of Vivienne giving me a silk scarf with a floral pattern in the same blue, so I rifled through my drawers until I found it and used it to push my hair back off my sticky skin.

There was time to kill until dinner, so I drew out the process of fixing my makeup by painting on elaborate flicks of eyeliner and rouging my lips. When I had finished I went around the room lining up my belongings so it would be more obvious if Vivienne moved anything in my absence, but there was nothing I could do to stop her from gaining access with the key. She laughed when I asked her to give them back, saying it had completely slipped her mind, and when she avoided the question again later I had to ask for a second set.

Eventually the long hand of the clock showed that it was an acceptable time to head up to the roof terrace to meet the others. I let myself out of the room and pulled the door shut firmly until I heard the useless, automatic click of the lock.

When I arrived at the lift there was a smartly dressed man with a briefcase waiting there. The doors pinged open, and he ushered me in first. He had a soft American accent and kind eyes, and we smiled politely at each other when we made eye contact in the mirror.

He looked like he might be about to say something, but he caught himself when the lift ground to a halt and the doors opened to reveal Vivienne and Robert.

'Good evening,' Vivienne said as she stepped inside, taking in my outfit hungrily.

Robert and I uttered a forced greeting to one other as had become our routine, and my gaze quickly returned to Vivienne. I was becoming less surprised by her new-found penchant for loose clothes, but she still didn't look herself without makeup on.

The lift doors closed behind them, but at the last second a man jammed them open for his companion and we all had to squeeze closer together as they folded themselves into the narrow space.

I turned around and found myself side by side next to Vivienne, our reflections staring back at us in the mirror.

An unsettling feeling of recognition made me shiver despite the warmth. It was as if we were standing back in the makeshift changing room in the market, my skinny frame refusing to fill out the dress and her beauty exaggerated by my lack of it. But now the roles were reversed.

Vivienne was studying our reflections intently in the mirror too, the whites of her eyes flashing as her gaze flicked back and forth between us. Eventually she gave a satisfied smile and I looked searchingly at the mirror, wondering what she'd seen there.

My blood ran cold as everything slotted into place.

What if Vivienne had engineered the reversal of our appearances so she could frame me for what she'd done?

The doors of the lift pinged open and I trailed behind in a numb state as Vivienne swaggered across the threshold, still walking as if she owned the room even with her modest outfit and bare face.

She disappeared through a set of doors and I followed, emerging onto a roof terrace that gave way to a twinkling view across the Athens skyline. The others had already claimed the table closest to the Acropolis, and Vivienne and Robert weaved through the other diners to join them.

The edges of my vision were swimming just as they had before I fainted, so I hung back and gripped the railings so hard my knuckles went white.

Fragmented scenes from the past few months flashed in front of me as I stared out unseeingly into the navy sky: Vivienne sweeping me away from the stables; patiently teaching me how to drive; bringing me tea when I was hungover and tenderly tracing her cool fingertips across my flushed skin.

I tried to cling on to these moments of affection, but the lies and manipulation were undeniable – the Vivienne I thought I knew disintegrated before my eyes, and despite everything my heart ached.

A movement in the corner of my eye caught my attention and I turned to see Anne waving me over to the table. The fuzziness was starting to recede, so I released my tight grip on the railings and focused on placing my feet one in front of the other.

Anne pulled a chair out for me, and I wanted to grab hold of her and tell her everything I knew. I wanted her to protect me.

'This looks gorgeous on you,' she said, reaching over to stroke my sleeve appreciatively. My gaze flicked to Vivienne and I saw her lips contort into a twisted smile.

The gifts of clothes and makeup had never sat quite right with me, but now they made sense.

Vivienne feared and maybe even knew that someone had witnessed her hit-and-run, and I was being offered up instead. She'd figured everything out so she could escape justice and compete in the rally without me should I be arrested before then.

This explained everything: the police tailing us; Vivienne asking me to run her through the course; her calm demeanour despite the horror of what she'd done. It all seemed so obvious now that I wanted to let out a manic laugh.

I tried to force a smile and quietly dismissed Anne's compliment. 'Oh, thank you, I'm borrowing it.'

'You keep it. It looks better with your bouncy youth anyway,' Vivienne said. She lit a cigarette and took a long drag.

I remained mute for the rest of the meal, looking out at the ghostly skeleton of the Acropolis as the others passed around wine and fava beans, aubergine dip and traditional chickpea soup. I could barely taste the food as I spooned it into my mouth and chewed mechanically, my mind elsewhere.

When I first met Vivienne she had seemed so concerned about whether there were people to look out for me, and I'd been happy to divulge this information.

I could disappear into thin air and nobody would care.

I laid down my spoon, no longer able to palate any of the watery broth.

The rally was too close for the others to think about anything else, and they discussed tactics with furrowed brows while I sat silently on the edge.

After the waiters had cleared away our meal Robert produced a pack of cards. Without discussion, we followed him to the lobby to claim a low table in a curtained-off area where we could spread ourselves out.

Robert called a waiter over to order some drinks, and Vivienne explained the rules while he shuffled the cards.

The game was Cheat, which hinged on players lying about their hand to get rid of all their cards, but this came with forfeits if you were caught out. She explained that we could only play cards that had a value the same, one up or one down from the previous player, and that we had to pick up all the cards in the middle if we incorrectly guessed someone was trying to cheat. If we were right, however, the cheat had to take the forfeit instead.

My mind was swimming as we were each dealt a hand, and when David pulled his cards in with a mock gasp I realised I'd been staring right at them.

'No monkey business,' he scolded, and I made myself focus.

Marie went first, calling two aces, and then the play moved to Mark, who called twos. The pile of discarded cards in the middle of the table mounted gradually until David incorrectly accused Hugo of cheating and had to pick them all up.

Anne was caught out several times for lower stakes, and when it was my turn I made an obvious bluff that Vivienne relished calling out. The waiter arrived with our drinks in heavy crystal glasses, and I took a sip of the sweet amber liquid to fortify me.

Vivienne won the first game and slapped her final card down gracelessly, but she wasn't as good as she thought she was. I'd studied her face for months, and I knew what made her tick. The way her nostrils flared slightly when she was lying, and the twisted smirk that appeared when she tried to suppress her glee at someone else's misfortune.

Robert shuffled the cards and I plastered a bewildered look onto my face as we started over.

I watched the game carefully as I sipped at my drink, the warming liquid trickling down my throat. Vivienne's thought process seemed as obvious to me as if it was written on her face, and I couldn't understand how nobody else was picking up on it.

Somehow she won again, and the crystal of her whisky glass gleamed as she rinsed the final drops and set it down heavily on the table. She saw me looking at her and dragged her chair closer. 'Jean, you're terrible at this. Do you need some tips?'

When I nodded she leant in close, and stage-whispered advice so obvious that it took all my energy not to retort with a quip.

'You need to hold your cards close to you – like this – so other people can't tell how many you have.' She grabbed hold of my hands and pulled them towards my chest.

I gritted my teeth and let her manhandle me into position.

'And you're never going to get anywhere unless you get better at bluffing. You just need to keep your expression relaxed.'

I looked into her dark brown eyes and saw complete contempt. She wouldn't realise it until it was too late, but I was already calling her bluff. She would regret having ever underestimated me.

TWENTY-FIVE

I spent the evening using the heavy hotel towels to swat mosquitos, caring little for the blurry commas left on the walls.

My earlier conviction that I'd be able to outsmart Vivienne was waning as I sobered up, and I was unable to decide on a plan. My first thought was that I might be able to get Yannis to tell the police what Vivienne had done, but I knew it was an outlandish idea. I didn't have enough evidence to force his hand, and there was no way he would come clean on his own.

My next option was Angela's letter. I still had it hidden in my holdall, but it meant very little without the passport to show it was in her writing. For all the police would know, I'd written it myself.

Another mosquito buzzed past my ear and I lashed out at it, catching the corner of a lamp. I lunged to right it before it could topple and made myself put the towel down.

My thoughts flicked to Angela's passport as I perched on the end of the bed. I wondered if Vivienne had brought it along when we left the last hotel, and where she could have hidden it now.

Most other people would have tried to dispose of evidence by now, but after finding the neatly catalogued collection of medals she carried around with her I had a hunch Vivienne would have held on to it. She liked collecting her little trophies.

The only chance I seemed to have was getting into Vivienne and Robert's room to look for it, and the thought filled me with dread.

I got into bed and kicked off the covers. I'd opened the window wide, but the heat of the still night was stifling. There was no other way, I thought to myself as I drifted off. Tomorrow I would have to find a way to get into Vivienne and Robert's room.

The next day was our last practice before the reconnaissance drive around the track, and because this would take up the final three days before the race Vivienne wanted to get as much driving in as we could.

We left early to get to the more rural parts of the course in good time, and Vivienne pushed the car harder and faster than she had before. I tried to formulate a plan as we sped past craggy limestone cliffs and dank forests, but when we reached the winding mountain roads I only had thoughts for the perilous drops on either side.

Vivienne was reckless that morning, playing up to the tight turns and sending loose rocks tumbling down the mountainside.

I knew she would only speed up if I challenged her, so I held tight. I spent the whole ride poised to fling open the door and jump if I needed to escape – though I knew by that point it would be too late.

When we finally returned to the cool of the lobby I had an insistent twitch in my right eye, and I flopped straight down on the nearest sofa. I noticed too late that Robert was sitting across from me, but I was too exhausted to move.

Vivienne perched next to me, but the rush of the drive seemed to have had the opposite effect on her. She was jiggling her leg up and down impatiently, and I could tell she was spoiling for a fight.

I was parched and my mouth felt as if it was coated with dust, so I begrudgingly heaved myself off the sofa to find a glass of water. I lingered in the cool of the high-ceilinged breakfast room, and when I returned Vivienne was pointing her finger up close at Robert's face. He grabbed hold of Vivienne's wrist and she shook him off, storming out of the lobby and into the street.

I hung back for a few more moments and then made my way over to the sofa.

'Where's Vivienne gone?' I said innocently, reclaiming my seat opposite him.

'Out,' he said bluntly.

'Will she be gone long?'

'Yes, she's gone to pick a fight with the mechanic.'

'That's probably for the best, she's been searching for her next target since we got back,' I said conspiratorially.

He looked up at me properly for the first time since the incident in my room, and I felt a familiar constriction in my chest. His eyes lingered over my figure-hugging overalls and I surveyed him steadily in turn, wondering where he had tucked his room key. 'I'm not sure about you, but I could do with a drink,' I ventured, and he nodded.

'That doesn't sound bad right now. We could go up to the roof?'

'Sure. Hopefully there'll be a breeze up there.'

Part of me had been hoping he'd offer me a drink in their room, but I didn't want to push him. Besides, I could hardly rifle through Vivienne's things while he was there.

I followed him up to the roof, and I was pleased to find that there was a rare breeze sweeping in from the sea.

The terrace was quiet at that time of evening, and we found a secluded table behind some plants with a view of the square.

A waiter fetched us a small bottle of ouzo, and Robert poured it into two glasses clinking with ice. The sweet smell reminded me of Igoumenitsa, and I felt almost nostalgic thinking back to the person I'd been then with the hazy summer still stretching before me.

My hand grazed his as he passed my drink and I resisted the urge to rub away the traces of his touch.

We clinked our glasses together and my heart sank as I noticed the outline of a key in the chest pocket of his shirt. I snapped my gaze back to his face and took a sip of my drink, trying to work out what to do.

At first we spent a lot of time looking out at the scenery in silence, but once I'd got him talking about his preparation for the race it was easy to fall back into the familiar pattern of his sarcastic back and forth.

'Vivienne will do that to you,' he said during a lull, and I wasn't sure what he meant until he indicated my twitching eye.

'It's the heat,' I laughed, knowing it was pointless to will the spasming muscles in my face to relax.

When the waiter failed to reappear, Robert went to the bar to get another round. The sun was still hot on the terrace despite the breeze, and the proximity of the early evening bathers around the stylish rooftop pool had encouraged several men to remove their tops. Once he had returned with our drinks Robert stripped off his shirt too and hung it close enough that I could almost reach the room key.

'Excuse me for one second,' I said, making sure to brush against his arm on my way past.

When I got into the bathroom I locked the door behind me and splashed some water on my face to cool down. I studied my dripping reflection and steeled my nerves. This could be my last chance.

When I returned to the terrace I sat down on a chair closer to Robert and pulled it towards him. I was so close to his shirt pocket now, I just needed a distraction.

Robert shifted his legs so that they were rested against mine and I let him, the familiar woozy haze of the ouzo settling over me.

Already my mind was skipping ahead to what I'd do when I got hold of the key. It would be tight, but I should have just enough time to slip into their room and search for the passports while they were out. I just had to hope they didn't return too soon.

Robert shifted closer, and all I could think about was the threatening bulk of his thigh pressing against mine. I placed my hand on his leg and leant forward to whisper in his ear, but when I saw Mark over his shoulder I pulled away. He must have seen us because he looked unthinkably awkward, but it was too late for him to turn around now.

'There you are,' Mark announced himself loudly. A look of annoyance slid across Robert's face before he jumped up and slapped Mark on the back.

'Sit down and I'll get you a drink,' Robert said, marching up to the bar again.

Mark sat across from me, eyeing me intently. I had been so close to the key, but I wouldn't be able to take it from the shirt under his watchful gaze.

I looked over to where Robert was leaning against the bar. I didn't think he'd be able to hear me talking if I spoke quietly enough – and once I'd explained to Mark why I needed his help he might even create a distraction.

'Mark,' I whispered, but when I shifted closer he pulled away.

'What?' he said coldly, and I flinched.

'It wasn't like that, I can explain . . .' but I stopped short when I saw the wary look on his face. The palpable disappointment.

'Maybe you're more like Vivienne than I thought.'

I opened my mouth to retort, but realised it was too late. I'd thought Mark was on my side, but even if I got him to believe me now there wasn't much he could do.

There was a sinking in my stomach as I realised: From here on out, I was on my own.

The conversation was stilted when Robert returned with more drinks. The two of them couldn't help but speak in an almost coded language from their decade of racing together, and I had to stop myself from taking frequent sips of my drink to numb the sinking feeling of despair. I knew I had to keep my wits about me, and I'd already drunk more than I'd intended to.

Mark looked at his watch. 'We ought to get ready sharpish if we're going to make dinner. We passed the restaurant earlier, and it's right at the other end of town.'

They both set their drinks down with an air of finality, but I indicated towards the remaining liquid in my glass. 'You go, it won't take me long to get ready.'

Mark nodded and strode off briskly, but Robert's eyes lingered on me before he turned and followed. I waited until they had disappeared out of sight before tipping the rest of the ouzo into a plant pot and marching to my bedroom to get ready for dinner.

In the bath I scrubbed and scrubbed but I couldn't wash the wooziness of the alcohol away, and when I re-entered my room I managed to knock my mascara so it rattled under the bed.

I got down on my hands and knees with the towel still wrapped around me, but when I peeked underneath I realised I'd have to shimmy under the bed to reach it. I lowered my chest to the floor and slid myself along the cold tiles, but I was startled by a jolt of déjà vu when my gaze snagged on something tucked under one of the slats. I lifted my hand up and felt the canvas of a bag, and I wondered if I had gone mad. It seemed to be the same one I'd seen tucked under Vivienne's bed in Igoumenitsa.

Grabbing the mascara and tugging out the bag, I eased myself out and laid both items on the floor.

Haltingly, I picked up the bag and shook out its contents. A passport tumbled out and hit the floor with a slap, followed by a pair of driving gloves.

I recoiled when I saw the dark stain on the fingers of the gloves and tried to drop them back into the bag without touching them.

I managed to manoeuvre the first glove in, but the second fell on the floor and I spotted the Saab logo. I leant forward to get a closer look, and I saw a name stitched just above the seam.

Jean.

I shuffled back. I'd never had any official Saab gloves, let alone personalised ones. I blinked hard and looked again.

Jean.

Eventually I managed to get the second glove back in the bag, and I leafed through the passport. It was Angela's, but Vivienne had ripped out the page with her identifying details, leaving just the stamps and the anonymous photograph.

My first instinct was to put the passport back in the bag and throw the whole lot away, but there was nowhere I could dispose of it in the hotel, and outside I risked being followed by the police.

I rolled up the bag tightly and hung it inside one of my dresses before pushing it to the back of the wardrobe. It seemed a much better hiding place than under the bed, but it wouldn't be too hard to find.

A peal of bells floated up from the street, and I knew my window for getting ready for dinner was growing thin. The thought of eating with the others sickened me, but Vivienne wouldn't let me miss it. I blindly selected a dress from the wardrobe and tucked the necklace I'd taken from the monastery under the neckline.

Although Robert hadn't been the answer to breaking into their room, I was sure I could find another way. It might just have to be a matter of playing Vivienne at her own game.

TWENTY-SIX

We left early the next morning for our reconnaissance drive around the course, but the churning in my stomach made it impossible to enjoy the clear morning light filtering between the monuments and tightly packed buildings.

The streets were buzzing with vendors and the first few city workers, but every now and then we would pass an open space with a handsome stone ruin and it would transport me back to what the city would once have been.

At one point I swivelled around to get a better look at a crumbling gate as it passed on our left and thought I spotted the wavy-haired policeman tailing us in an unmarked car. I squinted to try to make out his face, but the sun made it difficult to see past the glare on the windows. I kept an eye on the car for the rest of the drive, but when we reached the Glyfada neighbourhood it veered off in a different direction and I wrote the sighting off as nerves.

After about half an hour on bumpy roads that led us past half-built homes and rickety farms, we reached our destination and Vivienne killed the engine. We sat there in silence as the disused field that had been allotted as the starting point filled up, and Vivienne ran a shrewd eye over each car as they pulled in.

Anne and David parked their Mini next to us, and a few minutes later Robert and Mark appeared in their Saab. I didn't think they'd seen us because they parked on the other side of the wide dusty space – either that or Robert was still angry with Vivienne.

Without any warning Vivienne got out of the car. 'I'll be back in a minute,' she called behind her as the door was already swinging shut. I'd assumed she was going to talk to Robert or Anne, but she set out in the opposite direction and I craned my neck to watch her.

I waited until she was almost out of sight and then jumped out the car and followed, weaving between parked vehicles with oversized numbers and racing stripes slashed down the sides. A jumble of different languages and accents rang through the air as teams called out to one another, and every now and then a driver would rev an engine to assert their car's thunderous dominance.

Seemingly oblivious to the hubbub going on around her, Vivienne carried on walking all the way to the edge of the field and then stood behind a van to light her cigarette.

At first I thought she might have just gone all the way over there to have a smoke, but after a few moments I saw a familiar silhouette bouncing towards her. It was the mysterious brunette with the high ponytail Vivienne had gone to meet before the police arrived to question us.

Trying not to draw the attention of the racers sat inside their stationary cars, I edged around until I had a better view. From a distance the girl's immaculate hairstyle and gaunt face had given her an air of maturity, but close up I saw how young she was – more a girl than a woman. She accepted a cigarette from Vivienne and dragged on it uneasily, and I noticed how she was unable to stand still under Vivienne's intense gaze, sneaking looks at her whenever she turned away.

I'd been so intent on her expression that it wasn't until she shifted position that I realised the overalls she was wearing had a round company logo on like mine. I knew who most of our foreign Saab teammates were even if we weren't on chatting terms, so this girl must be with one of the other teams.

Intrigued, I crept closer. Was this my new replacement?

I wondered how Vivienne had approached this girl, and whether she had offered her an incentive to leave her teammate. But then again, maybe the girl had made the first move. Vivienne was a racing legend, and many ambitious young racers would trade in their loyalties for my job.

Now I was so close I could hear snatches of conversation between the revving of engines all around us, and I strained to work out what they were talking about. The girl raised her voice, and I peeked my head around the bumper to see her gesturing expressively at Vivienne. 'But Angela,' she said.

I held my breath, but the two of them fell silent, surveying one another. I wondered if I'd misheard, but I'd seen her lips spell out the words. This girl knew Vivienne's old navigator.

The unmistakable purr of Hugo and Marie's Ferrari pierced my focus and I ducked down as the white bodywork flashed into my line of sight. I saw Vivienne freeze in a moment of indecision, but when she realised she would be spotted she waved lazily in the direction of the car. When Marie and Hugo were out of sight she turned to the young girl and said a few more words before tossing her cigarette down.

I turned and darted back to the car before Vivienne could see me. Nobody paid me any attention, and I was glad for Marie drawing everyone's gaze as she made ostentatious laps of the field looking for somewhere to park.

When I was safely back inside I slumped against the seat. I thought back to what David had told me about Angela.

She had a sporty Mini and another young navigator with her, so I assumed she was going to try her luck as a driver.

Maybe this was the girl, here to find out what had happened to her friend.

Vivienne slipped back into the car without a word. When she slammed the door the smell of smoke lingered between us, and I was relieved when Marie appeared in the window. She knocked loudly, and Vivienne was forced to open the door again.

'Hello. Who were you chatting to?' Marie asked conversationally.

'Oh, some navigator. She wanted to use my lighter,' Vivienne said, wrinkling her nose. 'How are you two set up for today?'

The girl was quickly forgotten as they gossiped about the other racers they'd spotted, and when the starting horn sounded Marie hurried back to her car.

I clenched my fists in anger at Vivienne's lies, but once we'd joined the stream of drivers pulling out onto the route I had very little space to think.

It was my job to make notes to prepare for the race, so I scribbled down the state of the track and the severity of the corners as Vivienne calmly weaved in and out of the traffic.

As we neared the crest of the mountain the looming pine trees and choking cloud of dust made the visibility even worse, and I was relieved when I spotted the sea in the distance – an indication that we were getting closer to civilisation.

Vivienne was forced to slow down as we neared the coastal town of Varzika and normal drivers and buses joined the roads, but my body still hummed from hurtling across the rocky paths.

I used the lull to check my map for what was coming next, but when I looked up my view was blocked by a police car pulling in front of us. Heart pounding, I checked in the rear-view mirror and saw that there was another one hemming us in.

'What's going on?' I asked Vivienne. I could already feel beads of sweat breaking out on my forehead, but as always Vivienne remained unflappably cool.

The car in front indicated left away from the course, and I breathed a sigh of relief. But then a hairy arm shot out of the window and signalled for us to follow it.

'Do you think they're trying to signal to the car behind us?' I said doubtfully, but Vivienne gave a grim shake of her head and pulled off as we'd been instructed.

I thought we'd be stopped at the next verge and told what was going on, but the policeman in front merely indicated for us to continue following his car as we snaked back along the dirt track and into the city.

Inside the car Vivienne and I remained silent, the only sound the clunking where something had come loose during the drive.

Soon enough the landmarks became familiar again, and we circled around Syntagma Square a few times before finding somewhere to park. The policemen quickened their pace to reach the car before we could get out, and as we were escorted up the steps of our hotel I noted that none of them were the men we had spoken to before. The doorman raised his eyebrows when he saw their badges, but he said nothing and stood aside.

The air outside was soupy, and I was relieved to be enveloped by the cool marble of the hotel again, though the feeling was short-lived. As we passed the lift I realised how little was standing between the policemen and the items stashed upstairs and my heart began to pound.

The lobby was busy with weekend guests checking in, and mutterings of curiosity rippled through them as we were escorted past. When the concierge caught sight of us his face crumpled and he darted out to intercept us. 'This way,' he told the policemen curtly. He ushered us in the direction of the room where we'd been interviewed before, and I felt the inevitability of the situation wash over me.

I looked back to Vivienne and she gave me an encouraging nod. Maybe it was my nerves getting the better of me, but the policemen seemed to be giving her far more space than they were giving me.

The walk to the interview room was brief but torturous, and by the time we reached it I could feel sweat pooling under my top.

Lie to Me

To my dismay the policemen who had interviewed us before were already there waiting for us, and I didn't have the moment I had hoped for to compose myself away from scrutinising eyes.

'Sit down,' the handsome one said to me. His tone was more direct – more knowing and more judgemental than it had been the last time. 'You can wait outside,' he told Vivienne, and she disappeared without a word.

I took a seat and waited for the detectives to speak, but they just sat there staring at me. I tried to tell myself that it was an intimidation technique, but it didn't take long for the twitch in my eye to start up again.

'Please could you tell me what this is about?' I said, my voice cracking.

'What do you think this is about?' the tall man said evenly, and I caught a glimpse of his coffee-stained teeth.

I shook my head in confusion and he took out a cream envelope from a briefcase and slid it along the desk.

'Open it,' he commanded.

Keeping my arms clasped firmly by my sides to hide the sweat patches spreading across my overalls, I slid the envelope towards me and opened it.

A stack of photos tumbled out, the logo of the photo paper blinking up at me.

'Go on.'

My muscles felt like they were moving through treacle as I turned over one of the photos and studied it.

It was the picture the policemen had taken of me at the Acropolis – my eyes wide where the flash had stunned me.

I tried another. It was the same frame, but this time my features were blurry where I was pivoting to run away.

Before I could think of what to say, the handsome policeman leant over to leaf through the photos until he found the one he was looking for.

'Do you recognise this car?' he asked, pushing it towards me. I nodded, blood whooshing in my ears as I studied the crisp image of Vivienne's Saab parked in the garage.

'Have you ever driven this before?' the handsome policeman asked after he had given me some time to squirm.

'Yes,' I said reluctantly, and he raised his greying eyebrows at me.

My hands itched to fiddle with the comforting bulk of the monastery necklace tucked under my top, but I knew I couldn't let them see it.

'When?'

'A few times when we've been practising for the race.'

'Have you ever passed a driving test?' he asked, while the tall man made some notes in his pad.

'No,' I admitted. Nobody at the stable cared about licences, so I'd never bothered to take one.

'Did you enjoy driving the car?'

'I guess so.'

'Did you ever take it out on your own?'

'No. I wouldn't want to drive the car without Vivienne there,' I said, and he wrinkled his brow.

'Because it's hard to steer?' he asked, and I realised I'd walked into his trap.

'No, not at all,' I stammered. 'Because she wouldn't want me to drive it without her.'

'Vivienne said it would be a tough drive for a novice,' he said, emphasising the last word as he looked up at me. 'And the funny thing is – she said she didn't know how well you could drive it because she'd never taken you out in it.'

'That's not true, ask . . .' I started, but stopped abruptly when I realised Vivienne had never let me drive the car when anyone else was around to watch.

'The girl that was killed, the one we showed you the picture of, are you sure you've never seen her before?'

'No, I told you that,' I said, wondering if they still had no clue who Angela was.

'Are you sure?'

I nodded.

'All right,' the handsome one said with a sigh, arranging the photos into a neat stack and sliding them back into the cream envelope.

The tall policeman spoke next, and I heard his words as if in slow motion.

'You say that you haven't seen this woman before and that you wouldn't drive Mrs Fenwick's car without her permission, but we have an eyewitness who says he saw you at the scene of the accident.'

'I didn't—' I began to protest, but he stopped me with a raised hand and carried on.

'We've sent him these pictures and he's confirmed that you're the woman he saw in the car, even though you told us you didn't drive that night.' He flicked through a few pages in his notebook. 'It says here that you went out for dinner, driven to and from by a taxi, and then stayed at the hotel until the next day. Is everything you told us last week still true?'

'Yes.'

'We also have an eyewitness who was staying near the garage. She identified you as the person who returned to fix the car before daybreak.'

'But—' I said, and again I was silenced.

'We're going to interview your friend, and then we need to search your room. Sit outside and we'll come out when we're ready.' My body went numb as his words settled over me.

'Understand?'

'You've got it all wrong . . .' I said, but my voice petered out when they turned their beady gazes on me.

'I said, do you understand?' he repeated.

After a long pause I finally nodded, a lump forming in my throat.

TWENTY-SEVEN

Vivienne spent far longer with the policemen than I had anticipated, and when she came out she gave me a stiff smile.

I could only imagine the things she would have said to make me look guilty, and the quick squeeze of reassurance she gave my arm when the police weren't looking made me wince.

'Please show us to her room,' the tall policeman said to Vivienne, and she led the way while I followed behind, flanked by the other police officers.

The concierge was waiting for us by the exit to the lobby, and he shepherded us towards the stairs so we wouldn't disturb the guests by using the lift.

My room felt further away than it had before, and my vision blurred around the edges as we climbed the stairs. I grasped on to the banister, but by the time we'd reached my floor I feared I might faint again.

Vivienne led the way to my room, and when we got there the concierge pulled out the master key. He let the policemen in first, followed by me and Vivienne, and the room felt cramped with all of us in there.

'Is there anything you want to tell us? It's your last chance,' the tall policeman said, turning to me.

When I shook my head they made Vivienne and I step outside while they fanned out around the room.

The policemen were slow but thorough with their search, and Vivienne rapped her nails quietly against the door frame as we watched them open drawers and grab handfuls of my belongings before splaying them out on the bed. One of them pulled back the curtains to let in more light, and I squirmed at the sight of them sifting through the flimsy material of my underwear.

Next the policemen moved the clothes onto the floor and started on the bed. They ran their hands along the bottom of my mattress and stripped off the sheets, shaking them out aggressively and straining their ears to make sure nothing had dropped on the floor. Unsatisfied, they did the same to the pillows and the towels hanging over the doors.

Once they'd ransacked all the drawers around the edge of the room, the handsome one shut the door while they finished the search. Vivienne and I were left in the corridor with two more policemen and the concierge, who turned the key in his hand awkwardly, avoiding eye contact.

After several more minutes of muffled movements a volley of raised voices started up, and the door swung open to reveal the tall policeman triumphantly beckoning us inside.

It looked like the wardrobe had been turned on its side, the clothes and bags all scattered around the floor, but when I saw what the handsome policeman was holding I stood stock still.

It was the bag I'd stashed in the wardrobe.

I became aware of a buzzing in my ears as he unfurled it and flicked a look at Vivienne. She was feigning disinterest and looking out of the window, but it was clear from the glint in her eye that she already knew what they'd find.

He upturned it and the contents fluttered down to the floor. It took him a second to work out what he was looking at, but when the realisation dawned on him he called excitedly for the other policeman.

Instead of looking towards the commotion, I fixed my eyes on Vivienne. She took a deep breath to compose herself, then looked over at the floor and blanched.

Unable to contain his curiosity any longer, the concierge came inside to look at the item on the floor. He moved closer when the police didn't stop him, and I stood on my tiptoes to peek over his shoulder.

On the floor was the newspaper clipping with the picture of Vivienne and I after our win at the Tulip Rally. Even in black and white she looked glamorous – her lips painted dark and her glossy hair pulled back in a silk scarf – with her name printed underneath. My face was less obvious in the top corner of the frame, but it was undeniably me.

Vivienne's face twisted in confusion. She opened her mouth to say something but quickly shut it again.

'Do you have the pictures?' the tall policeman asked the other one, and he pulled out the cream envelope with the photos that he'd taken of me by the Acropolis. He found the one the witness had positively identified as the woman from the car crash and held it up next to the picture of Vivienne at the Tulip Rally. Even from where I was standing, the similarities were striking.

'Is this you?' he said to Vivienne, pointing at her picture in the newspaper clipping.

She paused for a split second as she worked out how best to play her next move, and then broke out into an uneasy grin. 'Why, of course it is.'

'And do you think our witness might have got the two of you confused?' He pointed to the picture of me and then back to Vivienne.

'How could they have done? We look nothing the same,' Vivienne said, walking over to me and opening her eyes wide in surprise.

'I would disagree.' The handsome policeman opened his briefcase and took out a neatly folded newspaper clipping. He held it up between us, and I recognised the photograph of Vivienne and I standing outside the hotel.

'They've swapped here. What do you think?'

He handed the clipping to the other policeman, who shrugged in agreement.

'We're going to search your room as well.'

'Of course,' she said pleasantly, but her lips were pressed together in a tight line, the skin turning slowly white where the blood was draining away.

We filed out and climbed further up the staircase to the level of Vivienne and Robert's room. A hush had descended across the group, and each squeak of the staircase was horribly pronounced.

This time the concierge led the way down the corridor rather than Vivienne, and he shot her an apologetic look as he fumbled with the key to her door. The police went in first, and we watched as they stopped and spun on their heels to take it all in, thrown by the opulence of the space.

Although technically one giant room, the king-sized bed was separated from the plush brocade sofas and heavy wooden furniture by a decorative partition wall, and the vast window provided views out across Acropolis Hill and Syntagma Square.

The maid must have been in that morning because everything was neatly squared away, but the policemen quickly undid her hard work.

They took all of Vivienne's jewellery out of its boxes, and although her wardrobe was stripped back where she'd given much of it to me, they still managed to amass a pile of clothes on her bed.

It took them longer to comb the vast room, and halfway through the door flew open and Robert marched in.

'Say, what do you think you're doing?' he said, snatching one of his jackets from the tall policeman's grip.

'Calm down, sir, we need to search your room in connection with this enquiry. It's all routine,' the policeman said, puffing out his chest.

'That's ridiculous. What kind of a hotel do you call this?' he said, turning to the concierge.

'They're almost done, Robert. It's fine.' Vivienne shot him a warning look.

'Move to the side please, sir,' the tall policeman said, and we watched in silence as he dropped down to his hands and knees to crawl under the bed.

He let out a muffled grunt, and when he shimmied out a few moments later he was clasping a snakeskin handbag, no doubt belonging to Vivienne.

'How did that get under there?' she exclaimed, but her voice sounded squeezed. 'Thank you so much for finding that.' She tried to take it out of the man's hand, but he held it high up out of her reach.

'Give it back,' Robert said, stepping in. 'You have no right to go through her handbag.' He looked like he might be about to take a swing at someone, so the policeman relented.

'Very well, here you go,' he said, handing it over. 'But I'd like you to turn it out.'

'This is absurd,' Vivienne said as Robert fumbled with her bag, the shiny clasp slipping between his fingers until it opened with a pop and a tote bag fell out, along with two blue passports embossed with gold.

Vivienne froze, looking down at the assortment of items on the floor.

'See. Nothing there but our passports and some jewellery,' Robert said, oblivious to the hush that had descended across the room.

'Exactly,' Vivienne said, regaining her composure. She tried to retrieve the passports from the floor but Robert got there first.

The policeman raised his eyebrows at her and then turned to Robert. 'Show us the passports please.'

'This is ridiculous, these are ours.' He was so confident that he didn't even peek at the passports before opening one of them out to prove his point, but it was not his or Vivienne's face staring back. It was mine – my pale face fading into the background.

The policeman frowned, and when Robert realised something was wrong he turned the passport around to face him and squinted in confusion.

'My mistake,' Vivienne butted in. 'I must have got it mixed up with mine.'

She felt around in her handbag for the passports, her final reserve collapsing when she realised what I'd done. She looked up at me – eyes wide open, mouth agape – and I held her gaze.

'Let's see the other passport then,' the handsome policeman said wearily.

Time sped up, until Angela's pale face and watchful, almond eyes were looking back at us, a piece of paper fluttering to the floor from between the pages.

The policeman lunged for the paper and opened it, trying to decipher the swirly writing, while his partner peered inside the tote bag. When he saw what was inside he darted over to the door to block anyone from leaving.

'Put your hands up,' he instructed Vivienne and Robert.

Vivienne did what she was told immediately, but Robert was slower to catch on.

'What do you mean? What's in the bag?'

The policeman drew his gun and Robert's face crumpled.

I was too far away to see what was inside. But of course, I already knew what it was.

TWENTY-EIGHT

A red mist had descended over me the night before when I found the evidence Vivienne had placed in my room.

As I attempted to style my hair, I thought with each yank of the brush about how she had used me and bought my trust. How she was willing to sacrifice me to get what she wanted.

I knew my attempt to hide the bag of evidence in the wardrobe wouldn't keep it safe if the police searched my room. I had to get rid of it that night.

As I started to layer on some makeup, I wondered if I should stop dressing like Vivienne if she was trying to frame me. I steadied myself against the sink, and as I surveyed myself in the mirror I realised that wouldn't be necessary. Her scheme could work both ways, after all.

Carefully, I took the tote bag out of the wardrobe and placed the gloves on the lip of the bath. I cut out the stitches spelling my name and checked the needle holes were no longer visible before replacing them and rolling the bag up tight. Stashing it under my arm, I marched out the door.

I took the stairs down to the lobby two at a time and arrived just in time to see Vivienne's favourite concierge disappearing outside twirling a cigarette between his fingers. A quick sweep of the lobby reassured me that I was the first one downstairs, and in that split second my vague idea crystallised into a plan.

As I drew closer I saw that the young girl was manning the desk, so I took a deep breath and flounced the rest of the distance across the lobby.

The girl didn't notice me at first so I checked over my shoulder once more and rapped my knuckles loudly on the desk as Vivienne would have done.

She twirled around in shock at the sound, her cheeks flushed.

'I left my key in the room and my husband has the other set. Please can you give me the spare so I can get in. It's Room 209. Vivienne and Robert Fenwick,' I added, tapping my nails against the desk to underline my impatience.

'Um, yes, I think that's OK,' she said, looking over her shoulder to see if there was anyone more senior she could ask. If the concierge came back he'd see that I wasn't Vivienne at once, but I knew I had at least a few minutes. 'I can call a porter to take you up to your room and unlock it?' she offered eventually, her uncertainty plain in the tenor of her voice.

'I'm in a rush. I won't be long. Can you please just give me the master key?' I said firmly.

For a nauseating second the girl looked at me slack-faced and I thought she'd seen through my ruse, but in the next moment she was reaching up to pluck the key off the wall of hooks behind the desk.

'Jean, there you are.' I jumped as Anne appeared next to me. 'I love this dress on you.'

'Oh, thank you. It's another one of Vivienne's,' I said, wafting the pretty fabric.

'Gorgeous.' She made her way around the desk and over to our usual spot next to the sofas. 'Are you coming?' she called over her shoulder.

'Sorry, I stupidly locked my key inside my room.'

'We can wait?'

I shook my head. 'Tell the others to go without me. I could be a while . . . no idea where I've left them.'

'Will do,' she called back cheerfully, and I turned to see the girl hovering at the edge of the reception desk with the key.

'Please bring this straight back,' she said as she handed it over, her voice lowered. 'I'm not really meant to give out this key.'

'Consider it done,' I assured her. Pivoting on my heel before she could change her mind, I made my way over to the staircase with the cold metal clasped tightly in my fist.

When I reached Robert and Vivienne's floor I hurried down the corridor and waited around the corner from their room. Once I'd heard them leave I waited a few minutes to make sure they weren't going to come back and then let myself in.

Locking the door behind me, I picked my way carefully across the floor.

Since we'd arrived at the Grande Bretagne I hadn't been invited into their room, and it was disorientating to see the familiar patterns of their clothes strewn around a different space. There was one thing that hadn't changed, though. The room was light and airy, but the heady scent of Vivienne's rose fragrance still overwhelmed the space.

I got to work turning out the drawers and looking under their clothes, the messiness making it easier to do so without a trace. After ten minutes I started to worry that Vivienne had covered her tracks, but then my fingers grazed a thick notebook with a grainy leather cover stuffed to the back of a drawer. I pulled it out, and it opened to reveal my straight nose and wide eyes looking up at me.

I dropped my passport into the tote bag with Angela's one and the gloves, and then squeezed the whole bundle into one of the handbags Vivienne wouldn't miss. With no time to look for a better hiding place, I dropped it to the floor and slid it under the bed with my toe.

When I got back down to the lobby and peeked around the drapes that hid the reception desk I saw that the concierge was back. I sidled over, making sure to keep out of his sight, and the girl gave me a wide-eyed stare begging me not to expose her.

I waited until the concierge had turned his back to help another guest and then slid the master key along the desk so she could snatch it up without him noticing. She did so quickly and hung it back up on the hook. I couldn't help but share a sly smile with her before I tripped out into the night.

ONE YEAR LATER

I rapped my knuckles on the edge of the kiosk and the shopkeeper woke with a start. From a distance he looked like the balding man who had served me the year before, but when he looked up his face was much younger than the craggy one from my memory. His features stirred in recognition, but I didn't react. I was getting used to the strange response when people realised who I was.

Everything else about the little kiosk was the same. It was still impossible to see the colour of the walls behind the chaotic display of newspapers, and some even carried the same front-page picture as they had last May. I plucked one from its peg and studied the photo of Vivienne being manhandled into a police car.

Word of the arrest had got out quickly, and by the time she had been questioned at the police station and led outside to be moved to Korydallos Prison there was a crowd of photographers waiting. Her snarl was caught from every angle as she twisted up to look at something out of shot. But none of them captured the rest of the scene; the defiant look on my face as I met her gaze.

I tucked the newspaper under my arm and studied the rest of the front pages. Only a handful showed me posing with the women's cup at the Acropolis ceremony the day before, but I was happy to share the limelight with Vivienne. She'd helped me get there, after all.

I picked up an imported English-language newspaper to read on the crossing and a few local ones, and the man gave a toothy grin as I fished out some coins from my purse to pay him.

'You?' he asked, pointing to my picture, but I turned away.

It was too early for anything in town to be open, so I carried the purchases to my old spot on the harbour wall.

Dangling my legs over the water, I held the newspapers tight as I watched the fishermen sluice down their boats and mend torn nets in preparation for the day ahead. My fingers automatically found the monastery necklace that had become my lucky talisman, and I fiddled with the chain.

I relished this moment of peace before the fishing boats cut through the calm, and then wandered the streets in search of a *kafeneio*.

When I'd found a quiet spot to order a bougatsa and some coffee I spread the papers out in front of me, feeling a wry smile steal across my face. Vivienne had always wanted to make history at the Acropolis, and in the end she had.

I still couldn't read much Greek, but I could only presume the journalists had taken the opportunity to use my victory at this year's race to rehash the story of Vivienne and Robert's demise the year before. Judging by the media frenzy that met me whenever I returned to the modest flat I was renting in London, the English tabloids had most certainly done the same.

After a short trial Vivienne had been placed in a rudimentary prison north of Athens, and to my knowledge that's where she remained. I had no interest in going to visit her, though part of me would have loved to tell her how everything had panned out.

The Saab executives had fretted that the notoriety of Vivienne's case would be a disaster for sales, but the opposite turned out to be true. Robert had decided to resign from the Saab team after his association with the scandal, or so they told me, but they soon offered me a place as a driver to keep the interest alive.

I'd taken to the role naturally – I'd learnt from the best, after all. But I still hadn't managed to find a good navigator, taking on whoever was free and willing to accompany me at the time.

As for Robert, I'd had no word of him since he left Greece. I could imagine him rattling around their Pimlico flat, bringing back young women and drinking himself into a stupor.

I flicked through the rest of the newspapers, and when I'd finished the final flakes of pastry and licked the sweet custard from my lips I made my way back to the port.

I made the mistake of taking the route that led through the weekend market, and I was jostled between groups of young children and burly men hawking fruit and vegetables by foot. Just as I spotted the exit someone bumped into me and I stumbled forward, but when I turned around I couldn't single anyone out among the seething throng. I thought I'd felt a hand on my bag, but when I patted it anxiously I could feel the reassuring outlines of my passport and wallet. Shrugging it off as an accident, I told myself to stop being so paranoid.

The crowds thinned out as I neared the port, and the proud hull of the *Appia* came into sight. Nikos had arranged to send my luggage ahead from the hotel, and when I was satisfied the porter had everything in hand I started to climb the ramp.

It was an unseasonably cloudy day for May, and as the morning wore on a lusty breeze had rucked up the surface of the water. My eyes watered as the ends of my hair whipped up into my face, and I wished I'd brought a headscarf with me.

A skinny teenager was checking tickets at the top of the ramp and he gave a start of recognition when he saw me. He lingered over the details on my passport longer than was necessary, stealing glances at my face before letting me through.

Anne and David had sent a letter to the hotel saying they would pick me up when I arrived in Italy. I hadn't seen them since they'd moved there several months before but I wrote to Anne often, and when I mentioned I'd be competing in the Acropolis she insisted I visit.

I heard someone call out behind me, but their words were lost on the wind and I began to climb the stairs.

When I reached the top deck I held on to the railing and turned to drink in the familiar details of Igoumenitsa; the shallow urban centre hugging the curve of the bay, and the mountains looming up behind the tightly packed buildings.

'Wait,' the voice called out again.

I turned to find a young woman trying to get past the staff checking tickets at the top of the ramp, and when she saw me looking she waved enthusiastically.

Clinging on to the railing as I climbed back down, I was surprised to see that the young woman was the brunette navigator I'd spotted Vivienne with the year before. I'd seen her now and then on the outskirts of races and done a bit of digging to find out that she worked for a second-tier team, but as the year had worn on I'd barely paid her a second thought.

She looked pale and vulnerable without her hair tied back in a severe ponytail, and like mine it whipped up around her face.

I indicated for the boy to let her through, and reluctantly he lifted up the rope so she could duck underneath.

'Is this yours?' she said breathlessly. She held out her hand, and nestled inside was a painted miniature on a gold chain, diamonds set into the metal around it.

My hand flew to the bare skin at the base of my neck.

'Where did you get that?'

'I saw it fall off before you went into the market, but I couldn't get to you through the crowds.'

'Thank you,' I said gratefully. I reached out to take it back, but she didn't move.

'Do you want me to put it on for you? To make sure it doesn't fall off again.' Taken aback, I drew my hand away uncertainly. She undid the clasp and I swept my hair off my neck as she fixed it in place, her cold hands sending a shiver across my skin.

'That's very kind,' I said, and she nodded.

'I'm Nicola.' She held out her hand in an oddly formal gesture and I took it, flinching slightly at the feel of her bones beneath her skin. 'Congratulations on your win.'

'I assume you know I'm Jean.'

'Yes,' she nodded, but she didn't elaborate.

'Are you staying in Igoumenitsa?' I asked, at a loss for what else to say.

'No, I'm going to Italy. Maybe I'll see you there. I heard you needed a new navigator.'

'No. I don't think so . . .' I said quickly. This was a chance for a clean break, and I didn't want anything getting in the way, though I admired her brazenness. 'Thank you again, I must be getting on.'

'I know what you did,' she blurted out as I made to leave, and I tightened my grip on the railing.

'What ever do you mean?'

'I saw you that night. What happened to Angela. How you covered it up.'

'I don't know what you're talking about,' I said, but my voice was shrill.

'With the paint. I won't tell, but just think about my offer . . .'

Before I could reply she turned and slipped into the crowd that was forming on the lower deck, and I realised she'd got on without showing a ticket.

I thought back to the policeman's words and shivered.

We also have an eyewitness who was staying near the garage. She identified you as the person who returned to fix the car before daybreak.

The ferry let out a cheerful honk of its horn and the water churned up around us. I watched the girl's slim form weaving between the unruly mass of passengers, and I gripped the railing so hard that my knuckles turned white. I saw her slip her hand into a man's jacket pocket and pull out a paper bag, and then she disappeared from sight.

I made my way unsteadily up the stairs to the bar on the top deck. The decor was a stark departure from the homely Greek style of the hotel, with Italian pegboard ceilings, polished linoleum floors and flamingo-pink chairs dotted around the room.

Perching uncomfortably on one of the pink bar stools, I ordered a Martini. When it arrived, complete with a bobbing green olive, I carried it carefully onto the deck despite the rising wind.

I felt the burn of someone's gaze on me, but it was only after some time that I spotted the girl in the crowd, calmly observing me from a spot by the railings as she ate flat peaches from a paper bag.

Raising my glass in acknowledgement, I took a briny sip of my drink. And then another one. I knew what I had to do.

I gave the girl a curt nod, and a wry smile slid across her face as the boat set off from Igoumenitsa with a jolt.

Acknowledgements

Thank you to my agent, Sam Copeland, for believing in my writing even from my first (never to be seen again) manuscript and making all of this possible, along with Honor Spreckley and the rest of the wonderful team at RCW.

I'm so grateful to Stephanie Carey and the brilliant team at Embla for seeing the potential in this story and helping me to really make it shine.

I don't know how I'd have got to this point without my fabulous mentor Sarah Bonner, writer of the twistiest thrillers and very generous giver of sage advice and encouragement.

Thank you also to Sarah Hilary and my wonderful coursemates from Curtis Brown Creative. Your early input on this story was invaluable.

To all my unfailingly supportive friends – thank you! A special mention goes to Bish, Caspar, Ele, Jacques, Pip and Ruta for making me laugh so much on holiday that I (almost) forgot I was waiting for book news.

As always thank you to Josie, Tacis and George for being my rocks.

Last but not least thank you to Edward for being my cheerleader, merciless first reader and partner in crime.

About the Author

Olivia grew up in Brighton and studied English literature at the University of St Andrews. She has a Journalism MA from City University, and lives and works in London as a journalist.

She is half-Greek and has been visiting the country with her family since she was a young child, when she first fell in love with the rich mythology, stunning scenery and of course the food. Returning to Corfu as an adult, she was struck by the dramatic – and often perilous – landscape and knew the island was the perfect starting point for a stifling psychological thriller.

About Embla Books

Embla Books is a digital-first publisher of standout commercial adult fiction. Passionate about storytelling, the team at Embla believe our lives are built on stories – and publish books that will make you 'laugh, love, look over your shoulder and lose sleep'. Launched by Bonnier Books UK in 2021, the imprint is named after the first woman from the creation myth in Norse mythology. Embla was carved by the gods from a tree trunk found on the seashore; an image of the kind of creative work and crafting that writers do, and a symbol of how stories shape our lives.

Find out about some of our other books and stay in touch:

X, Facebook, Instagram: @emblabooks
Newsletter: https://bit.ly/emblanewsletter